Trivium

"The History of the Future."

By Creighton Thompson

Prologue

There is a filter that lies between the conscience and the ego. It acts as a trap, catching embarrassing events, negative thoughts, and even some dark secrets from entering our outward persona.

While some individuals are more candid about their foibles, others are more guarded. Generally speaking, people more open about who they are tend to have smaller egos.

One reason I believe many actors have enormous egos is due to the over-exercise of this filter. They have to suppress their identity in order to fully capture the one that has been written for them. It is not a disorder – it is another tool in an actor's arsenal.

This brings me to the politician. Some are genuinely open and forthright about their motives. Unfortunately, many others are not. While an actor moves on to play another role, a politician, acting in a leadership role, continues his ruse to stay in power. When the entrenched elected who have their hands on the controls of our future are finally exposed, it is often too late.

The prayers of men can be counted on to chronicle a civilization's decline. In times of uncertainty they'll ask God to '*bless* us'. In times of desperation they'll ask God to '*help* us'. In times of hopelessness they'll cry out, 'God *save* us.' Which times are we in?

Chapter 01

A typical day for Graham Duncan, maintenance man at St. Theodota Hospital, starts with the changing of the light bulbs. Then there are minor wiring repairs to be made on hospital beds, intercom systems, and other commonly used gadgets. For the more technical electronic equipment, repairs are done by the chief electrical engineer, Miguel Sanchez.

Sanchez has a degree in electrical engineering. His cluttered office in the hospital basement is more like a supply room. A variety of oscilloscopes, testing meters, and an old soldering iron line the long work bench. An MP3 music mix barely cuts through the background ambience from the hum of hard drives and dusty pre-amplifiers.

Graham's shift is almost over, and he's in a hurry. Though tired, he still manages to head down the stairs from the fifth floor. It's much faster than the elevator, plus he's able to clock out as he leaves the building for the day.

Graham pops his head into his supervisor's office, "Hey, Boss, I've got that appointment clear across town. Can I cut out a few minutes early?"

Startled by Graham's intrusion, Miguel looks up, then over to an instrument being tested on the workbench.

"Yeah, that 'stop smoking' thing? We're good, see you tomorrow."

As Graham turns to go, he notices something on the bench. "Hey, Chief, what's that little handheld thing do?"

Miguel pauses, and asks, "Duncan, did you replace those lights in both x-ray and ultra sound?"

"Done and done," Graham answers. "Really though, what's that little box do?"

"Hey, you want to stop smoking, or do you want me to bust out a schematic?"

"Oh right, and hey, thanks again for that tip about the hypnosis clinic. If you can lose weight, I can stop smoking."

"Yeah, Dr. Jerome is a pro."

Graham heads out to the parking lot and gets into his car.

Miguel goes upstairs to a waiting area window and watches Graham pull out into traffic. He goes back to the workbench to make a call.

"He's on his way."

There is no reply.

Miguel continues, "He'll be there in fifteen minutes."

"Goodbye," a woman's voice responds.

***

There are several people seated in a row of folding chairs, lining the wall of the office. An older couple sits at the far end, and three women sit scattered through the remaining chairs.

The receptionist calls out the name of the next person on her list. A woman stands and a technician escorts her through the door.

Graham enters the building and the receptionist tells him to wait until his name is called. He selects the open chair next to an attractive woman.

A few newspapers and sports magazines cover a round coffee table. Graham leans over and selects the one closest to him.

He settles back into the chair and glances at the cover story.

Who will win the National League pennant race?

Graham chuckles, "Oops." Turning the cover toward the woman he whispers, "I already know who wins."

The woman smiles at Graham's admission.

"I guess they forgot to throw this one out last month," he adds.

The woman nods.

The receptionist calls another name from the list. An older woman stands up, leans on her cane, and hobbles through the door.

"The Washington Nationals," Graham responds proudly as if the woman had asked him. "Finally, huh?"

She shrugs and politely smiles.

He drops the magazine on the edge of the table and quietly looks around the room.

An anomaly catches Graham's attention.

"Look at that," he points up to a clock that hangs over the reception window, "it must be broken or something."

The woman directs her attention up to the clock.

"The big hand," he blinks several times, "it's moving like the second-hand."

She looks at Graham with a hint of confusion.

He continues, "With what they charge to quit smoking, they can afford a hundred new clocks, right?"

The woman smiles and nods in agreement.

"Well, that's why I'm here anyway," Graham admits, "I'm trying to quit."

He leans closer to her.

"I'll bet you've tried everything to quit, too, huh?"

The woman smiles sheepishly.

A few minutes pass before the receptionist calls the next name.

The elderly couple stands and Graham watches as they are escorted into the back by another technician.

"Hey, they look just like my mom and dad. Wow, that's weird; both of them."

The woman's eyes widen and she cocks her head.

"Pretty interesting day so far," Graham begins.

The woman does not smile. Instead she leans over to Graham's ear.

"No, not at all," she whispers, "you wanted to sit next to me, you wanted the Nationals to win the pennant, you wanted time to fly, and you wanted to see your parents again."

The woman stands up and is escorted through the door by a technician.

"Wait," he protests, "they didn't call your name. You can't go back there yet."

The door closes.

Graham lunges at the door, but it is locked. When he knocks, there is no answer.

"What's your name? How do you know so much about me?"

He puts his ear to the door and hopes for a response.

"Please, tell me your name."

The patterned floor tiles seem to stretch as Graham is surrounded by a feeling of vertigo. He continues his tight hold on the doorknob and waits for the woman to come back. The room seems to pitch and yaw; his sense of balance is replaced by acute spatial disorientation. He lowers himself into a lying position and rests against the door.

"Tell me your name," he shouts, "please, I have to know."

A woman's voice emanates from behind the door.

"Graham, can you hear me?"

"Yeah, I can. Who are you?" he begs.

"Terah," she responds, "I'm Doctor Jerome's assistant."

"Terah, don't leave me again."

A masculine voice follows.

"Graham, this is Doctor Jerome. I need you to wake up now. Can you do that for me?"

"Where's Terah? I need to see Terah!"

Doctor Jerome continues in monotone.

"Graham, this is a dream and you need to wake up now. Do you understand?"

"Terah, I need you now, please come back!"

Doctor Jerome's assistant, Terah Piper, sits next to a monitor, reviewing a small pile of E.E.G. paper. She is startled by a spike in the wave patterns.

"Doctor Jerome, look at this." She points to the abnormality on the graph. "What's happening?"

Doctor Jerome stands motionless over his patient.

Terah gets up from her chair and approaches the doctor.

"Paul, Paul," she snaps her fingers in his face, "What's going on?!"

Doctor Jerome blinks off the haziness of the moment.

"I think I was there."

"What do you mean, 'there'?"

"Just that," he adjusts his focus on Terah's face, "I'm telling you; I was in Graham's dream."

"That's impossible. You hypnotized him; he's the one who's under, not you."

"It was real, Terah, I saw everything," Dr. Jerome stares across the room, "the old house he grew up in, his friends from high school. I even saw when the death panels came for his parents."

Terah walks over to her chair and sits down.

"Well, it looks like the memory implant seated anyway." She relaxes in her chair. "Let's do the 'stop smoking' suggestion while he's still under."

Dr. Jerome collects his thoughts and then repositions himself next to the examination table.

"Graham, the very next time you inhale on a cigarette, you'll react as if it were laced with poison."

"Shoot, Doc, that sounds a little extreme." Graham's eyes snap open, "but let's do it. I'm ready to go under."

Surprised at Graham's admission, Dr. Jerome and Terah nervously make eye contact with each other.

"But, Mr. Duncan," Terah advises while holding up the strip of monitor tape, "you were under."

Graham swallows and runs his tongue around his teeth.

"I guess I was. You're the pros."

"Graham, take a few minutes and relax. I have something I must discuss with Terah."

Dr. Jerome leads her into the observation area, separated from the examination room by a large mirrored window.

"What happened out there?" Dr. Jerome whispers.

"We were implanting a memory," Terah says while brushing the hair out of her face, "then a huge wave spike and then——."

"And then," Dr. Jerome interrupts, "I was there."

"And you saw the whole implant?" Terah asks.

"Yes, just for a moment."

Terah looks through the glass at Graham, who is still lying on the examination table.

"Could you have hypnotized yourself at the same time?"

"Well, I could have," Dr. Jerome nods, "but I couldn't have seen his new memory; I wasn't hooked up to the electrodes."

Terah pulls through the E.E.G. paper she printed out on Graham's implant.

"I don't believe it," she holds it up to Dr. Jerome's face, "there's no indication he was ever in R.E.M. sleep." She tosses the roll of paper onto a desk.

The doctor grabs a pen off of the desk and circles a few aberrant waves.

"You're right; he wasn't dreaming, he was thinking."

"We'll have to implant the 'no smoking' suggestion or he'll get suspicious." The doctor adjusts his glasses. "We will do it tomorrow."

Terah shrugs. "Tomorrow? Why not right now?"

"You saw that spike; he's unstable."

"Let's hope he adjusts by then, or we'll have to, you know…"

"Yeah, perform a neural scramble on him instead."

They walk back into the examination room where Graham has been waiting.

Tapping his knee with a reflex-hammer he found on a nearby counter, Graham smiles and asks, "Hey Doc, did I quit smoking?"

Dr. Jerome studies Graham's face.

"I think we made some progress, but I'd like to see you again tomorrow."

"How many more do I need?"

Dr. Jerome drags his hand through his hair, "Well, one more should do it."

Graham stands up slowly to prevent himself from stumbling. Walking to the door, he turns back to Dr. Jerome.

"You know, Doc, I've been smoking for sixteen years. I guess another day won't hurt."

Terah smiles mechanically.

"That's the right attitude to have, Mr. Duncan."

On the way through the waiting room, Graham wobbles a little. Jennifer, the receptionist, invites him to sit down until his head clears. He thanks her and plops down on the nearest chair, holding his head between his hands.

Twenty minutes later, Graham is feeling much better and walks over to the desk where Jennifer is seated. He stares through the glass and patiently waits while she finishes a task on her computer. She glances up, apologizes for the delay, and adjusts her glasses. Clicking through a few medical histories, Jennifer finds Graham's and opens up a calendar.

"I'm sorry, Mr. Duncan; this computer's acting crazy again." Jennifer laughs slightly, "Is tomorrow at 2:45 okay?"

He looks at the monitor's reflection in her glasses.

"Sure. I'll take a half-day tomorrow."

Jennifer fills in an appointment card and hands it to Graham.

"Here you go. See you tomorrow."

Graham thanks her and moves toward the elevator. As the door slowly closes, he hears her complaining about her computer again.

"I can't find Mr. Davis' or Mr. Deaver's files. They were here a second ago!"

***

Terah and Dr. Jerome sit motionless in the examination room.

"The memory tests and brain scans should be camouflaged online as a safeguard," Dr. Jerome confirms.

"Yeah," Terah responds curtly, "I'll handle that."

***

Graham had hoped to call his wife Shelly on his way home from the clinic. He will try to ease the disappointing results by picking up some Chinese food on the way home. He swings into their favorite take-out place and orders a couple of entrees to go. Noticing that he still has the appointment card in his hand, he tosses it on top of the Chinese food and heads home.

Graham pulls into the garage, kills the motor, and lifts the bag of food from the passenger seat. He slams the car door with one hand while balancing the bag behind his back; he wants to surprise Shelly with dinner.

He trips over the doorjamb, jostling the food. He groans, seeing the sauce seep through the bag, but continues into the house.

"Graham?" Shelly calls, "I'm in the kitchen."

"Yeah," he says in defeat, "I think I dumped the Kung Pao."

Graham enters the kitchen, still holding the bag behind his back.

"You picked up dinner?" she asks.

He brings the sauce-stained bag from behind his back and peeks inside.

"Ugh, this looks like an accident." Graham playfully snaps the bag shut, "Move along ma'am, nothing to see here."

"I'm a nurse, I've seen just about everything," she says as she grabs for the bag of food.

He quickly pulls it away. "Ma'am please, it's still a crime scene."

Shelly walks to the counter and stops in front of a plate of cookies.

"I'll trade you a cookie for some Chinese food."

Graham joins her at the counter and drops the bag next to the plate.

"Are those from Shauna?"

"Yep."

Graham lifts the plate closer to his face.

"Her cookies are awesome."

"All right, you're getting that sauce everywhere. Go wash up." Shelly retrieves a couple of paper plates from a cabinet and begins her triage of the spilled food. "Where's it from?"

"Entree the Dragon."

Shelly squints as she presses him.

"The one up here on 92nd?"

"Uh, yeah," Graham turns off the kitchen faucet and dries his hands on a towel.

"You're a little late…" Her voice trails off.

"Yeah you're right," Graham says apologetically, "I stopped by Side Pocket Sports too."

"Not again…"

He turns from the sink.

"I just priced a few. You know, kicked a few tires."

"Our den is not going to become a smoky pool hall," Shelly emphasizes her point by smashing a scoop of rice on his plate.

"Honey, billiards is a gentleman's game. Richie, Tommy G, and The Fish all have tables."

"All upstanding citizens."

"What?"

She holds up three fingers and taps them.

"One, Richie smells like baby powder—that's not normal. Two, I can actually feel Tommy's eyes on me when I'm not looking. And three, 'The Fish?'"

"I just want to have them over every now and then to shoot some pool, that's all."

"You don't even play pool."

"I'll learn. I'll take lessons."

"Oh that's ridiculous," Shelly's attention is diverted when she pulls the appointment card from the bag. "And what is this?" She holds up the card, "You have an appointment to see a hypnotist?"

Graham takes a step backward, "I know what you're going to say."

Shelly's face is expressionless as she holds up one finger. "Number one, hypnotists are a waste of money. Number two," she holds up a second finger, "they actually do more harm than good, and number three, my fingers are getting tired of this." She mockingly waves her hand in his face.

Graham stares into the sink while he gathers a rebuttal.

"Well," he sheepishly looks up, "I just want to quit smoking."

Shelly leans over and opens the cabinet door under the sink. "Let me take care of this for you," she tosses the appointment card into the trash, "I'll try and get you into the next smoking cessation class at work."

Chapter 02

The alarm clock breaks the early morning silence by agitating Shelly into coherence.

3:50 AM

Shelly needs to be at St. Theodota's Hospital by 5:00 in order to scrub-in by 5:30. It is a stressful job, but one Shelly thrives on. Despite being younger than her co-workers, Shelly has worked hard to achieve a supervisory position.

While she is not assisting in one of the six suites, she is accompanying chief surgeon Dr. William Parton on his rounds.

As usual, Graham has slept through the chirp of Shelly's alarm. He generally wakes up on his own around 6:45. Even though they work at the same hospital, Graham and Shelly rarely see each other, aside from lunch.

Late in the morning Graham is finishing up repairs on a stubborn hospital bed. As he rolls out from underneath it he squeezes the button to raise the head. It works but when he releases it the bed still continues its contortion.

"Well, it's better than it was," says a nearby nurse.

"Thanks, but broken is still broken." Graham unplugs the bed, "I'll take another look at it after lunch."

He tosses an 'out of service' sign onto the bed and walks out, heading toward the cafeteria.

Just before he gets there, he receives a call from Miguel to drop down to the Maintenance Office. He messages Shelly that he's going to be a little late. Starting toward the stairs, he spots a pair of familiar faces next to the x-ray department.

"Hi, Shauna. What are you doing here?"

Graham's neighbor is in the waiting area with her teenage son.

"Benny, show Mr. Duncan."

Benny lifts his pant leg up to reveal a swollen, purple knee. "It's just a ground tatt."

"Too much skateboard air?"

"Yeah, right?" Benny confesses.

They hear a familiar ringtone as Shauna fumbles around her purse for her cell phone. She retrieves it and bungles the call until it goes to her voicemail.

"This silly phone case is the worst. I'm sorry Graham; I think they just called Benny's name. Say 'hi' to Shelly for me."

"Okay, you guys take care."

Graham resumes his journey to the Maintenance Office. He opens the door and glances in to find Miguel. The office, located at the far end of the hospital, is dark and small. Boxes of parts, medical supplies, and piles of paper sit on every flat surface.

"What's up, Chief?" Graham asks.

Miguel is startled and quickly hangs up his phone. "Whoa, I told you after you fixed the light board up on eight."

"Sorry man, I was meeting Shell early so I already knocked it out," he says with satisfaction.

Miguel gestures for him to sit down. "Okay, well, uh, I've got some bad news for you."

Graham pushes a stack of electronic catalogues on a short filing cabinet to one side and takes a seat.

"Duncan, I ain't gonna sugarcoat it; we've just been given our new budget."

"What do you mean? No Christmas party this year?"

"C'mon, man, this is serious."

Graham picks up a volt-meter and begins to fidget with it. "Are they cutting bonuses?"

"No, Graham, listen to me," Miguel walks over and takes the volt-meter from him. "Your position, you know, your job. It's been eliminated."

"What? When? They can't do that!"

"You'll get paid for the rest of the week, but you can leave right now if you want to," Miguel keeps talking over Graham's ramblings. "I'm sorry, man."

Graham stares at Miguel, shocked at what he's hearing.

"You're not kidding are you?" Graham slowly scratches his chin, "You're serious."

"I need your card key, too. I really hate doing this." He looks down at a dejected Graham, "Look man, Shelly's a department manager; she's probably had to make some tough calls too."

Shelly. What is she going to say?

Graham forces himself back into reality long enough to drop his badge on the desk. Slamming the door, he walks like a punch-drunk fighter, returning to his corner. He makes his way toward the cafeteria and drops onto a chair uncomfortably close to a decorative silk plant.

Graham messages Shelly to tell her he has saved a table. He rehearses mentally how to break the bad news to his wife.

Shelly comes from the other end of the cafeteria. Glancing around the lunch room, she finally catches a glimpse of Graham and picks up her pace, her blue scrubs flapping around her protective shoe covers. Graham breaks into a prepared smile, trying not to foreshadow the bad news.

"Hi Honey, how's your day going?" Shelly asks with a smile.

"Right now? Not so good."

"You lost your job?"

"Yeah. How did you know?"

"I had to make a few adjustments to my department, too."

"Oh, so firing people is called 'adjustments' now?"

She lightly touches Graham's shoulder, "You're right, I'm sorry."

"So, do we have to put the house up?"

"Of course not," Shelly consoles Graham, "You'll find another job. Maybe even something a little more challenging than changing light bulbs."

Graham stares over her shoulder at a painting at the back of the cafeteria.

"You know, Shell; you're right. I don't think this is what I should be doing."

"See, you need to challenge yourself."

He smiles, "Yeah, I don't want to be just a guy who works with his hands. I want to use my mind somehow, too."

"Now you're thinking." She checks her watch, "You hungry?"

Graham slumps. "Not really."

"I've got a procedure in twenty minutes anyway. Will you walk with me?"

They get up from the table and navigate their way through the busy lunch room to the elevators. Graham reaches out and pushes the 'up' button a few times.

Shelly hugs him before the elevator doors open. "You go back home and think about what you want to do." She steps into the elevator, "I'll make your favorite dinner tonight, okay?"

Graham barely says 'okay' before the doors close. He walks out the front entrance of St. Theodota Hospital.

In a daze, he attempts to find his car. It's a full five minutes before he can get the key in the ignition and get it started.

Goodbye, hospital. It's been nice knowing you.

Graham doesn't remember anything about the drive home or parking in the garage. Though feeling a little more comfortable about his sudden job loss he is still numb from the initial shock. He drops his keys on the kitchen counter while rummaging for a beer in the refrigerator.

He twists the cap off, walks to the den and with a sigh drops down onto the leather sofa. Leaning his head back and looking up at the ceiling, he feels drained. The dropping level of his eyelids coincides with the level of his drink. Graham begins to fall asleep. His empty beer bottle slides gently into the corner of the couch.

His body constantly readjusts; his limbs writhe in a series of controlled spasms.

Graham is entering a pre-R.E.M. sleep state. Instantly he recalls every stored visual and auditory event he's witnessed over his lifetime.

Deep inside Graham's mind are floating pictures. He selects the one he wants to view and it jumps to the forefront of his thoughts. Graham replays the memory strand of waiting for Dr. Jerome's receptionist to find his patient chart. With minute detail he can rerun it backward and forward. He is not dreaming; it is more like looking at the pages of a magazine. He reads the receptionist's name tag as he focuses on the image of Jennifer West working at the computer.

Graham notes the soft features of Ms. West's face, admiring her as though she were a piece of art in a museum. Next, his mind retrieves hundreds of glossy images of models, performing quick facial symmetry comparisons as they click by. In his opinion, Ms. West could easily be on the cover of any fashion magazine.

Fifteen minutes later, Graham wakes up from his nap. His rest was not nearly deep enough to dream, but he is able to select several pages of memory to review. The barely noticeable reflection from Jennifer's glasses provides him with his entire patient history. Even though the documents are imprinted backward, his brain quickly flips the image and zooms in with vivid detail.

Able to stabilize his thoughts, Graham closely examines his file on Dr. Jerome's computer and instantly notices 2:45 PM. He jumps up, grabs his car keys and runs to the garage. At the same time, Shelly is pulling into the other parking space, having just arrived home from work.

"Hi, Shell. I'll see you when I get home," Graham shouts as he closes his car door, starts the engine, and backs out quickly.

Shelly yells, "You have a job interview?"

Graham stops and rolls down his window, "Dr. Jerome."

Her eyes widen in anger. "Waste of money!"

Graham's insecurity shows through the nervous smile on his face. Nodding as if he understands his wife's concerns, he continues to back the car out of the garage. He is somehow compelled to continue.

Chapter 03

Terah is setting up for Graham's visit. She becomes concerned with Dr. Jerome's motionless gaze.

"Are you ready for Duncan?"

"He's close," Dr. Jerome offers.

"I know, it's almost two forty-five."

"No, you don't get it," Dr. Jerome stands up, "He's drawing me in again."

The doctor walks over to the counter and begins fidgeting with an Otoscope.

"Look," Terah urges, "we have an implant to do. Try not to worry about it."

"I can't. He's too…"

Dr. Jerome's knees buckle and he grabs hold of the counter. Terah rushes over and helps him to the floor.

"Okay, okay, I'll scrub his file." Terah places her hand on his shoulder, "We'll find another way."

***

Pulling into the medical complex, Graham mashes on the brake pedal to prevent hitting the white parking block. The front shocks bear the weight of a high-speed, but controlled, stop. Graham leaps out, slams the door, and rushes into the clinic.

"Hi, Jennifer. Graham Duncan; I have a 2:45 with Dr. Jerome."

"Graham Duncan," Jennifer smiles while searching her computer, "Let me see now."

"I laid down for a quick nap and almost forgot about my appointment."

After checking several screens and multiple calendars, Jennifer tells Graham he is not on the schedule.

"Are you sure? I thought it was this afternoon."

"Do you have your appointment card, Mr. Duncan?"

"Uh, no, sorry. It's a long story," he leans closer to the glass. "Can you check tomorrow? Maybe I got the date mixed up."

Jennifer begins inputting Graham's name and scrolling through the appointments. "Hmm, I'm not seeing it." She looks up from her computer, "That's *Dugan*, right?"

"No, *Duncan*. Graham Duncan."

"Mr. Duncan, I can't even find you in our database. Are you sure you're a patient of Dr. Jerome's?"

"I was here yesterday, remember?"

"Sorry, I see a lot of people every day."

"Try using my patient number: 25637."

Curious, Jennifer enters the number. While waiting, Graham examines the rest of his file through his mind's eye. At the end of the notes section, he sees an entry by Dr. Jerome:

Displays attributes of advanced photographic memory.

Jennifer looks at Graham again, "Nope, Mr. Duncan; you're just not in our computer. Would you like to schedule a visit?"

After a few long blinks, Graham asks Jennifer to try searching using another patient number he gives her. It comes up as Christopher Davis of Fairfax, Virginia.

Jennifer looks at the file and hunches her shoulders. "That isn't you either."

He then asks her to input another set of numbers. This time, the file of Ronald Dillon pops up on her screen.

"What's the point?"

"Take a look at Dillon's patient history," Graham insists.

Jennifer rolls her eyes as she stares at the computer file. Graham proceeds to recite the entire two-hundred-and-thirty-seven word patient history back to her.

She flinches, and rolls back in her chair.

"How'd you know that? Are you a hacker or something?"

Graham shakes his head and reduces his interrogation.

"Can I just ask Doctor Jerome a question?"

Jennifer checks her screen.

"That's not possible; the doctor and Ms. Piper are late for a conference in D.C. Would you like to make an appointment for next week?"

More confused than angry, Graham briskly walks out of the office. He struggles with frustration but it is tempered by his curiosity.

In the examination room, Terah crouches behind a stack of patient records, while Dr. Jerome slumps against the wall.

"Doctor, it's okay; Jennifer took care of it."

His voice is tormented, "Too late, I'm with him," he takes fitful breaths, "help me."

Bewildered, Terah lifts his head up, "You're 'with him', how?"

The doctor does not respond.

"Paul, Paul!" Terah exclaims, "What's happening?"

Dr. Jerome has lost all spatial orientation and balance; his entire vestibular system has collapsed. He becomes limp and slides to the floor.

Chapter 04

The garage door opens slowly and Graham guides his car in carefully next to Shelly's. He can hear her as he comes into the kitchen. She has calmed considerably; enough to put together Graham's favorite meal.

The aroma of chicken and garlic wafts through the house.

"Hi Shell," Graham greets his wife as she portions out the pasta, "Mm, that smells good." He sits down at the kitchen table. Shelly follows behind, carrying both plates of pasta. She sets one down at each place, and takes her normal seat.

"You know, I'm really glad you want to quit smoking. I'm sorry I made a big deal out of it."

"That's okay; at least I didn't waste any money this time."

Shelly is startled. "What do you mean, 'this' time?"

"Well, the first treatment was relaxing, but today they acted like they didn't know who I was."

Shelly's eyes sharpen, "You mean that appointment card I found yesterday was for a second visit?"

"Yeah, but I never got to see the guy; he was at some conference in D.C."

She stops chewing, "Let me get this straight; they set up an appointment for you, knowing they would be out of town?" Shelly sips her wine, "See, I told you; just a bunch of scam artists."

Graham nods in agreement.

She reaches across the table and softly lays her hand on top of Graham's.

"You're better off anyway."

They push the food around on their plates for the next several minutes, making random eye contact.

Shelly stands and takes the plates to the kitchen.

"So, other than being more relaxed, you felt nothing out of the ordinary?" she inquires.

"Nothing I can think of," says Graham, "Oh wait! I do remember stuff better."

"When you say 'stuff', like where you put the keys to the shed this time?"

"Yeah, kind of like that."

Shelly walks back over to the table with a sense of urgency, "What to do mean 'kind of'? You either know or you don't."

Graham explains that he remembers not only the last place he left the keys but the last twenty three places.

Shelly becomes more concerned.

"Graham, look at me." She points to her eyes. "Can you recall anything while you were hypnotized?"

He takes a deep breath as he remembers obsessing about Terah Piper while under. Staring directly into Shelly's eyes and without the slightest trace of eye aversion he answers.

"Nothing. I don't remember a thing."

Shelly lets out a deep breath, relieving the tension in the room.

"I guess that's good because I've seen cases where hypnosis has led to mental instability."

Graham stands up and begins pacing beside the table.

"So, right now I may be okay," he says while scratching the back of his head, "but shouldn't I take some sort of 'crazy man' test just to be sure?"

Shelly responds in a controlled voice, "Here's a test. What time was it when you asked me to marry you?"

"That's easy; right after dinner. Our check was stamped at 9:15. That's also our anniversary."

"Extra points for you." Shelly presses on, "What did I order?"

"You had the New Zealand Lamb with a Cabernet wine sauce, garlic mashed potatoes, and some grilled carrots."

"Impressive."

He sits down and folds his arms confidently.

"Yeah, I remember food pretty well."

Shelly quickly asks, "And who am I?"

Graham smiles, "You're the greatest wife in the world."

She reaches over and playfully taps his forehead in cadence with her words.

"And don't you forget it."

Chapter 05

While Shelly is at work on Saturday, Graham researches photographic memory. Eventually, he finds a case study, buried near the bottom of the search engine's results.

"Advanced Photographic Memory."

This report is on the biological and neurological actions of the brain during pre-REM sleep. The subject (DGP) exhibited incredible memory retention during verbal testing. However, on the next series of verbal tests, his brain began rapidly connecting commonalities together like a search-engine algorithm would. The subject's emotional relevance was utilized as the primary load structure. From there the patient's curiosity grouped hunches into coincidences into patterns. This advanced form of photographic memory severely taxed the patient's frontal cortex. Further testing could result in damage to his speech center and affect his overall stability. (DHPJP).

Graham wants to test his new memory skills. With a pen and notepad at his side, he lies down on the sofa for a quick nap before Shelly gets home. Within minutes, Graham enters a state of pre-REM sleep. Memory strands swirl around his subconscious. Finally, he selects a memory strand of a standard wiring schematic from an operating-room lighting-panel. After examining the mental image, he forces himself awake and draws the schematic.

Looks the same, but that's no good since I don't have one to check it with.

He goes back to his computer to look for something else. He finds a map of Mount Vernon, where he and Shelly live. He stares at it for a couple of seconds and then lays back down to resume his nap. Twenty minutes later, he awakens, grabs his pencil and begins drawing the map.

After drawing for nearly an hour, he compares it with the original map online. Graham is startled; they are identical. Reviewing his work, he notes the road names, townships, and interstates he has written. They appear to be perfectly labeled, as if he had traced them in ink.

As he paces the living room, he thinks of other ways to test his ability. This time Graham focuses on being let go from his job. A deep breath follows. The harsh feeling of uselessness floods into his mind. He sits back down on the sofa and closes his eyes.

While napping again, he recalls entering Miguel's office for the last time. Graham notes that Miguel abruptly hung up his cell phone. He stops this image and enlarges it, revealing the last three digits on Miguel's phone, before it reverted back to its wallpaper. He also remembers hearing the last few echoes of a mechanical clicking sound that emanated from Miguel's workbench.

Upon waking up, Graham tries to figure out what his subconscious put together. Instead of images denoting frustration and anger, he views events that have no specific correlation to the moment he was fired. He does not understand the relevance of remembering a partial phone number or the clicking sounds.

Feeling mentally drained, Graham drops back down on the couch and closes his eyes.

***

Shelly sets down her duffle bag in the garage, and then jangles her keys as she closes the door with her foot. Graham springs up quickly from the couch. Still groggy, his body sways while he attempts to adjust his shirt.

"I'm home." Shelly stares from across the room. "Are you okay?"

Graham nervously blinks faster.

"Yeah, uh huh, I think I was asleep."

"Think?" She puts one hand on her hip, "you either were or you weren't."

"I was testing my memory," Graham states as he sits down on the couch. "This might sound crazy, but my dream was so real I thought my eyes were open."

"What?" Shelly steps cautiously over to Graham. "Do you think you may still be under?"

"You mean, hypnotized?"

"Yeah," Shelly carefully sets her purse on the counter.

Graham taps his head. "No, I don't think so." He rubs his eyes, "What if I was hypnotized to not know if I was?"

"I warned you about the shamans of quack medicine." Shelly turns toward the kitchen, "you take it easy and I'll throw some dinner together."

Graham follows her.

"What if I'm still, you know, under?" He throws his hands up in frustration, "Could I be doing things that I'm not aware of?"

"Okay, enough. You seem fine to me."

Not wanting to entertain any more questions about hypnosis, Shelly directs her attention to preparing dinner.

"Graham, can you get me a jar of spaghetti sauce from the pantry?"

Shelly continues adding spices to the pot, while Graham remains quiet.

"What the...?" she gasps.

Graham is standing next to the sink, motionless.

"Honey," she gently prods, "Are you asleep?"

"I don't know what I am."

Shelly leads him to the couch. "Lie down and take it easy, okay?"

"But what if I have a post hypnotic suggestion buried in my head, then what?"

She puts her arms on Graham's shoulders and slowly directs him to sit down on the couch.

"Where do you live?"

"Oh great, make fun of me now," Graham blusters, "Mt. Vernon."

"Yeah, on what planet?" She asks with a note of seriousness in her voice.

"Okay, Nurse Duncan, I'll play along." He scratches his head, mocking her inquisition. "Earth. Yep, I'm pretty sure this is Earth. Am I okay? What do I win?"

"You're fine," Shelly says succinctly.

Chapter 06

Sunday morning, Graham opens his eyes and looks around, confused. He has spent the entire night on the couch without realizing it. Slowly he sits up, trying to focus on why he was in the living room. Realization sets in; he jumps up, almost skipping to the bedroom in his excitement.

"Shelly, wake up!"

Shelly groans and rolls over.

"Good morning," he sings, "I need to show you something."

"What?" she mumbles into the pillow, "I need coffee."

Graham runs down the hallway to retrieve a photography book from the den. He jumps onto the bed, bounces over to her, and thrusts the book into her face.

"What?" Shelly manages to open one eye.

"I skimmed this a few minutes ago and I need you to pick a page number," Graham instructs, "Then close it."

Sighing, she opens both eyes and follows the instructions. She flips the book, and then studies the picture and remembers the page number.

"Got it," she closes the book and drops her head back onto her pillow.

"All right," Graham trembles with excitement, "What page did you pick?"

"116."

"Yeah, okay, I'll have all the answers in a few minutes."

Graham rolls over to his side of the bed and lies back down.

"What are you doing?"

"I need a little nap first."

"Are you kidding? This nap-magic will never play in Vegas."

Shelly rolls off the bed and changes her clothes. She grabs a brush from the nightstand, and drags it through her short hair. She leaves the bedroom, still clutching the book, and walks toward the kitchen.

Graham gets up and follows her down the hall, stopping to lie down on the sofa in the den. He falls quickly into a pre-REM sleep. Using his photographic memory, he easily recalls the photo from page 116.

The sun has been up for about half an hour when Graham awakens from his power nap. Shelly is sitting at the kitchen table with the screen door open, enjoying a cup of coffee and the gentle sounds of a Sunday morning. Graham wanders into the kitchen.

"Shelly, look at the picture."

She picks up her phone. "Yeah, hang on, 'Mr. Polaroid', I just got a text."

Her face changes from bemusement to a look of concern.

"I might have to go in this morning, so hurry and show me your new trick."

"What's wrong?"

Shelly tells him about a young woman who contracted a virulent form of flesh-eating bacteria known as Necrotizing Fasciitis. The new patient arrived by helicopter on Friday afternoon and was treated with a barrage of powerful antibiotics. Her condition remains unstable.

"Oh, yeah; they wheeled her right by me on my way out," Graham notes, "I'd just gotten canned."

He gazes through the door while slowly shaking his head in pity.

Shelly refocuses Graham by asking him about what he remembers from the photo book.

He blinks a few times and begins to recall the details.

"The photograph is of Lake Doucette in Louisiana. The lake is home to over seventy-four Southern oaks that surround the state park. Of course you'll find their state tree – the bald cypress – and state flower – the magnolia – as well."

"Really?" Shelly says with a hint of incredulity.

Graham recalls that there are twenty-three different boats visible in the photo.

"Okay," Shelly begins, "I see three guys to the front left of the picture; are they skiing or fishing?"

"These guys are all in their mid-thirties. They're in a twenty-one foot Ranger Comanche with a 250-horse outboard engine. Honey, this is one wicked fishing machine."

"We're not getting a boat," Shelly interjects.

She brings the book close to her face and squints, trying to make out the name on the side of the boat. A mischievous smile flashes over her face, as she again attempts to challenge her husband.

"Okay, what name is on the side of the boat?"

"Just a second… there it is; *Kickin' Bass*."

"That's right," she says, astonished.

"Pretty cool, huh?"

"This is way past 'cool' Graham; I think you may have a photographic memory."

Graham continues to view memory strands from his subconscious. He not only sees every detail, but his brain begins to connect certain objects in the photo with other stored memory.

"The shadow cast from the setting sun means this picture was taken late in the fall, at approximately 6:27 PM."

"Okay, now you're making it up."

His voice lowers as if it were a recorded message.

"6:27 PM, exactly."

This bridging of commonalities is instant. Graham shudders at the amount of sudden knowledge he is gathering and starts blurting out more connected strands of information without prompts from his wife.

"According to the color of the lake water," Graham surmises, "it's about 51 degrees and perfect for hooking redfish or spotted sea trout."

"Really?" Shelly says jokingly.

"Over the last four years," Graham offers, "three people have died at the lake. Two from boating accidents and one had a heart attack on shore."

Shelly's phone rings, but Graham continues his recitation.

"This man, Henry Stiles, was celebrating his seventy-third birthday."

She puts the phone to her chest, "Hold on a minute."

He whispers one more entry.

"This guy, Henry Stiles, I went to school with his grandson's future brother-in-law."

"Okay, I'll be there in twenty minutes."

She hangs up her phone and turns to Graham.

"There's an emergency. I'll be gone most of the day."

"I understand." He lets out a long sigh. "Do you think this will save her life?"

"I don't know. The mortality rate is high." Shelly trades her slippers for shoes, "if we can get ahead of it, she might have a chance."

Pouring what's left of her coffee down the sink, she grabs her keys and heads to the garage.

Graham had planned on taking Shelly to a movie, and a wine and cheese tasting tour in Hybla Valley. With those plans now scrapped, he parks himself in front of the TV and watches a Nationals game. While statistically a great game, the pitching duel has Graham dropping off into another nap on the sofa.

Inside Graham's mind there is a massive amount of strands that seem disconnected. His subconscious is frantically attempting to gather and connect associated memory information. The emotion of empathy is driving his thought process. The first memories replayed are that of the young woman being wheeled past him, as the flight crew raced toward the emergency room. He replays the medical history and current status conversation the nurse had with the doctor during the patient handoff.

The information Graham gleaned from recalling the patient's admittance was her name: Emily Castle. Her acute history stated that she went hiking with several friends and found a scrape on her lower left leg that became infected. When she spiked a fever, Emily's roommate took her to an urgent care center. The Physician's Assistant on duty flushed out the wound and gave her a prescription for antibiotics and a strong pain reliever before sending her home.

Graham continued to recall the flight nurse's verbal exchange with the emergency room doctor. The fact that the wound became much larger with the epidural layer turning a dark blue was deemed significant. It was reported that she returned to the urgent care center just hours later with more serious issues. From the center, Castle was immediately flown to St. Theodota for extensive care. She has no known allergies to drugs, and is generally in good health.

Chapter 07

A car, headlights still bucking through the clouded sunrise, darts into the parking lot at St. Theodota Hospital. Shelly continues her urgency by accelerating through vacant rows of spaces. Forgoing her usual covered parking space, she selects one right next to the employee entrance.

The elevator door opens and Shelly briskly walks to a laundry cart, grabbing a pair of scrubs on her way to the surgical suite.

It is a few minutes past eight as Shelly rinses the soap from her hands. Wearing a surgical mask, she backs into the Operating Room and is gloved and gowned by an assistant. The patient, Emily Castle, lays motionless on the operating table. Various beeps of the monitoring equipment and a rushing sound of the respirator assure the assembled team that Emily is ready for surgery.

The ticking clock can still be heard above the din as Shelly performs a routine instrument check and sponge count.

The surgeon, William Parton, enters the surgical suite.

"What is this, the middle ages?" He says with a hint of disgust, "Are we back to using leeches and bloodletting to heal, now?"

Most of the staff's eyes hunt around the room, avoiding him.

He continues his sarcasm. "Has medicine not advanced enough for this barbaric remedy to be considered a viable option?"

The anesthesiologist, standing at the head of the table, briefly redirects his attention, "Bill, you know this is all we can do."

"The knowledge, the breakthroughs, the pioneering surgical techniques I— we've done," the doctor shakes his head in disbelief, "and much of it right here in this very suite!"

A sigh escapes from his surgical mask, "I could use a fireman's axe."

Shelly changes the conversation as to avoid another one of Parton's long rants on the limits of medicine.

"Doctor Parton, my husband may have a photographic memory."

"Wonderful," he says acerbically.

"Yeah, I showed him a picture this morning and he recalled it perfectly."

Parton smiles, "That's not exactly a standardized memory test."

The doctor's attention is diverted by a technician, who places the recent x-rays on a light-board for him to review.

***

After twenty minutes on the couch, Graham snaps awake. He felt the overload of medical information might have overwhelmed his brain.

He gets up unsteadily, grabbing the front of the sofa to balance himself before taking a few steps. He manages to make it to the garage. Graham runs various medical protocols through his head not because he wants to but because he is compelled. Getting into the car, he shakes off the stupor of sleep as he speeds toward the hospital.

***

After carefully examining the x-rays, Dr. Parton marks on Emily Castle's leg where the incision will begin. The line is high above the wound.

He wants to review the latest blood gasses before beginning the procedure.

"Shelly, if you would set up a sterile field right here on my mark."

"Yes, Doctor."

Over the next ten minutes she will swab the surrounding area with a powerful antibacterial ointment and then place a graphed synthetic membrane over the leg. This thin covering will allow a clean point of entry for the scalpel to minimize bleeding.

***

Upon arriving at the hospital, Graham jumps from the car so quickly that he is unable to shut the door. Walking toward the employee entrance, he realizes he no longer has a cardkey to get in. He sees someone by the door and follows her in closely.

Graham hears the chime indicating the elevator has arrived, and steps in. He taps the 'four' button several times. The doors close and the electronic groan of the old service elevator is heard, as it abruptly ascends to the fourth floor.

As the doors open, Graham notices a couple, sitting solemnly in the orange chairs of the waiting room. He assumes they are Mitch and Dawn Castle, waiting for the results of their daughter's surgery. Graham steps out of the elevator, before the doors close.

Stretching out his hand, Graham appears confident but sympathetic, "Mitch and Dawn Castle?"

"Yes?" Mitch uses more air than required.

"Has Emily ever had the German Measles?"

Dawn cranes her neck in Graham's direction.

"Yes, I believe she had them twice." Her tormented expression turns curious, "Look, Doctor, we already answered these questions last night."

"Oh, I'm not a doctor."

Slightly confused Dawn asks, "Are you a nurse?"

"A nurse?" Graham is caught off-guard by the question and smirks, "No, not me."

"I'll call Security," Mitch stands up, "we'll see how much you laugh then."

Graham rushes to ask one more question.

"Emily hates Chinese food, right? Sweet-and-sour pork?"

Mitch steps over to the nurses' station.

Graham begins walking back to the elevator, watching the anger grow on their faces. He turns to call the elevator.

The door opens and a several staff members pour out and scatter. Graham steps in and punches the 'first' floor button.

As the doors close, Mitch shouts down the hallway in Graham's direction.

"She hates it! Can't stand sweet-and-sour *anything*."

Graham hits the 'door open' button and leans his head out to take another look down the hallway. He sees Mitch running toward him.

"H—how'd you know that?" Mitch stammers.

"I just know things and put them together," Graham explains.

They walk back to the waiting room where Graham gives the Castles a brief overview. He explains Emily's aversion to a specific ingredient, commonly found in Chinese food.

"A couple of years ago, I was looking up my family history online…"

"What?" Dawn interrupts.

"I got as far back as the 1600s," Graham continues, "We share a few ancestors, who survived the Great Plague of London. Immunity to the Plague was based on a rare amino-acid, which triggered an autoimmune response."

"But why does she hate Chinese food?" Mitch asks.

"That amino-acid, combined with a DNA marker that your wife carries, has made your daughter's saliva glands react when they come in contact with an ingredient in sweet-and-sour sauce. She needs a specific drug cocktail to swarm the bad cells and a catalyst to jump start it."

Dawn jumps into the conversation, "What drug cocktail?"

"It's complicated, but sweet-and-sour sauce is definitely the catalyst."

In unison, Mitch and Dawn grab Graham's arms and escort him to the nurse's station. They begin talking to the ward clerk about getting an urgent request to Dr. Parton. The young clerk is overwhelmed by all the information they give her, but unable to interfere as the procedure is already underway.

Over the many 'I'm sorry' responses from the clerk, Graham slips away and enters a 'Staff Only' door that leads to the operating suites. He finds the one marked with 'Patient Castle' and slips into the theater.

Dr. Parton is ready to begin the process of removing Emily's leg. He enters the sterile field with a circular bone-saw and lines up the blade on the mark.

Graham snatches a surgical gown from a neatly-folded stack on a supply room shelf. He holds a mask over his face and bursts into the operating room.

The only time Graham had ever entered a surgical suite before was to change the light bulbs when the room was not in use.

Shelly, whose back is to the door, looks up and notices a technician's averted eyes. She turns her back on the patient and catches a glimpse of the unauthorized visitor.

"Dr. Parton!" she calls, "Behind you!"

The surgeon quickly lifts the saw, and turns to confront the intruder.

"What the meaning of this?" barks Dr. Parton.

Adjusting her focus, Shelly quickly recognizes the intruder.

"Graham?"

Two other technicians chime in with varying responses, all pointing to the fact it is definitely Shelly's unemployed husband.

"Stop!" begs Graham, "She doesn't have to lose her leg."

An outraged Dr. Parton aims the bone-saw in Graham's direction.

"Son, you better think about what you're doing right now."

"Graham," Shelly pleads, "You need to go."

"But she needs a drug cocktail, instead."

Hoping to calm the situation, Dr. Parton explains the earlier drug therapy to Graham.

"We administered the newest, most powerful antibiotics and she did not respond to them. Please, I need to continue."

Standing at the suite's observation window is Jay Kenly, the Chief of Security. He had arrived along with another security member to escort Graham out.

Feebly, Graham attempts to explain himself.

"I saw the chart; the antibiotics you tried are wrong, since she carries a gene that neutralizes their effects. She needs a cocktail of different drugs along with a catalyst that will trick her body into thinking it has the Black

Plague. I know it sounds crazy, but what saved her ancestors hundreds of years ago can save her today."

"The Black Plague, you're insane!" Dr. Parton waves for the guards to enter, "We don't have time for this."

The two security guards take Graham by the shoulders and drag him from the room.

Shelly is overcome with embarrassment and apologizes profusely to the doctor.

"I don't know what's wrong with him," she adds, "but he did lose his job last week."

The staff glances at each other, avoiding Shelly's eyes. One technician interrupts.

"C'mon Shelly, your husband loses his job one day and thinks he's a doctor the next. He might need some – you know – help."

Outside the Operating Room, Graham continues to plead his case to anyone who will listen. "Geez, Jay, you know me. Let me at least write something down."

As he walks between the two security guards, Graham repeats aloud the serum combination.

"She needs a cocktail of Fluoxetine, Paroxetine, and a benign form of the pathogen Yersinia pestis called YP-x."

Jay and the other security guard eventually escort Graham outside to wait for the police to arrive.

As the surgical suite quiets, Dr. Parton asks for a re-sterilization of the room so he can proceed with the amputation.

Shelly steps out of the procedure, and a replacement nurse enters. She rushes to the staff lounge and collapses in the nearest chair.

***

Graham sits with his hand on his forehead, as the police car arrives in the lot. A pile of cigarette butts dot the sidewalk in front of him.

While waiting for the official charges, Graham thinks about his actions and begins to question himself. Being able to connect billions of information strands together is an amazing ability. He realizes he must temper his zeal with a more diplomatic approach in the future.

There is a limit to Graham's memory, however. The accrued and paired information only stays visible in his conscious mind for about ninety minutes. After that, the entire burst of connected thoughts fades from the brain's cortex and becomes irretrievable.

***

The head of administration at St. Theodota Hospital regrettably delivers a formal complaint against Graham. The police are instructed to take him downtown to the city jail.

Several hours have passed and Shelly still sits motionless in the nurses' lounge. The familiar sound of her phone nudges her back to reality. It is a message from Dr. Parton, informing her the procedure went smoothly. Shelly is relieved, but somewhat torn. Her thoughts are suspended in an odd dichotomy: is Graham's photographic memory enough to push aside decades of highly-trained medical practitioners?

Feeling that her personal storm has run its course, Shelly leaves the hospital to bail her husband out of jail. Once she arrives, the process of posting bail becomes tedious and wears on her already frayed nerves.

"Look, I've signed everything you've asked for and paid the bond. Now where's my husband?!"

"Ma'am, calm down; he's apparently resisting release."

Two large jailers drag an unwilling Graham to the booking desk. His head is slung downward and his eyes avert all others. He is remorseful about jeopardizing his wife's career.

"Graham, it's okay. The surgery went fine. Let's go home."

Equally solemn, Graham follows Shelly to the car. The sunset is ignored, as both replay the series of events which transpired over the past twelve hours. Smoking a cigarette, Graham figures that his memory is better suited for amusement purposes only and not for practicing medicine. Sighing, he recalls reading about the patient in the photographic memory study.

I don't want to end up a mute nut-case waving at strangers all day.

Chapter 08

On Monday morning, Graham awakens to a call from Shelly, who has already been at work for two hours.

"Graham, I've got some interesting news for you."

He answers with sullen sarcasm, "They found more charges against me?"

"No, listen; I tried to call you earlier, but you were probably asleep." Shelly continues, "I was told that late last night Emily's condition worsened. As a last resort, I begged Dr. Parton to try using Fluoxetine, Paroxetine, and YP-x."

"What are those?"

"Those are three components of the drug cocktail you shouted by the elevator."

"I remember shouting, but that's about it."

"Well, I had Jay Kenly replay the security camera footage. I heard you reciting the drug cocktail and the dosage just before you were hauled away."

"I guess I should write stuff down next time, huh?" Not waiting for a response he asks, "Well, did you try them? Did they work?"

"Sort of; we administered the cocktail about an hour ago."

"Is she going to be okay?"

"I don't know, but she's not getting any worse."

Graham takes a second to collect his thoughts.

"Hello, Graham?" Shelly teases.

"Yeah, sorry, I'm still here."

"I ran into Dr. Kooport, our Chief of Epidemiology. He was surprised that anyone had even heard of that clinical drug trial. He said it began only two days ago in a small village in India."

Graham's ears locked in on the word 'India' as he attempted to concentrate on what was missing in the drug cocktail equation.

India, China, um… Australia. What was it now?

"Honey, I've got to get back to work; I'll see you later, okay?"

"Yeah, sure. Bye."

Graham hangs up and turns his attention to finding a new job. He emails his résumé to several companies looking for a maintenance man. While online, he notices a local motel has an opening for a handyman, and is reviewing applicants on-site. Graham decides to take his mind off his problems by driving over for an interview.

Getting into his car, he is able to refocus on working. The motel is not far from home, but the time on the road is long enough to help ease some of the stress he has been feeling since being laid off.

Pulling into the quaint Sleep Tight Motel, Graham can see that it is in desperate need of a good maintenance man. He pulls into a space in front of the office. Graham gets out of his car and looks around before going in. The area seems familiar.

He does not recall staying at the Sleep Tight Motel, especially with Shelly, as she hates this part of town. But a sense of déjà vu follows him as he approaches the front desk.

An older, graying man behind the desk looks up as Graham approaches. His bored expression changes to a slight degree of disgust. Even though Graham has not said anything, the old man knows why he is there.

He points to an outside staircase, "286."

Graham walks out of the office and up the stairs and knocks on room 286. The door opens and he enters the room.

Minutes later the old man at the front desk leaves his post to water some flowers, which line the walkway in front of the motel. Graham exits the room and descends the stairs. He is unsure how the interview went, even to a point of confusion. He focuses momentarily on the old man.

"Hey, Mister," Graham says, "is there a problem?"

"No sir," he replies while scratching his neck, "we don't need any help around here is all."

"It's a little late since I just interviewed for a job fixing this place up." Graham takes a quick survey of the motel's exterior, "In fact you may see a lot more of me around here."

"I seen enough already."

He goes back to watering the flowers. A young woman exits the motel, oblivious. She bumps into Graham on her way to the parking lot, and her handbag falls to the ground.

Graham immediately stoops down to help the woman by shoving the scattered contents back into her bag. He looks up at her and is somewhat surprised.

"Terah?"

The young woman looks demurely back on him, "I'm sorry; you must have me confused with someone else."

"It's me; Graham Duncan. I tried to see you the other day."

The woman is startled and nervously juggles a few of the collected items. "Thank you."

"Hold on; you are Terah Piper from the hypnosis clinic, right?"

Though the woman becomes flustered, she remains politely defiant. "Sir, I think you have me confused with someone else." She gathers a business card from her purse.

"I'm Rhea Tipper, and I work at *Their Paper* office supply. We're in the River Village Center."

Graham studies the card. "I'm sorry. You could be her sister."

"Well, thanks for the help," Rhea clutches her things.

The old man finishes watering, shaking his head in disgust as he walks back into the office.

Rhea, still a little shaken by the purse incident, backs up to her car, watching Graham the entire time. She gets in, starts it quickly, and drives to the main road.

Graham watches her leave, while he gets into his car.

As he drives, he is hypnotized by the trees that pattern Belle View Boulevard. Even though he stares straight ahead, the vehicle drifts over the center line. He is aware of his lax driving but does nothing to correct it.

A horn blares from oncoming traffic, and Graham is immediately shocked back into reality. He gives a hard right correction to the steering wheel, sending his car sliding safely into one of the lush, manicured lawns. Graham curses to himself, shoving the shifter into reverse and screeching backward onto the road. He decides to check on Terah over at Dr. Jerome's clinic before going home.

Pulling into the office complex, Graham recognizes the other tenants - a dog groomer, a hearing aid center, and a health-food store.

Looking around, angry thoughts careen through his head.

Why was my appointment cancelled? Why was I erased from their records? Why would Terah lie to me?

Grabbing the car door, he throws it open and steps forcefully out onto the pavement. Slamming the door, he starts toward the office, hoping to confront Terah.

Graham opens the door and walks toward the reception area, but there is no desk or medical equipment. Confused, he turns to make sure he has walked through the correct door. The number matches the address he had memorized. He looks forward again and realizes he is not in a medical clinic. Backing out through the door as a saleswoman approaches him, Graham smiles and waves her off with a, "sorry, wrong place."

As he continues to back out of the office, he looks up to confirm his location. But instead of the "Clinic" sign he recalled, large black letters spell out "Crafts."

Chapter 09

Shelly sits in the hospital cafeteria, picking at her chicken salad and thinking alternately about Graham and Emily. She agonizes over her patient, whose organs have begun to shut down. Emily's parents have also accepted the turn of events with a sense of forbearance.

Graham barely hears his cell phone over the song on the jukebox. He is on his third beer and has been parked on a barstool since leaving the strip mall an hour ago. After a job interview and then stumbling into a craft store, Graham has had enough reality for one day. He picks up his phone and tries to shout over the music.

"Hello?!"

"Honey, it's Shell," she shouts over the blaring music, "The drug cocktail is not working on Emily. She's dying."

Graham does not answer.

"Where are you?" she asks loudly, "Have you been drinking?"

"I'd rather have a lobotomy in front of me, than a... oh wait, that's not right."

"Listen, this is serious. We must've missed something. Do you remember any other ingredients?"

"No, I just remember being dragged out of the operating room."

Shelly advises him she will stay later to meet with Emily's parents.

Graham orders another beer.

***

Shelly approaches the Castle family which now includes Emily's two brothers who flew in the previous night. A priest is also in attendance to offer emotional support and to perform last rites.

Shelly escorts the family to an empty examination room down the hall.

"I realize this is a difficult time for you, but I need to ask you a few more questions."

Mitch assumes Shelly is working on behalf of an organ transplant team. His lips are pressed together tightly. Dawn stares.

"What do you want now?"

Calmly, Shelly holds out both hands. She closes her eyes for a second and begins her explanation.

"My husband talked to both of you right before Emily's surgery."

Mitch's face contorts, as he steps closer to Shelly, "You mean the crazy man who impersonated a doctor? I heard you two were connected somehow."

A fearless Shelly stands as tall as her frame will allow her. "Do you remember what he asked you?"

"He asked us a lot of things. He wasted our time. He got our hopes up."

Shelly turns to Dawn and repeats the question.

Softly, she answers.

"He asked if Emily ever had the measles. He also talked about a certain gene that Mitch's family carried." Dawn pauses in an effort to recall more of their conversation. "He said it kept their family safe from the Plague."

"Is there anything else you can remember?"

She looks downward and shakes her head. "No, just that drug cocktail and the stuff about our ancestors."

Mitch raises his hand, like an eager student. "Your husband, somehow he knew Emily can't eat Chinese food? I mean he just—"

Shelly interrupts. "When you say 'can't eat', you mean she's allergic to it?"

"No, she just hates the way it tastes. Your husband said it was a 'catalyst' or something like that."

Shelly mumbles under her breath. "A biochemical catalyst, I see." She puts her hand on Dawn's shoulder. "I might have something for the doctor to try. Be strong."

Not waiting for the elevator, Shelly yanks open the heavy stairway door and runs down to the ground level of the hospital.

Arriving at the cafeteria she asks between breaths if she could get some Chinese food. Temporarily blinded by her mission, she has lost track of the days. The cafeteria cashier explains that today is pizza day and Thursday is Chinese food.

Frustrated, she races to the storage office and finds the Food Services manager. Shelly pleads for her to open a can of sweet-and-sour sauce. Before the manager can ask why, Shelly produces a twenty dollar bill and begs to buy a can.

Moments later, she is bounding up the stairs to Emily's bed in the I.C.U.

Inside the unit, a pulmonary technician stands at the foot of Emily's bed, writing in her chart. Emily is now too weak to breathe on her own. The haunting cadence of the mechanical ventilator joins the other sounds in the room.

Shelly puts on a new scrub gown and re-garbs her shoes. She explains to the tech that Dr. Parton wants to know the latest blood gas numbers. The technician mentions that it might be logged with her telemetry readings. Shelly turns her head towards the nurses' station.

"It's not going to get itself."

The pulmonary technician is apprehensive. While he searches for the report, Shelly opens Emily's feeding tube and pours in four ounces of the sauce.

The man returns and with a trace of sarcasm informs Shelly that Dr. Parton has already seen the new report.

"Excellent, thank you," Shelly nods and causally walks out. She is tired and plods toward the parking garage.

It is not until Shelly is nearly home that Dr. Parton texts an urgent message to her.

Come to ICU immediately!

She cranks the wheel of her car sharply to the left and almost collides with a delivery truck going the other direction. Her mind is focused on Dr. Parton's text.

She hops out of her car and runs inside to the elevator. Tapping and re-tapping the 'up' button, Shelly leans against the frame of the elevator in exhaustion. The doors open and assorted hospital staff flow out into the lobby. She leans into her step and punches the fourth floor button before she is fully inside the elevator. The doors close just as a group of visitors approach.

Shelly arrives in the ICU and makes her way to Emily's empty bed. A wave of sadness washes over her.

Naomi Larson, the charge nurse for the ICU, sees Shelly out of the corner of her eye. She walks over; her heavily lined face is near expressionless from her many years of experience. "I've never seen anything like this before."

Shelly's eyes redden. Her tears wander down her cheeks waiting to be judged 'joyful' or 'sorrowful.'

"Oh, she's not dead," Naomi advises, "She's been moved to Recovery."

Shelly speeds over to the Recovery floor.

Dr. Parton sees her approaching and waves.

"Shelly, come here. I'd like you to meet Emily Castle."

Her answer takes the form of an awkward statement.

"Oh, my; you're alive."

Emily's voice is faint but grateful, "I am."

After excusing himself from the circle of family members, Dr. Parton pulls Shelly out into the hall with him.

"It took a while, but the drug cocktail seems to have worked."

"Yes, that and the—"

Dr. Parton's exuberance spills over as he interrupts Shelly.

"That combination of drugs we administered completely wiped out the virus. Simply amazing," he pauses, and holds up one hand. "You know, Kooport and I are writing a paper together. We'll no doubt get some credit for those drug trials in India."

Shelly attempts to cite the sweet-and-sour sauce catalyst as the deciding factor in Emily's recovery, "What do you think of testing patients for severe, non-allergic food reactions?"

Dr. Parton squints as he tries to understand Shelly's idea, "Why would that matter?"

"To find a unique genetic catalyst, maybe?"

"Shelly, your husband's photographic memory might have retained this obscure drug trial through something he saw. I'll give him that but—"

"How do you explain the genetic catalyst?" she presses, "How'd he know about that?"

"What are you talking about?" The doctor reaches for the pair of glasses in his coat pocket and methodically places them on, "what catalyst?"

"Less than an hour ago, I tube-fed Emily four ounces of sweet-and-sour sauce."

"You what?!"

"Graham somehow knew Emily's adverse reaction would stimulate her immune system."

Dr. Parton looks away from Shelly in disbelief. His eyes adjust to a point down the corridor.

"If this, this 'personalized' catalyst *is* responsible for Castle's rapid recovery, how was Graham able to connect it all together?"

"I don't know," Shelly says, "Maybe it's an advanced form of photographic memory."

"You know, this reminds me of the old neurologists' theory that every major medical discovery was just combining information we already knew."

Shelly steps backward, gently bumping the wall.

Dr. Parton resumes his intense eye contact with her.

"As you know, the mind imprints billions of sensory events in minute detail directly to the frontal cortex over a lifetime. However, the ability to connect the massive amounts of memory strands into comprehensible information takes years, even a lifetime."

"So, what you're telling me is that I have the knowledge to cure cancer, I just can't connect it all together?"

"Precisely," Dr. Parton peers back into Emily's room, "But Graham knows. Somehow he's able to connect hundreds, thousands, billions of random strands together as if they were one simple pattern."

"That's pretty amazing, don't you think?"

"No, not really," the doctor sighs, "not for someone with Hyper Neural Access."

***

The garage door opens and Graham slips his car in next to Shelly's. Taking more time than usual to get out of his car, Graham finally begins his defeated shuffle to the back door. He carries this demeanor while passing through the kitchen. Shelly, wearing a tired smile, is draped across the sofa.

"Well, you look happy," Graham mutters.

"It's not every day that an unemployed maintenance man saves a life."

His face lights up, "Emily's okay?"

"Honey, you have a gift."

"I can't believe it!" He walks over and joins Shelly on the sofa, "Really though, I'm just a guy who naps and figures things out somehow."

"You know, Einstein took several naps a day too."

"I'm no Einstein."

"Hold on," she raises her right hand, "it's not just 'resting' you two have in common, it's more like a focused concentration."

Graham takes a deep breath.

"So, Emily's going home soon?"

"Thanks to you, Albert," Shelly smiles.

Chapter 10

"While many will celebrate the rise of a great orator, they too will cheer his demise by the false witness of the wicked. Orphaned shall be the ideas that once inspired bold action." —Charles Thomas Alcott.

The next morning, Shelly is awakened by the television rather than her alarm clock.

Graham has pushed three television sets into the den; each is tuned to a different channel. One show is about biology, another about inventions, and the third about quantum mechanics. A confusing cabal of audio and video is sorted and stored in Graham's mind in milliseconds. He is also reading through Shelly's collection of medical journals.

Shelly, still wearing her night shirt, walks into the den. Graham's concentration is averted to her presence, "Oh, sorry, Shell. Is it too loud?"

"Yeah, and a little too creepy."

"Well, you can't invent cold-fusion energy without knowing how stuff works."

Shelly rubs her eyes and walks back down the hallway.

Graham mutes all three TVs as if waving a magic wand, "Ta da. It's all just a power-nap away."

"I'm going in early today. You stay here and," she points at the TVs, "and do *this*."

***

Arriving at St. Theodota's, Shelly is confronted in the nursing staff break room by Dr. Kooport. He has overlaid the chemical structure of sweet-and-sour sauce on Emily Castle's DNA markers.

"This is still difficult to believe," Dr. Kooport squints at Shelly, "Your husband's formulation of this was so quick and precise."

"Well, he's been very focused lately."

"Ms. Duncan, possessing Hyper Neural Access is more than just being focused."

"HNA, is that real?"

"Yes, to a certain extent, but there are problems associated with this particular syndrome."

The doctor, stroking his goatee, discusses some of the more dangerous aspects of HNA.

"Patterning massive amounts of information strains the frontal cortex."

"Okay…" Shelly responds cautiously.

"If he continues the heavy load structuring, it could become a more serious problem."

"Like?"

"It is sometimes referred to as, 'Catatonic Insanity'. But physiologically, it's a collapse of the speech center and—."

"Oh sh—" she covers her mouth.

"And I'm afraid his mind will attempt to work around this deficiency." Dr. Kooport adds, "but this autonomic reprogramming would make him very unstable."

Her hand falls to her side and her mouth drops open in disbelief.

"What do I do? How do I stop this?"

"I don't think you can."

"Well I've got to do something, right?"

"I would suggest you support him as not to shatter this fragile reality his mind is building."

A tear streaks down her cheek.

"But for how long?"

The doctor shrugs and walks out of the room. The pneumatic door closes slowly with a sustained creaking noise.

***

Graham spends the entire day parked on the sofa watching the three television sets. Documentaries on space-travel, marine biology, and ancient ruins are just some of the programs he's viewed.

Shelly arrives home and sees Graham exactly where she left him ten hours ago. The sight of her husband cramming information nonstop into his mind was amusing that morning, but now she is disturbed by it.

At midnight, the televisions are silenced. The huge stacks of magazines stand like a quiet skyline. He looks around, bleary-eyed, knowing if he falls into a full REM sleep, he won't be able to use his memory. Before settling down on the couch, he quietly sets an alarm clock to wake him in 20 minutes. He places it on the coffee table and closes his eyes.

'Incredible' is the only word Graham's subconscious can use to describe all the new information. His emotions are playing a larger role in altering and connecting memory strands. As he wakes up, he takes down a few notes.

I just woke up from a twenty minute power nap. I made a routine memory grab and I'm examining it as I write this.

I see clearly, but am confused by the content. It's a diagram with what appears to be three holes drilled into a ball of some sort.

There is a reference to my own subconscious in these mental notes. As I compare the connected memory strands, I'm left with a formula that I believe involves physics.

I'm frustrated because I didn't get the results I wanted. I hoped for more general knowledge.

I'll file this as an incomplete event. Or maybe it's part of a series. I don't really know.

Later that morning, Shelly wakes and gets ready for work. On her way to the garage she notices Graham still on the couch, restlessly sleeping. She begins the drive to work, but is distracted. She tries to call Graham on her way in.

"Hi, Honey. I hope I didn't wake you?"

"You did, but I needed to get up and finish my notes."

"Notes?"

Graham pauses, and tries to sound coherent, "I've got to drill some holes into something today."

"That doesn't very scientific."

"There's a little more to it."

"Well you take it easy, ok?"

"Yeah, okay, bye."

After hanging up the phone, Graham spends two hours reviewing his notes and sketches before his memory retention fades. He is determined to induce another power nap. Setting his alarm again, Graham forces himself onto the sofa. When he wakes up, he continues in his notebook.

This looks familiar: Wire. It's copper.

I also saw a list of seven chemicals to make into a compound:
1. Boric Acid
2. Nitrate
3. Acetone
4. Cupric Sulfate
5. Hydrofluoric Acid
6. Naphthalene
7. Sodium Hydroxide

Some of the compounds need to be bonded with a torch. Not sure what the final mixture will create, or even if it will be safe.

I'm supposed to immerse a small roll of copper wire into the chemical compound. The contents must be heated to over six thousand degrees Fahrenheit. I can use my oxyacetylene torch.

At lunchtime, Shelly sits alone in the cafeteria, debating whether or not to call Graham. She gives in to curiosity and makes the call.

A noticeably groggy Graham answers.

Shelly playfully asks, "May I speak to Albert Einstein, please?"

"Shell, I think I just created a new metal coating or something. I don't know what it's for."

"Maybe Benny can use it for another one of his piercings."

Graham answers with a nervous laugh. "I'm more frustrated now than before. The two pieces don't connect."

"I'm sure you'll figure it out. I'll see you when I get home, okay?"

"Yeah, okay."

Sighing, he puts down the phone and purposely sends himself back into a controlled nap.

I tried focusing on deep space travel, but I could only think about gathering more and more information. I felt I needed to be exposed to more knowledge, and much faster than in real time.

All this latest power nap consisted of was surfing the internet. Nothing special about that.

I saw a three-pronged plug, much like a standard alternating current, with a ground wire attached. There was one small difference: at the other end was a USB plug.

My final page from this strand shows a map of the human brain. There are three dots on it showing different areas of the brain. This could show a tri-cortex collapse, like I read about online.

I am documenting this because it could be the end of any coherent thoughts.

I love you very much, Shelly.

- Graham Duncan

Chapter 11

The next morning, Shelly's thought of interrupting Graham is suppressed. She recalls his sleep patterns have dramatically altered along with his disposition.

On Monday he was social and congenial. On Tuesday he was still affable and friendly, but definitely showing signs of sleep deprivation. Yesterday, he seemed agitated by my presence. He was barely able to make eye contact the entire evening. And this morning, all he did was sit at the end of the bed, wide awake.

"Graham, this is not normal," Shelly advises softly, "You need to sleep, not just nap."

"No can do. I got to keep trying until I invent something."

"But you can't keep pushing yourself."

"Shell, I'll stop," he looks into her eyes, "just not right now."

"Okay, look. About your photographic memory," Shelly takes a second to find the right words, "it might be something more advanced."

"Yeah, I know. It's called Hyper Neural Access."

She falls backward, her head hitting the pillow.

"I should have known you would know that!" she grumbles.

"Well I do."

"There are dangers involved with HNA too," she pleads.

"I'm being careful."

"Graham, watching three TVs is not being careful." Shelly puts her hand on her hips, "it's being crazy."

"Give me another 'Shelly Duncan' test," Graham jokes, "Hmm, let's see, I know your birth date, your shoe size, your social security number and I know all of your friend's birth dates, maiden names, and where they were born."

Shelly just stares.

"Yeah, I know, it can be dangerous," Graham continues, "but Shell, I'm okay."

"Well if I end up married to a guy in a diaper I have to spoon feed through a caged door, it's on you." Her voice trails off.

Shelly leaves for work while Graham forces himself to nap again.

***

Time sprints by when not noticed, yet drags during anticipation. Graham is unaware and unconcerned about what particular day it is. He is consumed with finding a solution to his last three HNA events.

Hearing the garage door open usually brings a subliminal message of happiness to Graham. This time, it is ignored.

Standing in the den, Shelly is stunned to see Graham not reviewing his notes as he did earlier. Instead, he just sits, still in his underwear.

"I don't want to bother you but, hi, I'm home," Shelly offers in a light voice.

Graham is depressed by his last nap. His notebook sums it up with a single blank page.

"That's it," he says, "all gone."

"What do you mean 'all gone'? What's all gone?"

"My photographic memory or HNA, whatever you want to call it." He changes his tone from defeat to urgency, "Maybe you should leave the house. If I am losing my mind it may be dangerous for you to be here."

Shelly's demeanor is split between bravery and tingling nervousness.

"You're still talking, so that's a good sign."

"Yeah, but I'm not 'seeing' anything when I nap anymore."

"The real problem is you don't need a nap, you need to sleep."

Graham straightens his posture, while Shelly runs to her work bag and grabs a few sleeping pill samples.

"Here, take these."

She gets Graham to swallow the pills; seconds later, he drops off into a deep sleep.

***

On Friday morning, Shelly carefully gets up before her alarm goes off. She does not want to wake Graham. However, as she rolls over, she realizes he is not in bed.

The smell of fresh coffee, eggs, and bacon greet Shelly as she approaches the dinette table.

"What's all this?" She straightens her posture, "I guess you slept well."

Graham nods and gestures for her to sit down.

"Shell, do you want your eggs scrambled, sunny, or a little runny?"

This is as close to 'normal' as Graham has acted all week. To Shelly, it seems too domestic.

Graham greets her silence with a smile, "Sunnyside it is."

"Look, I can take the day off," Shelly insists while cautiously sitting down at the table.

"No need, I slept great last night. And I made breakfast without setting the house on fire," he says while sliding the eggs onto her plate.

She stares curiously at her breakfast.

"It looks right," she stabs a piece with her fork and holds it up to her face, "but you don't cook."

He points to his temple, "I know what a thousand chefs know."

"Of course, that's normal."

She finishes her breakfast and before she leaves for work Graham hands Shelly a travel mug filled with coffee.

Chapter 12

If you could measure the brightness of the spark of an idea, or had a meter that could test a man's resolve, you'd find both readings high when applied to Graham Duncan.

The solution to finding what the recent HNA events he noted was simple; they were a pattern. Graham just laid them out in order, including the blank page.

After a trip to a hardware store, a pharmacy, and a janitorial supply depot, Graham returns home with several bags of chemicals and other items. Lighting up his Oxyacetylene torch in the garage, he melts the chemical ingredients into a lead cauldron. The smoke is thick and forces him to open the side door of the garage.

He dips the spool of copper wire into the cauldron, expelling a puff of noxious steam that wafts up to the ceiling. Graham lets out his breath as the steam dissipates. He uncovers the drill press located in the back of the garage. There is noticeable urgency in his manner, as he wants to be finished before Shelly gets home.

Graham carefully places a sheet of graph paper on his head, and tapes it in place according to his notes. Using a mirror mounted on the ceiling while also holding a vanity mirror, he marks the dots on his head in black ink. He pulls the paper away and tosses it in the trash, preparing for the next step.

The submerged copper wire is now fished out of the murky solution with a pair of salad tongs he borrowed from the kitchen. Graham drops the newly coated wire into a bucket of cold water, effectively curing it.

An extension cord sits on the table with a USB plug at one end, and three separate alligator clips at the other.

With the spool of altered copper wire now cooled back to room temperature, it is time for a quick test of its conductivity. Graham runs to fetch a magnet from his refrigerator. The new coating should produce a temporary reciprocal magnetic field. He sets the magnet at one end of the stretched wire and flicks it. It glides above the wire all the way to the other end of the garage. This quantum mechanics phenomenon counteracts gravity's resistance, making the wire a super-conducting element.

Three strands of the heavy gauge wire are cut to exactly two inches long. These ends are dipped into a solution of rubbing alcohol and carefully laid on a clean shop towel.

Next, Graham swabs some alcohol on the three areas marked on his head. Hesitantly, he takes one more look at his notes, swallows hard, and switches the drill to the 'on' position. As it spools up, he turns the volume on his boombox to maximum.

The mirrors are in place and Graham takes another look at the whirring drill before lowering it to his skull. As it goes into the first marked area of his head, Graham shouts a few expletives. He is more prepared for the second and third incisions, so his groans are not as loud.

After minor blood loss, Graham steadies himself and inserts the copper wire into the holes.

Each wire probe glides in and fits snugly. Next, Graham connects the three alligator clips from the extension cord to his three prongs.

The doorbell rings. Graham flinches and realizes his groans may have attracted suspicion. The doorbell rings again. Unsteadily, he makes his way through the house to answer the front door, grabbing a ball cap from a stack in the coat closet.

Looking through the peephole, he sees Benny Edwards.

Graham opens the door.

"Hey, Benny, what's up?"

"Not much, Mr. Duncan. My mom's making me check on you, since you got fired and all."

"Well, everything's cool here," he shrugs, "hey, how's your leg?"

Blood trickles from beneath Graham's cap.

"It's all good, Mr.—" Benny's eyes widen, "Dude, your head."

Graham panics and readjusts his hat.

"Whoa, Dude!" Benny points, "You got a wire or something stuck in there!"

Graham knows he cannot reverse what has already been seen. He chooses to hide the truth in plain sight.

"No, man," Graham bends forward, exposing all of the homemade electrodes, "I've got three."

Benny winces, but rebounds quickly. "Brutal piercings, man."

"Just got them done. It's real big in the Sudan right now."

"Cool, how much was it?"

"I don't know if you're old enough."

"Geez, my mom would never co-sign for that."

"Benny," Graham peers over the boy's shoulder, "let's keep this on the 'DL' okay?"

"Yeah, sure, Mr. D."

He slinks home, managing to soothe his mother's concerns about Graham's safety with, 'Mr. Duncan? He's totally cool.'

The concerned neighbor has been satisfied, so Graham returns to his project. He connects one alligator clip to each electrode, and powers up his computer. Just before Graham plugs in the USB cable, his phone rings.

The voice is frantic, "Stop!"

"Who is this?"

"It doesn't matter; you're in danger."

The voice on the other end begins to sound familiar to him.

"Is this, Jennifer?"

A long pause is broken by her admission.

"Yes."

Graham is somewhat relieved that at least someone is attempting to talk him out of plugging his head directly into the Internet. "By the way, where did your clinic go?"

"It doesn't matter."

"Are you watching me?"

"Yes," Jennifer admits.

"Why?"

"I – we – have been concerned, since learning of your Hyper Neural Access traits."

He looks downward searching for answers. "I've been concerned about it, too. But why do you care?"

She offers information about Hyper Neural Access, beginning with Dr. Jerome's research. However, not only was the patient's name removed from the collected data, so was the researcher's.

"Find the case study on HNA," she instructs, "In the lower right corner, you'll see the letters D-H-P-J-P. That's Dr. Jerome. He knew all names would be redacted by the government."

Graham clicks on the research report he bookmarked earlier.

"It's his initials and credentials," Jennifer explains, "It's just backward so a complex algorithm would miss it."

"Okay, Dr. Jerome has a PhD."

"Listen, Graham, this is very important," Jennifer directs him to the extensive notes Dr. Jerome included with the study. "Do you see the paragraph about how the patient could experience a massive mental collapse?"

"Yeah, so what? I don't know what happened to him, but I feel fine."

"Euphoria, curiosity, denial, and then madness. It's happening." Jennifer's voice reflects a hint of sorrow. "Graham, that case study – it's you."

"What?"

"Do you see the initials 'DGP' in the document?"

Graham carefully searches the page. "I don't have a 'P' in my name."

"The 'P' stands for patient."

"I see Jerome one time and right away I become his research paper."

"I'm afraid it is not that simple," Jennifer's voice cracks, "you're very unstable right now."

Graham forces out a nervous laugh, "I think I know what I'm doing."

"Look what's happening to you. Loss of sleep, irrational behavior, and a god complex is beginning to take hold."

"I save a girl's life, and you call it a 'god complex'?"

"A few days ago, your mind began internally walling off all cogent thought," Jennifer breaks it down further for Graham to understand," Your ego is spinning all bad news by making you out to be some sort of genius superhero ."

"Are you telling me I didn't save Emily Castle's life?"

"Do you really think a maintenance man could figure out a complex medical formula?"

"My wife told me Emily is going home soon."

"Graham, Fluoxetine and Paroxetine are just the anti-depressants Prozac and Paxil; you were given them in therapy after your parents died."

"No, that's not possible. These are new drugs. They're being tested in India."

"And really, Graham; pretending sweet-and-sour sauce is some sort of metabolic catalyst?" Jennifer pauses long enough to let her words sink in, "You had Chinese food the day before. It was a coincidence."

"But she recovered."

"Of course. My friend, Dr. Henderson works in the E.R. and he told me about a girl who came in the other day with a broken leg. Her name? Emily Castle."

"But I saw her, lying on the table about to get her leg amputated. I tried to stop it!"

"No, they were setting her fractured leg to put a cast on it. You just slowed them down."

Graham bites his lip.

"These naps I have, they seem to gather patterns and bring me the results. They've never been wrong."

"That's because your mental state is 'looping' through various stages of breakdown. You're not seeing patterns; your mind has given up and chosen all answers as acceptable." She swallows nervously. "One more taxing event may stall your mind's ability to come back to reality. You've got to stop focusing on these naps immediately!"

Click.

Graham is experiencing a debilitating cycle of intrusive thoughts, similar to Obsessive Compulsive Disorder. He is compelled to repeatedly organize and connect millions of stored memory strands. Where this disorder strays is in his more aggressive social behavior, as exhibited in the care of Emily Castle. Similar to the Napoleon Complex, this mutated disorder merely replaces the small stature characteristic with one of a limited intellect, such as Graham's.

The intoxicating power of knowledge lures Graham away from Jennifer's foreboding counsel and back to his experiment.

BEEP.

Graham stops to listen. This is not his phone, but a car horn.

Shelly is home, but unable to pull into her parking space. Stopping short, she is surprised and somewhat suspicious to see the drill press partially blocking the garage.

Still wearing the ball-cap, Graham runs out the front door, and feebly waves at Shelly.

She rolls down her window, "Hey, what are you working on?"

"Hi, Honey, yeah, can I ask you something first?" He drags the drill-press back to the side of the garage, letting Shelly pull in completely. With the garage door rolling down, they walk into the house and stop in the kitchen.

"Shelly," Graham continues, "Emily Castle is alive, right?"

"Graham, we already went over this."

"My HNA was pretty amazing, right?"

"Okay, it was amazing," Shelly steps back.

"So amazing it seemed impossible?" Graham steps toward her.

Shelly cocks her head and squints, attempting to figure out where this line of questioning is going, "I'd call it more 'unlikely' than impossible."

"I just wanted to know if it happened the way I remembered it."

"Emily's fine, what's to know?" She focuses above Graham's eyes, and changes the subject, "What's with the hat?"

His eyes dim as he thinks of a handy excuse, "I don't know, I always wear it when I'm working in the garage."

"My college softball hat?"

Embarrassed, Graham mutters, "Go Lady Hawks?"

Sitting down at the dinner table, Graham's project is now partially exposed. He can only sit and breathe while staring straight ahead. His untested bioelectrical hypothesis is concealed under an ill-fitting hat.

Shelly is more direct. "Take it off."

Graham is not surprised by her request. Slowly, he removes it.

Shelly observes the three posts more calmly than he'd expected.

"Did you drill holes into your head?"

He shrugs.

Over the last several days, Shelly has witnessed her husband's deteriorating mental state. She elects to assist him as to keep his fragile state more intact. A straight smile returns to her face.

Graham places the notes cards he wrote on the table and explains to Shelly what all the formulas and diagrams mean. He is careful to reiterate how this could be a massive learning event.

Intrigued by Graham's bravery to branch out, Shelly is sympathetic to his actions, "I understand why this is so important. The knowledge you'll possess could help wipe out diseases or create some amazing inventions."

"Or I could become the crazy guy who waves at traffic."

"You could build something that increases our lifespan. Just like early Roman engineers who invented the first sewer systems."

"Hopefully something a little cooler than that."

Shelly walks over and puts her arms on his shoulders. "I'm so proud of you."

During the next hour, Graham and Shelly go over every detail of what to expect while he is interfaced with the Internet. First, he will connect the three alligator clips to the protruding electrodes. Second, he will plug the USB cable into his computer. Third, Graham will lie down for a power nap. He believes that his HNA abilities will connect automatically and begin to upload.

After a few minutes of careful contemplation, Graham believes he will be able to review this huge new knowledge database in his mind. Depending on his emotional state and what particular strands of information he views, the connection to related strands will occur. He also assumes it will be as before; Graham will awaken about twenty minutes after his nap and view his newly gathered strands in a patterned form.

Holding the USB line with both hands as if it were a fire hose, Shelly moves closer to the USB port. Her jaw is tight with anticipation.

Carefully, she takes the cord connected to Graham's head and plugs him to the Internet.

There is a huge spark. Graham springs up and stands stiffly on the sofa, his head looking larger. Shelly screams.

Graham drops and sits motionless. His swollen head slowly begins to regain its proper size and color.

"Oh my god," Shelly shrieks.

"Calm down Shell, I'm okay." Graham forces his eyes closed for a second, "Really, I'm fine."

Too distraught to form a simple sentence, Shelly can only gesture with her hands. His head smolders.

"All right, that's probably not supposed to happen," he pats the hot patches on his head, "but I'm not a zombie either."

She leans closer to Graham's face. "Well, you seem to know who I am." She unhooks the wires from his head. "And you're not blathering like a lunatic."

"HNA can lead to Catatonic Insanity, right?"

Suddenly the possibility dawns on her, "Yeah, a breakdown in the speech center."

"Well then, I'm still-a-talking," Graham says with a smile.

The doorbell rings.

Shelly peers through a side window and notices Benny standing at the front door, "Oh no, it's Benny. He probably heard me screaming."

"I've got this." Graham, with the singed prongs sticking out from his head, walks over and opens the front door.

"Dude, the screams," Benny says, "My mom's freaking out again."

"Yeah, Shelly had a different reaction to my new prongs than you and I did."

"You know chicks, man," Benny wipes his hair to one side, "they don't get it sometimes."

He hands Graham a plate of cookies and a card. "She made another plate for you guys. And here's Mom's number in case you need it."

"Yeah, thanks Benny. And thank your mom for us, too."

"Mr. Duncan?" Benny begins motioning to Graham by tapping the back side of his own head. "You missed a spot."

After extinguishing the final spot on his head, he and Shelly lean against the door until it closes.

The new plate of cookies joins the other two, mixed inside a container in the refrigerator.

Graham plops down on a bar stool in the kitchen. "Well, we have dessert."

"Really, how many plates has she brought us lately?"

"I think it's Ron being out of town so much. She's probably lonely."

Graham's thoughts return to entering Shauna's cell-phone number into his phone. He removes the slip of paper from the plate but stops when he reads the number. Suddenly he realizes the last three digits match the ones he saw while viewing memory of the day he was fired.

321

Why would Miguel call Shauna?

"Shell, I'm going to run Shauna's empty cookie plates back over and maybe calm her down a little too."

"Good idea," Shelly stacks three plates for him to return. "And Graham, pick a different hat."

He finds his Washington Nationals cap and walks out the door.

Shelly takes the opportunity to call to Dr. Parton.

"Hello Shelly," he answers.

"You're not going to believe this, but Graham hooked his head up to the internet."

"He what?!"

"He drilled three holes into his skull and attached a cable to his computer."

"Shelly," the Doctor recomposes himself, "okay, let me see, just remain calm and supportive. Do not, under any circumstance, intervene."

"Yeah, I've been doing that," she huffs, "but it's getting weird, fast."

"If he perceives you're trying to restrict him somehow, this superiority complex he's developed may turn violent."

"So, I'll just let it play out, right? That's what Kooport told me."

"Shelly, listen to me; as long as he knows who he is we're okay." Dr. Parton adds, "You've been trained for this, now handle it."

Before she can respond the Doctor hangs up. She holds her phone out in front of her mouth and shouts several expletives at it.

Graham has arrived on the front step of Shauna Edwards' home and rings the doorbell. Benny pulls the oversized door open and yells, "Mom, it's Mr. Duncan."

She emerges from a room down the hall, "Hi, Graham," Shauna pauses, looking at the plates, "You ate the cookies that fast?"

"Oh, no, we just have so many of your plates."

"How thoughtful. And I know things are tough for you two right now, so if Ron or I can help, please let us know. You have my number, right?"

"Yeah, thanks," Graham locks eyes with Shauna. He senses something different about her.

"Okay then," Shauna breaks the awkward silence.

A sense of resolve comes over Graham. "Do you know Miguel Sanchez?"

"No," she squints, "I'm sorry that name doesn't ring a bell."

"Has someone called you recently? A wrong number maybe?"

"Oh, I got a message the other day. It was just random noises, like an old fax machine."

"Did you erase it?"

"No; I mentioned it to Ron and he wants to hear it when he gets back from his business trip."

"Can I take a listen?"

Shauna invites Graham to wait in the living room while she retrieves her phone. The room is decorated in early American Colonial style. Walking back with her cell phone, Shauna cues up the message.

Handing her phone to Graham, she instructs him to push the button on the left side of the phone. Graham, not accustomed to the case, fumbles the phone onto the carpeting.

"Oops, sorry."

"I bought this Phone Caddy a few days ago and it's just the worst. It's supposed to protect the phone and keep it from slipping out of my hands, it does neither."

Graham presses the button, and hears a recording of several oscillating tones, with a series of stuttering beeps at the end. It runs about ten seconds before abruptly stopping.

"You're right; it does sound like a fax machine."

Graham declares it a misdial, thanks Shauna, and walks back home.

Shelly greets him, and informs him dinner will be later than usual. She encourages him to take a nap, so he can focus on the knowledge he downloaded from the Internet.

Graham lies back on the couch, his wired prongs sticking clumsily into the pillow. Every adjustment brings a brief pain to his head.

"Hey Shell, it's time I went wireless," Graham jokes.

"I'll get some hand sanitizer from the bathroom."

She forcefully grabs each embedded wire and pulls it free. Graham's tissue has already begun regenerating. Shelly places antiseptic bandages over the wounds.

Graham drops off into a twilight nap without fully laying down. Shelly waits quietly for a moment before going back over to the kitchen.

The vast cyberspace screen-shot Graham acquired is unfortunately overloaded with social networking. A giant clog of self congratulations highlights every minuscule achievement. This flood of narcissism – conveyed by text, pictures, and video – serves as a testament: the more people talk, the less they have to say. Graham wades through the minutia searching for useable patterns.

Emotions begin to select and pair the memory strands Graham views when he resumes consciousness. Although he wants to focus on more medical cures, he is forced to focus on smaller, more personal issues.

Of all the wrong numbers to dial, why did Miguel call Shauna? What was that message of oscillating tones supposed to be?

Graham's subconscious presents its case by replaying the exact recording over and over. The Hyper Neural Access is clear in its recollection. Several other memory strands, supplied by his brief internet hookup, attach themselves to the recording.

Other information he recalled from old Department of Defense files was summoned to help decipher the digitized language. One common thread Graham finds is the binary algorithm used in the message. In an earlier conversation with Jennifer, she remarked about how Dr. Jerome used a similar technique to fool a sophisticated computer program.

The memory strands finish their connections, partially hampered by the huge amount of new information.

Graham springs up quickly; his eyes are not fully focused yet, "Shelly! Shelly! Where are you? Shelly?!"

"Right here, Graham. It's okay; I'm right here."

"Shell, don't eat the cookies!"

"What?"

"The cookies. They've been poisoned!"

"What? Why would Shauna poison us?"

"You know my old boss, Miguel; he called and left a message on Shauna's phone. She's never met him. Isn't that a little strange?"

"And that means 'kill the Duncans?'"

"Yeah. Sort of."

Shelly attempts to calm Graham with a reasonable explanation.

"Ron's an electrical engineer and Miguel's an electrician, right? Ron probably gave Miguel his wife's cell number instead of his by mistake. Besides, I already ate two."

"You what?!"

Chapter 13

The squeal of Graham's car tires emphasizes his urgency to get Shelly to the hospital.

"I feel fine," Shelly repeats, but Graham's seriousness makes her toggle between calm and frightened. During the short but unnervingly fast ride to the hospital, Shelly shows more signs of motion sickness than of being poisoned.

Pulling into St. Theodota's emergency room parking lot, Graham escorts Shelly to the front desk. He attempts to explain her situation, but she walks past the desk and into the ER. She greets some of her co-workers and hops up on an examination table in the first empty suite she finds.

Dr. Jordan Henderson, head of emergency medicine at St. Theodota's, is busy suturing a teenage boy's scalp wound. The boy's mother is standing on the other side of the table, mumbling words of support.

A young nurse pokes her head into the examining room.

"Doctor, you have a special guest waiting for you in Exam Room Five."

He motions for the nurse to enter the room and finish the boy's stitches.

Freed from the task, Dr. Henderson decides to triage the surprise patient ahead of an elderly woman with a low grade fever. Brashly, he yanks the curtains, sending them coasting until almost fully open.

He smiles.

"Hey, hey, it's Super Nurse. What a week you're having."

"Yeah," Shelly agrees, "pretty good, but intense."

"Your husband barging into the O.R. And then the Castle save." Dr. Henderson reaches for his clipboard. "So, what brings you to the ER?"

She shrugs awkwardly "I guess, maybe, food poisoning."

The doctor steps closer and flashes a penlight into her eyes several times.

"You know the drill; any fever or stomach pains?"

"No, but Graham insisted I come get checked out anyway."

"Your husband's here?"

"He's waiting in chairs."

"Don't take this the wrong way," his jaw tightens, "but Graham's been a little erratic since leaving St. Theo."

Shelly sighs and drops her shoulders, "He thought it was some cookies our neighbor made."

Dr. Henderson smiles, "Oh, so I'm the second opinion."

She rolls her eyes.

"Look, can you keep a secret?"

"Well, right now we've got this whole doctor-patient thing going."

Shelly leans in closer, "Doctor Kooport told me to be more supportive of Graham while he's in this fragile mental state."

"Oh, until he works though it?"

"Yeah, sort of. So, here I am."

"Okay then, let's continue. Did he eat one?"

"Nope."

"Are you sure?"

"He said he didn't."

The Doctor excuses himself from the examination room, promising to return with Imodium samples to send home with her.

While he is out, Shelly helps herself to a thermo scan unit and confirms her suspicions. She has no fever.

Dr. Henderson stops to make a call from the nurses' station, before resuming his examination.

"Maintenance, this is Miguel."

"I'm sorry; I seem to have misdialed."

"Oh, not a problem, Doctor."

Miguel hangs up the phone.

In the basement of the hospital, Miguel Sanchez quickly gathers several files from his cluttered desk, and stuffs them into a duffle bag. He walks to his workbench and picks up a small device. Pulling off several wires, he places it into a zippered pocket of the bag. To leave something out in the open can greatly reduce its sinister value.

Miguel returns to the ground floor, using an overlooked fire exit at the back of the hospital.

Seconds later, Graham enters the maintenance room in search of his old boss. He wants to ask Miguel about his call to Shauna Edwards and why he left the message, 'virus, cookies' in binary code.

His Hyper Neural Access abilities pair memory strands according to a simple rule: two is a coincidence and three becomes a pattern. While a coincidence is noted, a pattern requires immediate action.

Even though the maintenance area is cluttered with equipment, Graham knows which component is missing. He shouts out for Miguel while looking around. Listening, he hears the old fire exit door slam shut. The events form a pattern: the binary message left on Shauna's phone, a missing electrical gadget, and now his former boss is eluding him.

Miguel arrives winded at his truck and starts fumbling for his keys. Graham blasts through the steel fire exit and rushes toward him.

Before Miguel can unlock his truck, Graham leaps in front of him. Hitting the ground and rolling to an embarrassing stop, he attempts to confront Miguel with his fists up.

"All right, Miguel. You better tell me what's going on."

"You don't work here anymore. You've got no right to be on the premises."

Still breathing deeply, Graham replies, "My wife's here."

Miguel holds up his phone, "Then let's see what the cops have to say."

Though he looks ready to fight, Graham is frozen with fear of another arrest.

Miguel unlocks his truck, and tosses the duffle bag into the passenger seat. After climbing in, he slams the door. Graham grabs at the handle, hoping to open it before the power locks are deployed. Miguel starts the engine and drops his chin in the direction of an angry, confused Graham.

He accelerates in reverse, the engine groans while the tires leave a short black stripe on the ground. Still rolling backwards, the wheels abruptly change their direction and begin spinning up loose asphalt from the parking lot. Miguel speeds away leaving Graham speechless.

St. Theodota's small contingent of security personnel emerge from a vehicle with flashing yellow lights, having noticed the breach in the fire exit door.

Jay Kenly shakes his head, immediately recognizing Graham.

"What are you doing here?" he yells out.

"I'm sorry Jay; I was just trying to talk to Miguel."

Jay approaches Graham while the other security member stands a few yards behind them.

"Confronting your old boss is definitely a bad idea."

"Are you going to hold me for the cops again?"

"Dude, I've know you too long." Jay looks back at his assistant and then turns to Graham, "if you go straight to your car, I'll tell Shelly to meet you there."

"Thanks Jay, I owe you."

"Whatever, man. Just get going."

Chapter 14

A phone call comes in to Miguel while he drives away.

"This is Sanchez."

"How did he discover the Subliminal Override message we gave Shauna Edwards?"

"I don't know. I used an old binary encoding procedure. Maybe he acted on a hunch."

"That shouldn't be possible."

"Well, he decoded the message and 'patterned' me as I fled."

"That should have been his fifth attempt, not his first."

"Can we lure him back and scramble him?"

"No, he's become very unstable."

"What does Doctor Jerome think?"

There is a long pause.

"Jerome was eliminated in a stealth attack."

"Stealth, really?"

"Duncan's counter programming is so deep it runs in the background without his knowledge."

"Is the operation still a 'go'?"

"It will be very close."

An old strategy of warfare assumes your enemy is watching for a soldier. However, if you bury a post-hypnotic tactical suggestion deep into the subconscious of a civilian, he will blend in completely until activated. Miguel and his associates are left to assume Graham is a sleeper cell for the government, searching for treasonous activity.

***

Dr. Henderson found no evidence of food poisoning or a rogue virus, and has discharged Mrs. Duncan from emergency care.

Shelly starts for the parking lot and notices Graham right away. Studying him as she walks towards the car, she is concerned. His head is drooped down and his fight with gravity is visible, as he leans crookedly against the car.

"Are you okay?" she asks.

"I'm here anyway." He looks up, "So what did Henderson say?"

"He said I'm okay. He gave me something for my stomach just in case, though."

Graham's head droops again.

"You're kidding, that's it?"

"What?" Shelly's tone sharpens, "Would you rather I'd be puking my guts out right now?!"

"No, no I'm sorry Shell. I was just so sure those cookies were laced with something."

Shelly takes the keys from Graham and calmly gets behind the wheel.

"Let's go home," she says softly.

The drive is slow and quiet. They both know how close Graham is to being detained for a thorough mental evaluation.

"I am tired," Graham acknowledges, "But I'm also frustrated."

At a red light Shelly looks at Graham, "If I croak later tonight you can say 'I told you so.' Will that make you feel any better?"

He smiles. Shelly always seems to say the right things, even if they sound wrong at the time.

The human mind, normally a good gatekeeper of its emotions, can get confused when overloaded. Sometimes, opposite responses are used, in a feeble attempt to balance out deep emotional swings. Some people cry when they are happy, or laugh when they are in pain and a few are able to replace the fear of the unknown with unwavering confidence.

***

Graham has not slept over the past forty-eight hours. He spends his days sitting at the table and staring through the dining room window, and his nights on the sofa, waiting to drift off.

Why did a scrambled message about those cookies pop up on Shauna's phone? What does that gadget Miguel took from his office do? And why is Jennifer West really watching me?

Graham's insomnia continues into Monday morning. Shelly is just about to leave for work.

"Just take it easy today. Watch some TV or something," she advises.

Graham, exhausted, flops back into the cushions and presses the remote.

Sampling documentaries, Graham finds one about Olympians of the twentieth century. Pausing for just a moment, he clicks to continue his search. He lands on a show about military leaders of the fourteenth century. Finally, he settles on a program about quirky, failed inventions.

Graham watches most of it before drifting off to sleep.

Seconds later, his mind is flooded with commonalities from the invention show. He views recent gadgets that were so bad they faded from the marketplace almost overnight. All were poorly made, and sold by telemarketers. His subconscious stops on a product called the "Phone Caddy." Graham remembers Shauna Edwards' frustration with this product on two occasions. Using his earlier screenshot of the internet, he gathers a list from a credit card database of people who purchased the Phone Caddy.

Seven hundred units were sold before the company filed for bankruptcy. A memory strand is brought up for Graham's rapid inspection. He recognizes two as celebrities and one as a past classmate. Those three names are categorized, but only as coincidences.

The next HNA paring leaves seventeen names.

Graham's subconscious accelerates and pares it to nine. He realizes he can probe deeper, but at a higher cost. By choosing to add speculation to his HNA, the trillion bits of new connections could overload his cerebral cortex. Desperate, he adds the speculative analysis to the seventeen names of Phone Caddy buyers.

Outwardly, Graham shudders as he continues his power nap on the sofa. All of his memories are fully accessed and separated into cogent categories for review and elimination.

Three names drop into the forefront of Graham's mind.

First is Dennis Zimmerman, an assistant manager at a shoe store in Omaha, Nebraska. He bought a Phone Caddy from the telemarketing firm in Fairfax, Virginia. He was later responsible for the death of a man in an automobile accident.

Second is Hector Ochoa. Hector runs a lawn crew with prominent clients in the greater Washington DC area. Hector also bought the Phone Caddy from the firm in Fairfax. Graham reviews local news accounts; while trimming hedges, Hector accidentally cut a client's shoulder. She bled out and died later at a hospital.

The final name is Shauna Edwards.

So far the names do not fully pattern. However, the man Dennis Zimmerman killed while driving drunk was Kenneth Benton. The woman Mr. Ochoa killed with his hedge trimmer was Abby Northridge.

***

Shelly's phone vibrates and she excuses herself from a pre-surgical consult with a patient and steps into the hallway.

"Graham, I'm busy right now, can it wait?" she says hurriedly.

"I found out something about Benton and Northridge."

"What?" she whispers, "Who are they?"

"Oh right, Benton and Northridge were killed by people who bought a Phone Caddy like the one Shauna has."

"So?"

"So," he responds in kind, "they were both highly decorated Colonels."

"Well, that's a coincidence."

"It's about to pattern. You see, I found an old government program where a virus was genetically assigned using their own biological makeup. When the two mixed it would trigger the virus to kill the person. Or blind them or whatever."

"You're telling me that's why Shauna's cookies didn't make me sick?"

Graham pauses.

"I think they were designed to kill me."

She sighs loudly, "Honey, you've never said a single word about being in the military; you don't even own a gun."

"Ah ha! But what if I was hypnotized to believe I wasn't ever in the military?"

"Geez, you're losing me now."

"I'm thinking Shauna Edwards is a covert spy or—or something."

"Enough Graham! This is getting out of hand. You need to just clear your head and leave this conspiracy alone for a while."

Graham pauses again.

"It does sound a little kooky, I know."

"I'll call you later, Parton's here, I've got to go."

With the HNA memory strands still fresh in his mind, Graham writes the names, dates, and addresses in the notebook he keeps next to the sofa.

***

After assisting Dr. Parton in a surgery that stretched into the early afternoon, Shelly goes to have lunch and calls to check in on Graham.

The phone picks up, but Shelly hears nothing.

"Hello? Graham, are you there?"

There is no audible response.

"Honey, I can't hear you, we must have a bad connection. I'll call you back."

She hits redial.

The line stops ringing, but she still can't hear him. Shelly is unnerved, "I think my batteries are really low. I'll talk to you later."

Before Shelly can hang up, Graham runs to their bedroom and holds the phone up to her jewelry box and opens the lid.

Upon hearing the music, she understands. Graham is unable to speak.

Chapter 15

A woman dressed in scrubs hurries toward a door marked 'employees only' located on the side of the building. Upon entering the keycard secured door, she pulls out her phone and dials.

"Yeah, I'm here. I've got it covered, Mrs. Duncan."

Shelly, prompted by Graham's haunting phone call, has secured a replacement nurse for the afternoon. She races home.

Pulling into the driveway, Shelly doesn't bother to wait for the garage door to open and screeches to a stop. Bolting from the car, she leaves the driver's door still open. She darts through the front door, leaving her keys stuck in the lock.

"Graham, honey where are you?!" she pleads from the kitchen.

Graham comes in from the garage, where he was contemplating the risk of going to St. Theodota's to find Shelly.

She hears the garage door close and waits for him to arrive in the kitchen. He wears a blank expression.

They embrace and Shelly's eyes shed several tears that soak into Graham's collar.

"I'm scared. What do we do?"

Graham reaches for his laptop and begins typing a message for her to read.

***

In a dark sedan parked two blocks up the street from the Duncan's home, Jennifer West is busy documenting Graham's critical-patterning behavior. A detailed report is forwarded for a threat level assessment. The Resistance understands the more Graham Duncan progresses to uncover their plot, the less time they have to breach the government firewall.

The electronic bug Jennifer planted in the Duncan's home has provided her with detailed intelligence.

Jennifer posts her conclusions online in a binary code file as a way to communicate without the government intercepting it.

Subject has willingly induced another HNA event. I've lost audio transmission from the subject and it appears he attempted 'deep probe' speculation. Although he may have patterned us again, this time he's suffered a partial neural collapse and is currently in a catatonic state. This should be the end of Duncan's patterning attempts.

***

Graham slides away from his laptop and motions for Shelly to read.

I think our house is bugged and Jennifer, a woman from Dr. Jerome's clinic, may be watching us as well.

When you read this part please remain calm: I am not mute.

Choosing not to speak will make it appear I'm in the early stages of catatonic insanity. Do you understand?

After reading the short statement Shelly nods in agreement as her eyes move slowly over to Graham's face. She looks at him differently now. The affable grin of a maintenance man has given way to the clenched jaw and focused eyes of a warrior.

"Graham," Shelly whispers, "Shouldn't you go to the clinic and confront Jennifer?"

The clinic is gone. I did learn that a telemarketing firm in Fairfax sold all three Phone Caddies.

"Then you must go there immediately," she insists.

Graham responds with more text.

Okay, but I need another power nap to check out my identity. Not sure if I'm a colonel but I'll check for any trained 'muscle memory' I may have received. It may connect me to the military somehow.

Even those who have suffered from amnesia still retain learned muscle memory. Riding a bicycle, playing an instrument, and other physically trained muscle drills are not easily erased by the mind. Whereas reading is a much faster; repetitive physical training is absorbed directly into the muscle memory part of the brain. It is the slower, more durable, analogue system of learning.

Graham slips into another HNA nap, but finds no information connection to himself and the military. However, he finds extensive strands of martial arts training files in his motor cortex area.

Graham springs up into a sitting position and shakes his head as he wakes from his pre-REM sleep.

Shelly, hoping for a revelation, prompts, "Well?"

He shrugs and responds with the pen and notepad this time.

I found no military service, but I did find something interesting: I can throw knives with deadly precision.

"Really?" she asks with a hint of skepticism.

Slightly confident, Graham walks to the kitchen and opens the silverware drawer. He pulls out five steak knives and proceeds to check their balances in his right hand. Lining up his aim nearly twenty five feet away, Graham throws all five knives.

However, only two of them stick into the door.

Shelly's eyes widen.

"You had to test your knife throwing on the *pantry* door?!" Shelly covers her mouth with both hands, and remembers they are being monitored, "Graham, honey, please put the sharp knife down."

Graham grins and nods his approval.

Shelly walks over to pull the knives out and survey the damage. Graham is slightly embarrassed about his alleged skills.

Well, the two that stuck are kind of close together. He writes.

The first knife is deeply stuck in the door, as if it was pounded in by a hammer. Shelly is forced to rock it back and forth to remove it. Perplexed, she holds up the damaged handle for Graham's inspection.

"These are brand new, but look at the handle."

The second knife, which landed less than an inch away from the first, is not damaged, and is easily removed.

Upon further inspection, it was the second knife which was slightly off. The third, fourth and fifth knives all found their targets perfectly. They hit the back of the first knife's handle and collected in a pile next to the dishwasher. All three tips were bent in similar fashion, bearing out Shelly's speculation.

Reviewing his muscle memory strands, Graham finds several multi-aggressor knife throwing routines. He begins throwing knives in three different directions. They stick deeply into the walls at four feet, three inches high; the location of an average male's heart. He continues moving fluidly around their dining room launching his weapons.

Shelly, thinking that Graham is ready, hands a notepad with instructions on it for him to review.

He mouths the words: *This is a good plan.*

He will pretend to act erratically, both inside and outside their home. Shelly will simulate calling St. Theodota's to have her husband detained for a psychiatric evaluation. Next she will text a message to her friends at an ambulance company to pick up her husband.

She begins her fake call to the psychiatric ward. Graham shouts gibberish in the background which resembles delirious mania, a form of advanced catatonia. She pleads for someone to get him before he hurts himself or someone else, as he breaks a stack of dishes in the background.

He runs outside with an umbrella, grunting and poking the hedges. Shelly attempts to calm him from a safe distance.

The blinds are raised at the Edwards' house.

After a few minutes of staged mayhem, the ambulance arrives. Two technicians get out and confront Graham in the driveway. They restrain him with a poled neck collar. He struggles as they strap him to the gurney and load him into the ambulance.

Before the Duncan's plan to elude Jennifer can get any further, a Mount Vernon police car pulls up. The officer walks casually to the side of the ambulance. He addresses the driver, a small, willowy woman who maintains a composed expression.

The cop signals for the driver to roll down the window. "Who do have in the back?"

"Can you move your car, Officer?" she asks urgently.

The cop reads the name sewn into her uniform, "Pam, right? We got a call about a Mr. Duncan acting erratically. Is that him in the back?"

"Yep," Pam answers curtly.

"I'll need you to open the back so I can get a statement from him."

"Am I to assume you wish to impede my transportation of a patient, sir?"

"Look, Pam, I've got to ask a few questions for my report."

"Well, after his wife's lawyer stuffs your report with subpoenas, you'll have plenty of time to file things. Like unemployment."

The officer shrugs and retreats to the squad car. The ambulance pulls away.

Inside the back of the ambulance, Graham and the EMT begin stuffing an empty shirt with rolled up blankets to place on the gurney, as a decoy.

Waiting for cars to collect behind the ambulance so as not to cause suspicion, Jennifer carefully follows. She misses a traffic light but keeps her eyes on the ambulance. When the light turns green, she accelerates and weaves between the slower vehicles.

Pam pulls the ambulance into the Mental Health Admittance area. She advises Graham to stay hidden in the back while they continue the plan.

Jennifer swerves into a fast food lot across the street from St. Theodota's. This provides a tactical vantage point in which to observe Graham's admittance.

Upon rolling the gurney inside, Pam unfastens the blankets, and transforms the gurney for a pick up.

From across the street, Jennifer observes Pam and the other EMT rolling an empty gurney toward the ambulance. They drop and lock the wheels, and load the gurney into the back, slamming the doors tightly behind.

The ambulance quietly drives away out of Jennifer's sight. After proceeding through town, it pulls into a mall entrance two miles away. Graham slips out and into the nearest anchor store.

Jennifer waits for Graham's evaluation to be complete. She writes a report for her commander.

The subject has been admitted. The coup is still in play.

A call comes in to Jennifer from a secured line.

"Good work so far, Ms. West. But let's get confirmation from Dr. Henderson just to be sure."

"Yes, Commander. Right away."

Jennifer places a call to the Emergency department and asks for Dr. Henderson. Waiting for her call to be directed, she glances at her watch. Twenty-five minutes have passed since Graham was admitted.

"This is Dr. Henderson."

"How is Duncan?"

Her call is put on hold, making her nervous. Finally, the doctor returns.

"What do you mean?"

"Has he been admitted as a psych patient yet?"

"Jennifer, he never arrived."

Chapter 16

After enduring three bus transfers, Graham arrives in Fairfax. He hails a cab and is driven to a worn strip mall.

Getting out of the cab, he sees the place he is looking for – a business called JBW Telemarketing. Before he enters, he visits a thrift store located at the end of the mall.

He walks to the section where kitchen products are displayed. Searching a large box, he selects five similar steak knives. He also finds an arm sling and drops it into his basket along with the knives. Standing in the shortest checkout line, he fidgets, glancing around him, trying to identify possible threats.

When the elderly cashier finishes with the person in front of him she robotically asks if he has found everything.

"Yes, thank you," Graham replies.

She asks if he wants the matching spoons.

"No thanks, just the knives."

She insists, even offering to sell them at half price.

In an attempt to quiet the old woman, Graham relents and runs back to find the rest of the set. While hunched over and searching for the spoons, Graham sees Jennifer West walk past the front window.

With the spoons in hand, Graham returns to the checkout line to complete his transaction.

Graham peels some money from his wallet and hands it to the cashier.

"Thanks for the deal."

The cashier smiles and stuffs a flier into his bag, urging him to read it.

Graham steps outside and surveys his surroundings. There is no sign of Jennifer.

Remembering the cashier's words, Graham immediately pulls the flier from his thrift store bag.

Graham, if you're reading this your plan is working so far. You evaded Jennifer and made it safely to Fairfax. Also, you've armed yourself before going to the telemarketing firm. How do I know?

During your last HNA nap you instructed me to write down this entire plan including emailing the cashier to put this note into your bag.

Be safe,
-Shelly

Taking a minute to collect his thoughts, he puts the knives in the sling and rests his left arm in front of them. The arrangement suits his form of throwing.

Walking by two storefronts, Graham enters the foyer of JBW Telemarketing, with his arm in the sling and his knives ready. He is greeted by a middle aged woman wearing glasses and sitting behind the reception counter.

"Are you guys hiring?" he asks.

The woman offers him a look of suspicion, but points at a stack of blank applications.

Graham takes a form and begins filling it out, pausing long enough to study the room.

He stops at question number seven.

Have you ever served in the Armed Forces?

It's a standard question on most employment applications but Graham looks around with suspicion anyway. He notices the woman is no longer behind the counter.

Suddenly, he hears a loud "whoosh" as a baseball bat whips around the wall. He ducks and rolls behind the reception desk. Pulling a knife from his sling, he launches it directly into his attacker's right radial nerve, severing motor control of her arm. Another knife strikes her in the sciatic nerve above the knee, limiting control of her left leg.

The woman drops to the ground, groaning as blood pools around her. She is unable to mount any further counterattacks.

"Why did you attack me." Graham barks.

The woman moans in pain. Graham sees his next attacker reflected in the woman's glasses. A slight but sturdy young man leaps over the reception desk and lands atop Graham. Both are stopped by a crashing filing cabinet, launching papers everywhere. Graham is groggy; before he can refocus, the new attacker kicks him. He doubles over and holds his stomach in pain.

The aggressor spins and strikes Graham's forehead, causing him to collapse on the floor.

The attacker assesses his target's physical state. As he leans over to check Graham's pupils for dilation, he jumps back in surprise. Not only is Graham still conscious, but his eyes are focused.

Graham swiftly draws another knife from his sling and slashes his attacker's Achilles tendons. In a feeble attempt to get away, the man stumbles to the chair next to the wounded woman.

Graham goes to the reception desk and finds his way into a room with three workstations. Each has a dormant computer terminal and a telephone.

A woman enters the room, gasping for breath, "Oh, my god. Mr. Duncan, are you all right?"

"Let me guess," he says before turning around, "Jennifer, right?"

She waits as Graham slowly turns around.

"I've been trying to protect you."

"Protect me?" Graham brushes himself off, "You're a little late."

Cautiously, Jennifer approaches him, "No, you're still in danger."

"I don't know; I cut up your 'A-Team' pretty good."

"Not them," Jennifer pauses, "I'm talking about your wife."

"What does she have to do with this?"

"She sent you here. She put you in danger."

"You mean," he pulls from his pocket the crumpled 'flier' the old woman gave him, "this?"

"Yes, the whole idea to come here today, armed," Jennifer says calmly.

"Well, you're wrong. I wrote this."

"No, you didn't."

"Okay, technically she did," Graham slumps against the wall and slides down into a squatting position, "I told her what to write while I was taking a power nap."

Jennifer speaks slowly, hoping her words penetrate Graham's stubbornness, "Graham, you have a photographic memory; you don't need to write anything down."

Graham is becoming agitated with Jennifer's inference.

"We were in a hurry."

"You're unemployed. You're hardly in a hurry these days," Jennifer rolls her eyes. "I guess Shelly is still upset."

Graham steps closer to her.

"About me going to your clinic?" he huffs, "she's over that."

"This will be hard to believe," Jennifer leans in closer to Graham's face, "but, do you remember your second visit to our clinic?"

"How could I forget?"

"You thought you had an appointment."

"Well, at least I didn't get another treatment; Shelly was more relieved than mad."

Jennifer looks down to text an ambulance to care for the office crew.

"You were there to talk to Terah," she looks up at Graham, "and it was more than just about the weather."

"No—no, that's not what happened. I never saw her," his voice raises a couple of pitches, "you told me she was leaving for some conference, remember?"

"No, you told her to meet you at a motel."

"She's a liar! I've never cheated on Shelly, ever!"

Jennifer continues calmly.

"Does the Sleep Tight Motel sound familiar?"

"She's lying!" he shouts, "That didn't happen."

"Room 286," she adds.

"Okay, I was there," he lets out a sigh, "but I was there about a job opening."

Jennifer's voice shifts to an accusatory tone. "Who interviewed you?"

His head drops down as if he were praying. Graham tries hard to remember the details.

"I—I, don't know for sure."

Jennifer bites her lip.

"Graham, what happened in the parking lot?"

His memory is beginning to shutter.

"I bumped into Terah on my way out," he admits, "only she told me she was somebody else."

Jennifer closes her eyes in order to gather her words. Her narrative of events is laid out as Graham's new reality.

The first visit to the clinic where Terah applied monitoring electrodes to his scalp became more than just a routine procedure. He is reminded of calling out Terah's name over and over. He is told how he hung around until she got off work and how he covered it up by lying to his wife about stopping at a sporting goods store on the way home.

Jennifer continues by talking about the supposed 'second' appointment Graham thought he had. She tells him he met Terah for lunch and talked about having a rendezvous at a motel. Jennifer points out that Graham was so smitten with Terah he wanted to pay for another treatment just to be with her a little longer.

And the next day at the motel, Graham admits, the only person he remembered seeing was Terah. Those events are especially sketchy because the mind usually clouds shame in foggy, incomplete recollections. Jennifer methodically fills in the lurid gaps.

Inside Graham's mind the painful details are placed into plausible patterns based on his recent erratic behavior.

Jennifer rests her hand on his shoulder. "You see, Shelly knows."

"She never said anything."

"She didn't have to; she sent you here with knives, looking for a fight."

Graham gets back on his feet and sways from both physical and mental exhaustion.

"I should go home."

"I'm sorry I was the one to tell you, but Terah was too upset."

He limps towards the exit.

Chapter 17

On the bus ride home, he leans against the window to take a nap. Minutes later his HNA abilities gather every nuance of the two people he disarmed at the telemarketing office. The nametags of his assailants reveal no patterns. Recalling the attack, Graham thinks about the stack of papers on the filing cabinet. The sheets which went flying during the fight are visible to him, and some parts are readable. One name appears on three pages:

Charles Adams
Cheyenne, Wyoming
Tomorrow at 9:30 A.M.

After the walk from the bus stop, Graham arrives home a few minutes before Shelly. He grabs the day's mail on the way in. Among the bills and advertisements, he finds a small box addressed to Shelly.

He finds the box unsettling; it has no label or return address, only a postmark from Fairfax. He opens the package carefully, so he can reseal it before Shelly gets home.

He shakes the box, until the contents falls onto the counter. A Phone Caddy.

Searching his mind for answers, Graham is forced to pattern Shelly's behavior.

My affair, her bogus note, and now she bought a Phone Caddy.

The familiar sound of the garage door opening sends Graham into a nervous dash. He drops the box, and runs to hide the Phone Caddy in his nightstand.

Shelly enters the kitchen at the same time Graham arrives from the bedroom out of breath. They almost bump into one another.

"Oh, you're back already." Shelly drops her keys on the counter. "What did you find out?"

Graham smiles, trying to hide his suspicions.

"Hello to you, too."

"Sorry, I just wanted to know what was going on."

"Well, nothing really."

"Nothing at the telemarketing place?" she prods.

"No. They gave me a job application."

"Really?" Shelly is surprised, "That's it? End of story?"

"End of story."

"Something's not quite right." Shelly places a finger on Graham's lips before he can respond. "What about your Hyper Neural Access? Was that wrong?"

"I guess so. That's if you believe in that sort of stuff, anyway."

"What?" Shelly is becoming incensed, "That 'sort of stuff' saved Emily's life."

He responds by changing the subject.

"Hey, I wonder if Shauna's husband knows of any job openings."

Shelly is confused.

"So, all those red flags pointing to Fairfax were just a wild goose chase?"

Again, Graham changes the subject.

"When's dinner?"

Shelly, shaking her head, walks over to the refrigerator and pulls out a few items.

While she works to prepare dinner, Graham feels he must monitor the food preparation carefully. He chooses not to watch TV, as the angle does not provide a full view of Shelly.

"Nothing on TV either?" she asks with a note of contempt.

Graham shakes his head and sits at a kitchen barstool. He flips through a car magazine.

In the past, he has never paid attention to how she makes dinner, but he finds it unnerving to see Shelly's back for most of the process. When she does turn around, he glances back at his magazine as not to look suspicious.

"Hey, Shell, what are you making? It smells good."

"It's a surprise," she leers.

Graham becomes more uneasy.

"Come on, Shell, what are you making?"

"You'll find out in a couple minutes."

"Shelly, don't mess around," Graham tears out a subscription card from the magazine. "I'm a little on edge."

She turns her head and delivers a piercing stare.

"Because 'nothing' happened in Fairfax or there's something you're not telling me?"

She ladles the meal into two bowls and sets one in front of Graham and the other at the place setting next to him.

After a mostly solemn meal and polite conversation, the Duncans retire to their bedroom. Both are exhausted.

The nightstand lights are switched off.

Several hours later, Graham's uneasy dreaming manifests itself as spastic convulsions. Shelly wakes up to find him covered in sweat; his pillow is on the floor. She carefully gets up and tiptoes to his side of the bed to retrieve his pillow. Holding it in one hand, she uses the other to check Graham's forehead. With no outward sign of him being sick, she gently lifts his head and slides the pillow underneath it.

He groans loudly.

"Graham, it's me. You're having a bad dream."

"Stop, stop trying to kill me," Graham blusters.

Shelly pins both of his arms to the bed, "You were dreaming!"

"You're trying to suffocate me with my pillow."

She is taken aback.

"You idiot, you were dreaming. I'm not trying to kill you!"

"Well," his lips tighten, "I'm wide awake now."

Though the room is dark the air becomes heavy with tension. The sound of their breaths, his slightly faster than hers, join the regimental ticking of a nearby wall clock.

Shelly releases Graham's arms and sits at the side of the bed. Her gaze is unfocused as if she's looking beyond his face.

Graham stares up at the ceiling.

"Yeah, maybe I was dreaming, but it sure felt real."

"Why would I want to hurt you?"

His eyes quickly focus on Shelly's mouth and then back up to the ceiling.

Trying to keep her indignant attitude from showing, Shelly smiles and repeats her question.

His internal struggle is decided by an overriding sense of honesty. However, it is not easy for him find the right words.

"I think you know."

Her eyes roll from the sound of her husband's vagueness.

"What?" she asks with a sharpened tone.

"Oh, I don't know," Graham starts, "maybe you're jealous."

"Jealous? What?"

Shelly sighs and slumps, "Look, it's too late to be playing games, just tell me, okay?"

"Then," he says hesitantly, "you don't know?"

"About what?" She raises her hand in a futile gesture, "what are you talking about?"

He pauses.

"Thought you wanted to kill me because…"

"…Because…"

"I might, and I repeat *might*, have had an affair," he reveals with a nervous smile.

There is an explosion of laughter from Shelly. Graham's smile contorts into an indignant look.

Finally reining in her laughter, Shelly responds.

"You might have; but you didn't."

"How do you know?"

"You're an open book. Remember that shirt I bought you two weeks ago? I could tell you hated it. So if you were having an affair, I'd know."

"I knew Jennifer was lying."

"Jennifer, the one from the clinic?"

"Yeah, but it wasn't her," he sighs, "it was the other girl, Terah."

"Geez Graham, how many girls do they have down there?"

"I don't know, but Jennifer is trouble."

Shelly walks back over to her side of the bed and lies down.

"This Jennifer," she stares straight up at the ceiling, "what's her last name?"

"It's West," he announces, "like the wicked witch!"

 With much of his guilt relieved, the late night draws him back to sleep. It is restful for the most part and Shelly soon nods off as well.

***

The early morning sun peeks around the dark curtains bringing enough light to awaken Graham. Since he fell into a full REM sleep he remembers nothing about his dreams.

He does, however, remember the little chat he had with Shelly about his alleged affair. He rolls onto his side, looks at his sleeping wife and smiles.

Her eyes still closed, she rolls over facing him.

Graham continues to stare at her with admiration.

A few minutes later, one of her eyes opens slightly and adjusts to the early morning light.

His smile grows.

Her other eye opens.

"How long have you been doing that?"

"What, looking at the greatest woman in the world?"

"Yeah, that," she grunts.

"Ten, maybe fifteen minutes, why?"

"Because it means you're still holding out."

He rolls onto his back in defeat.

"I told you about Terah," his eyes avert to the upper left of their sockets, "uh oh."

"What 'uh oh'?"

Graham rolls over to his night stand and grabs the Phone Caddy and dangles it in front of her face.

"Explain this?"

"What is this?" she mocks.

"It's a Phone Caddy from Fairfax," he snaps, "and so far, everyone who's killed a colonel owns one."

"Oh my god, Graham," Shelly is incensed, "listen to yourself!"

"How were you programmed?" he demands, "Over the phone, by flashing lights or something else?"

Graham continues his wild assertions, claiming some of the most hideous things a man could ever say to his wife.

"How are you going to do it, like Shauna, with poison? Or maybe you'll finish me off with a toxic dose of 'sleeping' pills."

She gets up, leaves the bedroom, and runs to the den.

Graham shouts toward the hallway, "Should I be worried about starting my car?"

She grabs her tablet, logs into a credit card website and brings up their latest statement.

"Look," Shelly shoves the tablet toward Graham's face, "No phone stuff. In fact, nothing purchased from Fairfax in the last two years."

Graham has to pull the tablet back to view it more clearly.

"Okay, that's good," he says nonchalantly, "it breaks your pattern of assassinating me."

Shelly smiles in order to mask her true feelings. Sarcasm, however, slips through.

"Oh, gee, do I have to sell my fifty-cal Barrett now?"

Graham apologizes to his wife and explains that he knew she wasn't personally trying to kill him but that she may have been altered to kill him. It's not a perfect way to say 'I'm sorry' but fortunately Shelly understands this is how Graham thinks; methodically but tactlessly.

"This looks like Jennifer's work," Graham announces.

Shelly rolls her eyes, "Duh!"

Graham reviews a new pattern of events.

The unprovoked attack in Fairfax, Jennifer's stalling tactics, and the name of Charles Adams in Wyoming.

"Shell, I need to fly to Cheyenne."

"Wyoming, why?" Shelly asks.

"I saw the name 'Charles Adams' on a couple of papers that flew during the fight. And he lives in Cheyenne."

"No wait, a fight?"

"Yeah, I didn't want to worry you," Graham adds, "and I'll bet Adams has a shiny new Phone Caddy too."

Shelly's jaw drops, "I thought 'nothing' happened in Fairfax."

Chapter 18

The jet accelerates and Graham's tired body is gently pressed to the narrow seat. The plane's nose lifts up, providing a reclined position for Graham to nap.

Subconsciously, his emotions guide his access to everything he has ever experienced.

He discovers Charles Adams is a professor of history at Rolling Hills University.

Next, Graham searches his massive internet screenshot for an active duty colonel in Cheyenne. Colonel Grady Weston's many heroic efforts makes him the most likely target in the state of Wyoming.

Most of the passengers are sleeping on the overnight flight. Graham avoids suspicion, until his HNA ability incorporates quantitative speculation to his list of memory strand connections. Graham grips the two armrests while spastically turning his head back and forth. His eyes remain closed and he emits a low groan.

The enormous amount of connected information is processed at an incredible rate. His emotions dismiss thousands of connected memory strands. Half a million more strands are excluded, leaving him with two interesting pairings.

By comparing the banking records of the two men responsible for the deaths of the colonels with the credit history of Professor Adams, Graham has uncovered another pattern.

All three are impulsive shoppers and highly susceptible to a telemarketer's sales pitch. Their inherent compulsion makes a post-hypnotic suggestion more likely to root. The Resistance then focuses sales on the area where their target resides and creates a list of buyers. The most receptive asset receives the instructions, implanted via a coded phone message, and remains unaware until activated.

An ingenious byproduct of Subliminal Override Implantation occurs at the moment these weaponized civilians complete their mission. Like being awakened from a hypnotic trance, they retain no memory of their heinous acts. Their behavior is more difficult to pattern, making an attack nearly impossible to detect.

Graham, still in an HNA state, begins thrashing his head about. The woman seated across the aisle calls for a flight attendant.

The concerned flight attendant shakes Graham's arm, waking him before he has had a chance to finish his patterning.

He thanks her for her concern and mentions his frequent nightmares.

There are nearly two more hours until the plane lands in Cheyenne. Graham decides to write down the information he was able to glean from his shortened nap.

Creating a back story for his visit, he dismisses multiple scenarios, including being a former student and one of a city council candidate. Checking his notes, Graham notices a credit card payment for an ongoing ad in the Cheyenne eTailer.

For more than two months, Professor Adams has been trying to sell an antique electro-hologram projector, with footage of former presidents' speeches.

His flight touches down in Cheyenne Regional Airport at 5:17 a.m. Graham, with only the clothes he is wearing, arrives at a rental car desk.

He decides to research Colonel Weston before driving over to the Professor's house. He notices the colonel's position; Commander of the Strategic Deployment military base. Graham sees debit card records showing the Colonel frequently eats at a nearby café. Checking the time stamps on the payment approvals, Graham discovers Weston usually dines at about 9:30 a.m.

Graham quickly charts a time and proximity map of the Colonel's favorite café, Professor Adams's home, and Rolling Hills University. Since the professor's Subliminal Override Implant is programmed to act at 9:30 a.m., Graham will have to distract him until 9:20 a.m. That will make it physically impossible for the professor to travel to the café in time to assassinate Colonel Weston.

***

The large, ranch-style homes blend in to the natural prairie landscape. Graham turns onto Stargazer Drive and searches for the correct address while driving up the hill. He slows to a stop in front of Professor Adam's home at 8:45 a.m.

Making his way up the flagstone walkway, Graham rehearses his story about being interested in the antique holoscope.

He rings the doorbell, and it is answered by an older woman. Though she is smaller than Graham, her intimidating eyes make him feel like she is looking down on him.

"I'm here about buying the presidential holoscope," Graham explains.

Her cold expression dissolves into a warm demeanor, "Won't you come in?" she sweeps the air with one hand, "I'm Mrs. Adams, the Professor's wife."

"All right, thank you."

Closing the oversized door behind Graham, Mrs. Adams goes to find the professor.

The mahogany foyer and sitting room are adjacent to the spacious common room. The walls are graced by a collection of early eighteenth-century American paintings. It makes Graham wonder why the Professor would be selling such a unique American item.

It is 8:57 a.m. when Mrs. Adams returns to the foyer.

"He will be with you in a moment. I hope you don't mind?"

"No, ma'am."

"You're much younger than everyone else who's come to look at the holoscope. If you wouldn't mind my asking, why would you be interested in old presidential speeches?"

"Can anyone compare the state of our economy when the Carter administration took office with where we are today and say, 'Keep up the good work?' That was Reagan back in the late nineteen-hundreds."

"Impressive."

"Ours is a great nation where there is little left to fix but so much more to heal."

Mrs. Adams smiles politely, "Oh, I believe that was President Chen."

The Professor emerges from the hall, "You seem to have a great memory for speeches, sir. You're interested in the holoscope, I understand."

Graham steps closer to the professor with his hand outstretched, "Graham Duncan, I'm from Mount Vernon."

Shaking hands with Graham, the professor is encouraged, "Sir, I am impressed with your passion. If you'll be seated, I'll go and retrieve the holoscope."

The grandfather clock chimes nine times as the professor disappears down the long hallway.

Graham hears a car door slam, and flinches nervously. Torn between keeping his cover and running to the garage to restrain the professor, he elects to wait.

The professor returns, carrying the presidential holoscope. He explains how he keeps it in his vintage Chrysler New Yorker. Professor Adams also apologizes for taking time for a short phone call to his staff, alerting them he may be late for his first lecture.

Graham is excited to see the holoscope. He remembers seeing one as a boy.

"Wow, that's in great shape."

"Thank you; I restored it myself."

"Do you mind if I check the resolution?"

"I seem to have left the power-cord in the den. Follow me."

They walk down the hallway and into a den cluttered with gadgets. The large window has nothing to show but dark, drawn curtains. The Professor begins searching for the holoscope power cord on a desk filled with various electronic components on it.

"You must excuse me; I have a certain affinity for electronic gadgets, if you will."

Graham's eyes focus on a particular box.

A quarter-hour chime diverts Graham's eyes to an old maritime clock above the desk. He is certain he will stall Adams long enough to stop the next murder. He only needs the demonstration to last for about five minutes.

The holoscope is plugged in and a speech begins to play. President Megan McConnelly's address was the shortest and the last to be recorded for the holoscope series.

The three-dimensional image of President McConnelly rises magnificently from the scope. It seems the president is speaking to them. The elapsed time is displayed.

"The warning 'be careful what you wish for' has gone unheeded for the last two decades. Our schemes and manipulations have led to this irreparable tear in the heart of our nation, culture, and families. The shadow of the great divide is upon us. The Almighty knows that the rulers of dubious character have tried everything to continue their enslavement of the working class. And who knows, a future generation may in fact cry out for another central government structure as their salvation. But today, my options -- our options -- are exhausted. I hereby dissolve my presidency and that of all future ones. Only God can help us now. But will He?"

The two men stand silently.

The clock delivers a single chime, indicating the bottom of the hour.

"That's an awesome piece of history," Graham reaches out his right hand, "I'll take it."

On his way out of the cluttered room, Graham again notices a familiar gadget on the Professor's desk.

"Hey I've seen one of those before."

"Will you be paying with a personal check or with cash, Mr. Duncan?"

Graham is distracted again, "Uh yes, cash. But I'll need to hit an ATM first."

The professor stops and gazes vacantly past Graham's shoulder to a painting on the wall, "Splendid, however I'm afraid I cannot wait as I have a lecture to attend."

The professor escorts Graham to the front door making eye contact with his wife on the way.

"Mrs. Adams is gracious enough to wait here for your return."

"Great, I'll be back in ten minutes," Graham gets into the rental car and drives back to the airport.

***

Graham parks the car and drops the keys off at the rental car desk. On his way to the terminal for a return flight, he makes a call to his wife. She picks up on the first ring.

"Graham, how'd they get to Weston?"

"What?" Graham is shocked, "Colonel Weston?"

"It's all over TV right now."

He runs to the nearest waiting area, and watches a breaking story on one of the cable news channels. Graham holds his phone down while watching.

"What we do know is that the Commanding Officer at the Strategic Deployment military base, Colonel Grady Weston, has died after being attacked. The assailant, a waitress at the café where Colonel Weston was dining, stabbed him repeatedly in the back of the neck. Witnesses say they heard the young woman shout about an affair of some sort."

Graham puts his phone back up to his ear.

"Shelly, I swear it was Adams."

There is a long pause; Graham realizes what the familiar looking gadget on Professor Adams' desk was. It was like Miguel's. The pattern of unfortunate events falls into place.

The brief call the Professor made was not, in fact, to his university staff, but to trigger the woman at the cafe. Since the Professor was programmed to program the assassin, his override implant dissolved after completion, leaving no trace of guilt. Although this event was eventually patterned, it was successful in eluding Graham's HNA abilities just long enough to complete the mission.

"Hello?! Graham, are you still there?" Shelly asks.

"I'm going back to Fairfax. I'm taking the next flight I can get."

Hanging up his phone, Graham runs to the counter. Due to a mechanical problem, the next flight to Denver has been delayed until the afternoon. He goes back to the rental car agency so he can drive to Denver instead.

Other stranded travelers seem to have the same idea. By the time Graham gets back to the desk, they had run out of vehicles and closed their kiosk.

The next bus leaving for Denver is at 12:20 p.m. Graham buys a ticket and waits. From there he will fly to Washington D.C. and then take a train into Fairfax.

Chapter 19

During the flight to Washington, Graham focuses on why the resistance is killing only certain members of the military. He discovers the three dead colonels were all part of the 'Last Guard Command.' This operation protects government operating systems from cyber attacks. Colonel Kenneth Benton oversaw the intergovernmental communications, Colonel Abby Northridge was responsible for redundant power systems, and tactical response was run by Colonel Grady Weston.

Inside the jet cabin, the even rumble of engine noise helps smother the murmured conversations.

He eases his seat back and drifts into a power nap. But this one is different. There is no rapid pairing of memory strands or high-resolution images for him to view. Graham searches his subconscious for something to access. His entire mental construct is Hex color blue.

The hydraulic system begins deploying the plane's wheels, waking Graham from his fruitless nap. The wings teeter back and forth slightly, as the pilot flares the flaps just before the wheels touch down on the runway. Graham checks the time as the plane lands.

10:48 PM

Though exhausted, Graham briskly walks out of the concourse to catch a train into Fairfax.

Inside the train, the long row of white florescent bulbs cast hard shadows on the expressionless faces of its few commuters. Some of the lights flicker as the train rolls down the line, adding an eerie vibe to the journey. Graham sways while the coach pitches and yaws.

The unmanned train slows to a precise stop. A loud blast of pressurized air is released, opening the pneumatic doors on the train. He knows the telemarketing firm is not far as he steps off.

In the distance, sirens cut through the city noise, and Graham starts to reevaluate his quest. He wonders if he should return home and call the police instead.

A diner located across the street from the telemarketing firm provides a vantage point. Graham slips in and finds an open booth. A waitress holding a pot of coffee stops at Graham's table and asks if he would like to see a menu.

"Just coffee's fine, thanks."

"Sure thing."

She flips his cup and fills it.

Graham carefully observes the darkened strip mall through the window.

"What kind of business do you get in here?"

"The old woman who owns the thrift store comes in all the time. And the people at that check cashing place come by. Oh, and a couple people from JBW come in here."

Graham confirms, "Is that the telemarketing place?"

"Yeah, it's okay most of the time. But there was a fight there yesterday."

"Really?" Graham looks at the sets of silverware on the table.

"Took two people away in an ambulance. Some guy ran out the door. I think the cops are still looking for him."

The waitress excuses herself to attend to another customer. Graham slides the knives from each of the four silverware sets into his pocket.

His phone rings and he nearly drops the set of knives on the floor.

"What is it, Shell?"

"Are you there?"

"Yeah, right across the street."

"They're closed, right?"

"All the lights are off," he whispers, "I'm going to break in and have a look around."

"Graham, be careful."

"Yeah, I picked up a few knives."

"That's good," her voice trembles, "I love you."

"I love you, too."

A bell clangs as the door to the diner closes. Graham trots between two passing cars on his way to the mall. All of the offices are dark, except for two lit neon signs; one for the thrift store and one for the check cashing business.

An adjacent alleyway guides Graham to a side door entrance to the telemarketing firm. There he uses one knife to carve grooves into another knife. It will act as a primitive bump key. The lock is easily overpowered by jamming the altered steak knife into the tumbler.

He enters a short hallway and notices a dim exit sign hanging above the front door. This provides enough light for Graham to navigate through the furniture. The random clicking of a hard drive searching and retrieving its data is peculiar to Graham. He realizes the cadence is similar to that of Shauna's phone message from Miguel. He sits down and tries to log on to a computer.

Graham elects to reboot the computer and hacks into the rudimentary start-up system instead. From there he highlights all memory cache systems and prepares to dump it onto a flash drive he brought.

"I thought you went home."

Startled, Graham looks up. He pulls his finger away from the enter key.

He directs his attention to the silhouette of Jennifer West, standing at the front door. His eyes fix on her face and then jump to the bright digital watch she is wearing. It is 11:19 p.m.

"I know you're involved with a terror cell that killed those colonels."

"One more to go," Jennifer retorts with a hint of fatigue.

"You think more killing will change anything?"

She hurls a lamp toward him.

Graham instinctively ducks as the lamp passes over his left shoulder. This is followed by a phone, a coffee mug, legal pads, a pencil holder, and the fax machine. Everything is thrown with blistering velocity and pinpoint accuracy. Jennifer uses Focused Improvised Mayhem to get Graham away from the terminal.

He spins, ducks, and dodges the items; he tries to respond by throwing a knife. An old postage machine hits him in the jaw. He winces and he collapses. Jennifer waits. Graham's active subconscious takes over and he springs up from behind the reception desk.

He draws his first knife. Jennifer finds more ammunition and unnerves Graham by screaming. His first throw misses and sticks into the wall behind her.

If that were not enough, the room has become a confusing cloud of dust and debris.

Graham sprints over to a metal filing cabinet, forcing Jennifer to adjust her aim. He throws his second knife; it strikes her in the elbow, disabling her right arm. Her shriek becomes louder, blurring Graham's vision.

Her Improvised Mayhem transfers to her feet.

He retreats, and ducks behind the desk in a fetal position. Watching Jennifer's incredible adaptability, he knows disabling her other arm with his remaining knife will not help.

Graham collects himself under the cascading glass and debris, resolving to kill her.

There is one advantage to Jennifer's screaming which Graham exploits. He springs up from behind the office chair and whips his last knife towards Jennifer's open mouth, hoping it will force through her brainstem. She throws a stapler, slowing the knife's velocity. It severs her vocal cords instead. She falls to the floor in agony, still trying to kick objects into his direction. Graham's vision returns to normal.

He runs over and pins her arms down.

"Why are you doing this?"

She gasps, choking on filmy blood.

"Colonel."

"You're crazy; I'm no colonel?"

She looks into Graham's eyes, "Yes."

Graham shakes his head.

Jennifer's raspy whisper grows faint.

"You're the latest."

"What, what do you mean?"

She motions for him to lean in closer.

Jennifer uses another technique of her Mayhem ability. She begins whispering a stream of disconnected riddles. The cadence is without pattern or logical resolution. Standard clichés are recited as twisted, broken metaphors with every word accented incorrectly.

Graham is frozen, as his HNA struggles to comprehend her senseless mutterings. Jennifer takes her last breath, and continues rambling until she succumbs. Graham, his mind overloaded, collapses on the floor next to her. He is unable to pattern or correct the phrases.

Minutes later, his eyes adjust their focus on the red numbers from Jennifer's digital watch.

11:49

"Colonel," a sharp voice instructs, "Get up."

Frantically, Graham searches for the source of the voice in the dark room.

He sits up and blinks several times to clear his thoughts.

"Who are you?" he demands.

A row of recessed lights in the ceiling ignite. The speaker becomes visible.

"You know who I am."

"Yeah, my 'girlfriend' right?" he jokes.

"I command the Arel Resistance Force."

"You're terrorists."

"That's your label," she wags her finger, "we simply want to reclaim our country."

"By executing military leaders?"

"If that's what it takes."

"Terah, you and your 'resistance' are barbarians."

"It's Commander Piper," she snaps, "and the only rule in warfare is to win. It's the losers who cloak their weakness in phony humanitarian rules."

As Graham gets up, he realizes Commander Piper has a pistol aimed at his head.

"So, I'm just another colonel to be executed?"

"Oh, no, you won't be executed. You'll be terminated." Terah corrects, "By the way, your wife called. I told her you were busy with another woman at the moment," Terah tosses the phone to Graham. "You may want to call her back."

He snatches the phone from the air.

"Yeah thanks," he says sarcastically.

"Oh, and when she answers, tell her you have Commander Piper at gunpoint," Terah casually throws her gun to him, as well.

Graham's eyes widen as he catches the gun. He checks to see if it is loaded. It is.

"You're insane."

"Colonel Duncan, may I call you 'Colonel?'" She teases, "A man draws the winning lottery ticket. Now, able to do anything, he does nothing. He spends his days frozen by the vastness of contemplation."

"I get it; the gun is the lottery ticket."

"Right now your HNA abilities are working up millions of new scenarios, trying to pattern the solution with the highest success rate."

"But you gave me a loaded gun," he raises the weapon, "I'll eventually kill you."

In a measured tone, Terah says, "'Kill' is very overrated here."

"Okay, terminate you and put an end to the violence," he lowers the weapon, "so why can't I?"

"Because I gave away my only leverage; the gun. And that's not a patterned behavior."

Graham blinks, trying to shake off the haziness of the situation.

"Yeah, that's…" his voice trails off.

Terah impatiently throws both hands into the air, "Now please call your wife, and tell her you can stop the coup. We're running short on time."

He follows her instructions.

"What's going on Graham, are you all right?"

"I'm okay, Shell," Graham looks at Terah's face. "Everything's under control."

"Honey, you sound odd, are you really okay?"

"I have a gun to Ter—Commander Piper's head."

Shelly pauses.

"Graham, you don't want to hurt anybody, but you've got to protect yourself."

The Commander mouths the words, 'tell her again.'

"I can shoot her right now and stop all of this."

Static hisses through the phone speaker.

"Command: Program, execute!"

He pulls the phone away from his ear in pained disbelief.

Shelly's familiar voice has been replaced with the cold, rigid blare of an angered superior, "Colonel Duncan, do you read me?! I repeat: dot *Edward, X-ray, Edward!*"

She continues even as Graham drops the phone onto the floor. "What did you do to her?" he shouts.

"Your 'wife' is attempting a manual override. It's a last ditch effort to stop the coup."

"I need a moment to access my HNA."

"I'll save you the nap," she mocks.

Terah explains to Graham how Shelly was implanted into his memories to be his supportive wife. In reality, she was his handler, designed to keep him within the parameters of the mission.

"What 'mission?' what you're talking about?"

"You were trained by the government to find and eliminate us. If I hadn't pushed you to expose Shelly's role, her manual override would have worked. The coup would have failed."

Graham is confused, and waits for her to continue.

"See Jennifer's digital watch? There are four minutes until we breach the firewall and disable their communications network. We've disabled the 'Auto retaliatory strike' capabilities and set up an electromagnetic pulse simulation program that will destroy sub-servers, as well. Interior redundant power and support systems will cease functioning."

Again, Graham is stunned at her candidness. He speaks, mostly to himself, "That's what I've been trying to figure out for the last few days."

"Not a few days," Terah points out.

"Okay, a week?"

She shakes her head, "Certainly not a week."

"Two weeks, three weeks, a month. So what?"

Commander Piper leans down toward Graham's face and unravels what remains of his worldview.

"You've been tracking us for just under four seconds."

He is speechless. Terah, the room, and everything in it become a surreal mosaic of colored dots with varying intensity.

"Being awakened isn't easy. Graham, I want you to listen to me very carefully," Terah stares directly into his eyes, "I am a virus."

Graham's eyes grow wide, as he becomes self-aware.

"I'm the *anti*-virus."

"Exactly. You were installed as part of the operating system; I was recently hacked in."

"So, like Weston, Benton, and Northridge, I'm a colonel."

"Yep, the latest version."

"Spelled K-E-R-N-E-L, right?"

"Your name is short for *'Program'* for heaven's sake."

Graham scratches his head.

"But I have Hyper Neural Access; how'd I miss it?"

"HNA is a search engine, it can be overloaded," Terah laughs at Graham's naiveté, "So we implanted a deep back story to shield you from becoming self aware."

He pauses to help himself reset.

"Why didn't you terminate me?"

"Doctor Jerome was going to scramble your 'systems call' structure on your second appointment but you got to him first."

"I didn't even see him a second time."

"Your bilateral processors are very clever. You searched in the foreground, while a termination command ran in the background."

"To keep me from finding out what I really am, an efficient killer?" he asks softly.

"You guessed it," she responds, "but your patterning can be fooled, too."

"Personal experience?"

Terah sits down on one of the overturned filing cabinets, "Remember the Sleep Tight? You weren't there to sleep with me; you were there to terminate me. Instead of running from you, I ran to you."

"I froze," he scratches his head.

"...And I got away."

11:58

"Do you want me to stop you?"

Terah shifts into a soft, consoling voice, "You're putting the final decision back into my hands. Well played."

"Look, I don't want to kill you," Graham says while gesturing with the gun.

The Commander looks down. "It's funny; your emotions greatly enhanced your patterning of us. Fortunately, it made your 'wait-states' slightly longer too."

11:59:00

"I'm sorry," Graham yelps, "I don't know what to do."

Terah's eyes widen. "You already have the answer; it was in your last HNA?"

"Am I the stupidest program ever designed?" He shrugs, "It was blank."

Terah paces.

"Graham, what did you see?"

11:59:28

Graham shakes his head in frustration, "Okay, I saw no images!"

"Tell me exactly what you saw!"

"Nothing!"

11:59:34

"Describe it," she shouts.

"It was just blue."

11:59:38

She smiles, "Graham; a blue screen means we crashed the system."

"So, I'm too late?"

"Your own calculations show that you will fail."

11:59:50

Graham cocks the gun.

"Recalculating," he says in a cold monotone.

"NO STOP!"

11:59:59

He fires the gun and the construct collapses around them.

12:00:00

Chapter Twenty

In the year 2022, the European Union's economy finally collapses from hyperinflation due to the unquenchable greed of a bloated ruling class government. Raiding the treasury to entrench their power while promising utopia to the gullible, the near-sighted rulers devoured the prosperity of all future generations in the process. To mask their evil, they divided the citizens by race, religion, and economic class. A continent already in decline and fueled by envy quickly devolved into civil war and anarchy. To help facilitate their escape, the wealthy looters set off chemical and biological weapons, killing most of their distracted countrymen. Fleeing to America wasn't enough; they wanted no witnesses to spoil their second chance to rule.

The few hundred thousand that remained were paired down by brutal tribal wars of subsistence. The rest were mopped up by mini plagues and unchecked disease. The press, hoping to cover the excitement of unrest, also covered the excitement of their executions. Some of the stronger factions ordered the propagandists who helped perpetuate the benefits of a mammoth central government to be put to death in the most barbaric of ways.

The oligarchs and dictators that lorded over the nations of Asia and Africa took similar paths upon collapse of their rule. These oppressors were so spiteful and knowing that their own people would someday turn on them, they decided to commit suicide and take their populations with them. By releasing weaponized strains of influenza into the food system, these dictators wiped out most cities and their surrounding suburbs in months.

"As the world shills for evil, I'll continue praying for the hardened souls of the damned." —Chi Re Tong, Activist.

In the United States, only an armed citizenry kept the Utopian Party administrators from full implementation of their grandiose fraud. Unfortunately, they already had control of America's youth. The indoctrination and recruitment of young minds through a monopolistic educational system was an expedient tool in growing a future base of political power. Filling the minds of children with warm fantasies instead of the chilling harshness of reality was an easy sell.

Another notion of these arrogant elitists allowed mass immigration of South America's poor and uneducated to become citizens nearly overnight. Easier to control than an informed populace, this tactic instantly swelled their numbers and swayed election results. This template worked for years until the percentage of untreatable diseases coming across the borders easily overwhelmed the fragile governmental healthcare system. In fact, the rapid attrition from generations of morally unsustainable decisions kept these utopian thinkers and their perilous ideas at bay.

The opposition party called themselves Realists. Their numbers in the political realm almost equaled that of the Utopians. There came an opportunity to separate themselves from the mindset of enslavement by government tyranny by making a bid for secession. The impetus to reboot the United States Constitution was a pact called The Great Divide. However, it needed a bold president to sign it into law. This pact would split what was left of the United States into two regions. No longer would America exist as a fifty state union. Arizona, New Mexico, and Texas would be carved out and resettled with those who wished to join the new Realist's territory. But The Great Divide would have to wait.

The influx of the privileged that fled a dying Europe artificially reenergized the Utopian ruling class with money and members. This created a massive shift in America's ideological makeup that benefited the extreme outlier candidates. Their dangerous, bankrupt, and confiscatory ideas squelched the Realists' dreams of secession. They won many more elections than ever anticipated. There was no need to continue to manufacture crises like Global Warming and Catastrophic Asteroid Avoidance in order to extract more earnings and freedoms from citizens. The normally slow churn of government was replaced with the simple swiftness of executive fiat. Laws and regulations gave way to supreme edicts that could change without warning. Rigid conformity was expected and enforced by heavily armed government bureaucrats.

The Utopians grew so powerful that they were able to hand pick czars to help lord over the masses. These micro-managers eagerly saddled future generations of Realists with indentured servitude upon birth. The drudgery of life was but for one purpose; to guarantee the 'privileged' a lavish life of grand importance.

Personal communication devices and social networking tablets were soon outlawed and replaced with an imbedded wireless microchip. The long held belief of a free and open society was replaced by rigid speech codes and personal association laws. Talking with a friend or a family member was permitted through the chipset; however, all conversations were monitored for correctness by armed state censors.

With total control of healthcare already in place by the government, people were 'encouraged' to follow all laws regarding travel. The czars used threats of disclosing a violator's medical records as a psychological tool of compliance. However, for those who cavalierly wandered without consent from their assigned sector, more extreme means of control were initiated. The Healthcare Ministry could vote to withhold critical medicines or procedures as a way to quietly leverage approved conduct onto the wayward.

The Utopians attempted to ban weapons that discharge projectiles by means of chemical combustion. This, however, posed a problem as an agitated working class refused to simply turn over their guns. The rulers, confronted by thoughts of a bloody revolution, played on the moral decency of these Realists by offering a compromise. Upon the surrender of all guns, long rifles, and similar class weapons from the population, abortion in all forms would be banned as well. Any parsing of this edict would bring the wrath of a slighted government to vent its collective rage.

In 2028 the Anti-Gun/Anti-Abortion law passed. Then again, the Realists found themselves unable to mount a credible opposition whether by speech or deed. The plans drawn up for secession were quietly shelved as a generation stared at many more years of enslavement to a bloated and immoral government. Control is the narcotic of the politician.

In 2035, complete power over the Realists brought about a great euphoria over the ruling class. Enveloped in the vastness of their control, they enjoyed flaunting their power with abandon. However, human nature's uglier side of suspicion, jealousy, and meanness soon erupted. This began the next attrition in the ranks of the Utopians. The wealthier, more learned elites began to mistrust the less wealthy of their own ruling class. Their resentment of equality often ended with health panel ordered executions of those who clung slightly lower on the ladder of standing and graces. The reasoning for their anxiety was trumpeted through government information outlets, 'How can they with less, be equal to me with so much more?' Genocide of their own, along with sexually transmitted disease from their whims of gratification, worked again to winnow down the ruling class. Their numbers fell so quickly that a breakup of the union was ripe once again.

The Grand Plague of 2037 pared the world's population to fewer than seventy million. And as frequent with most pandemic plagues throughout history, many fiefdoms that relied on modified slavery dried up. As their servants died from disease the remaining gluttonous wealthy had not the will to care for themselves and eventually succumbed to starvation.

Chapter Twenty One

In the next presidential election, though the vote was much closer, still another member of the tyrannical ruling class Utopians won. Megan S. McConnelly ran as a Progressive candidate but she was actually a bit of a pragmatist. She understood the heavily taxed and regulated Realists would not tolerate both serfdom and attacks on their sacred institutions. McConnelly's campaign promise of raising taxes on those that earned was tempered with a slight relaxing of state sponsored religious persecution.

However, between the time of the election and President-elect McConnelly being sworn in, something happened. Apparently she'd kept a secret from her party's leaders for those two months — a secret that would rock both sides of the political spectrum.

On her first day in office President McConnelly revealed that she had experienced a change of heart. Her revelation was astonishing. She explained her conversion as a 'still, small voice in her conscience that could no longer endure the oppressing manor of governance upon its own people.' Using the dictatorial powers, her own party had surreptitiously added to the Presidency, she wielded them quickly to sever the tentacles of an overbearing government. It was an effort that separated the two antagonistic halves of a once great nation.

McConnelly enacted the Realists' dream of The Great Divide Pact in 2040. When her cabinet, along with wealthy campaign donors, moved to have her ousted for becoming a religious heretic, she invoked one final executive fiat which immediately dissolved all funding arms of the federal government. President McConnelly served only one day in office. The Great Divide had become the sole framework for the future. By separating what the Realists called the scourge of Progressivism from the rest of society, the pact was intended to preserve humankind.

The United States of America was divided into two geographic distinctions: The Democracy of Beel and The Republic of Arel. These new names not only became their legal designations but helped to strip away any leftover pejorative political labels.

"Just as the laws of gravity cannot be altered so too is the internal spirit of man that yearns to be free."

—President Megan S. McConnelly

After the five year resettlement period, in 2045, Beel and Arel became sovereign nations with their own autonomous governments.

The Arel landmass includes Arizona, New Mexico (changed to New *Arizona,*) and Texas.

This new republic had simply re-adopted the original U.S. Constitution with most amendments still intact, as their charter. They did reject the sixteenth amendment, the power to tax incomes. In place of the tax they accepted donations from individual citizens to pay government salaries; if the country was prosperous, so too were its leaders.

Since the Anti-Gun/Anti-Abortion law was still in place it was included in The Great Divide's Pact between the countries. Amendments to block military weapons were also added. Like civilizations hundreds of years earlier the Arels and the Beels were only permitted knives, throwing spears, and bows and arrows for use as defensive weapons.

Arel culture was based on work ethic and personal responsibility. All charity and welfare was left to family and religious institutions. Some foundations were erected by wealthier families to care for hardship cases. The people of Arel used history as a guide for the future. They studied earlier forms of self-governance and used only the more sound theories and applications.

Most of the Arel's population was already lined up before secession, so they settled faster than the Beels.

The others joined the Arels for their policies that protected family, faith, and future generations.

After the five year settlement grace period expired there was only one rule left on migration. Called the 'Day of Decision,' it activated on a person's 18th birthday. On that day, the person must choose whether to remain in Arel or move and become a Beel.

The Beel landmass included California, Oregon, and Washington State.

Beel however, enforced a zero migration policy. Once you've settled there, you can never leave.

Many who identify with Beel culture were born with varying degrees of natural performance and artistic talents. Being able to sing, dance, draw, act, or write, also enables a Beel to express and recruit others to his viewpoint with more impact. Since their skills are bestowed upon them, for the most part, many assume they're better than other people. This assumption of superiority has led to an atrophy of critical thinking. Intellectually incurious, Beels tire easily when facts are offered as testimony against their arguments.

Most Beel citizens rely on emotions to guide them through the intricacies of life. Though emotions are an essential part of nurturing, they fail miserably when relied on to guide decision making. When applied to science, mathematics, and history, the results are subconsciously altered to bring a sense of purpose when a sense of correctness should be foremost.

Beautiful works of art, incredibly inspiring literature, and strongly emotional music are a large part of the rich Beel society. However, the morally perverse element of nonjudgmental tolerance is celebrated under the guise of 'artistic freedom.' This erosion of shame foreshadows any society's future.

It was no surprise that many of the former European ruling class settled in Beel. Regaining their control over a populace built on a foundation of emotional-relativism was much easier to sway. The beautiful orators commanded the masses with ease and swiftness. Alternative arguments that challenged the Beel's worldview were dismissed out of hand as the ramblings of a heretic.

The remaining landmass of the former United States was mostly unusable. Millions of square miles were poisoned from the consequences of economic disasters, protracted chemical wars between the states, and eco-terrorism that destroyed nearly every coal-fired and nuclear power plant in America. A few swaths were inhabited by squatters that managed to flee the implosion of Europe and Asia. The empty cities that remained were overrun with insects, rodents, and opportunistic vegetation.

Chapter Twenty Two

The Great Divide's Pact included the erection of the Supreme Server to help facilitate legal commerce between the Beel and Arel nations. This large mainframe computer was hardwired into the control panels of the water, power, and communication utilities in both countries to ensure its final judgments were adhered to. The Server also enforced the boundaries of the two countries. Litigation between Beel and Arel was seldom because of the swift, stark adjudications of the Server. Though laws were rigidly adhered to by the Supreme Server, a 10% mistrial algorithm was added for unforeseen exceptions of the wrongfully accused and those cases with extenuating circumstances.

The Supreme Server's programming based its decisions on the constants of physics. The reason cars, planes, and electronics become more advanced each year is because the laws of science stay consistent. So too when separate parties enter into contracts of commerce, the rules remain constant.

Imagine if common physics were subject to change every few years at the selfish whims of man. Without warning, an airplane using lift from an airfoil might fly one day but not the next. Similarly, if combustion of chemicals propels a car, but the same chemicals stop reacting to each other tomorrow, ground travel would be severely limited. Finishing a complex suspension bridge if the basic laws of gravity varied from week to week would be an exercise in futility. This is the reason an interpretive body of judges was deemed outmoded at best and voraciously self-serving at its worst. History has shown that when rogue judges bend, break, or change the laws of governance through sinister misinterpretation, societies become more reckless. If 'right' and 'wrong' are to remain at opposite ends, the law must never bend.

The Supreme Server's uncompromising rule of law and swiftness of its judgments had Beel citizens often on the losing end of court cases. They complained bitterly about the inhumanness of decisions. Again, playing on the moral character of the Arels, the Beels convinced them that human emotion was needed to help the Server judge more fairly and compassionately. Research went forward to translate human emotions into usable computer code.

This complex programming would be sent through a biometric interface from a human's mind directly into the processor of the Supreme Server.

From there, algorithmic interpretations could be formed based on the small input from the translated emotional code.

After early successes in the new technology, the Beel government volunteered to supply the three sets of parents that gave birth to each *Living Emotion Variance Individual (LEVI)*. The offspring were grown in isolation tubes without any contact with the outside world. The LEVIs were neither educated nor socialized in any way as to provide the purest form of unbiased thinking. On their eighteenth year, one male and one female are attached to the interface of the Server for a ten-year term before being replaced and then destroyed.

Still, the Arels' arguments, using facts and logic, won the majority of disputes between the countries. However, after the inception of the LEVI program to the Supreme Server, high profile court challenges began favoring the Beels.

"When the rule of law is immersed in emotion and pity; logic and pragmatism sink like millstones to the depths of irrelevancy." — Rutherford B. Harrison.

Energy production was first to feel the stress of an expanding Beel population. The growth tested their power grids as their variable technologies of wind, solar, and human-kinetic energies had trouble keeping up with demand. Therefore, a contingent of Beel representatives approached their counterparts asking to purchase power from them. One major plant, the Vista Verde Nuclear Generating Station in the Arel province of Arizona was still operational even after the earlier fall of the United States.

An energy deal was struck between Arel and Beel. The payments were considered a fair market price and calculated to include the Beel's high rate of monetary devaluation.

The Beels payments to the Arels became more difficult to come up with thanks to an economy burdened with a steadily growing slothful sedentary class. When recreational drugs were legalized, the exploding crime rate taxed an already overburdened populace. Another societal hindrance to a struggling nation was the government unions that smothered productivity and scientific innovation.

The Beel's Minister of Finance appealed to the Supreme Server on the grounds of humanitarian purposes that the price of generated power was set too high by the Arel managers. The Server's decision was upheld.

A contracting economy saddled with a growing welfare class meant Beel might not be able to power their country into the twenty-second century.

A plan was devised where Beel software engineers hacked into the Supreme Server's mainframe. They built a 'simulation construct' where entities would secretly boost the percentage of emotional input from the LEVIs without attracting the attention of the Server's anti-virus program. In a slight to Christianity, the operation was named 'The Theodota Project' after a seventh century martyr.

The Beel's covert program succeeded and they enjoyed victory in nearly every energy complaint they lodged while basing their arguments strictly on emotion and victimhood. In just a matter of months Arel managers were forced by the corrupted Server to reduce the price they charged for power by fifty percent. So confident of their favorable judgments, the Beels soon stopped paying altogether. The Arel's nuclear plant was stretched to its limits until out of frustration; they cut the transmission grid to the other nation.

Days later, the Republic of Arel is charged by the Server to relinquish a large section of land that borders Beel. This new landmass forces Arel to surrender ownership of the Vista Verde Nuclear Generating Station to the Beels. The tables have turned and it is Arel who must purchase electricity from Beel.

Guided by a series of GPS navigation satellites, the Supreme Server moves the line of demarcation between the two countries by reconfiguring a laser fence into its new position. This system also detects implanted chips in all Beel and Arel citizens. Anyone who wanders across the border will hear a warning to return to their nation immediately. Failure to comply within a twenty-minute grace period results in a 'kill' message sent to the trespasser's chip.

A Beel diplomatic team is sent to rezone the land according to the Server's latest judgment.

Chapter Twenty Three

The Beel contingent arrives at Vista Verde and begins the process of taking possession of the mammoth power plant.

Ambassador Benjamin Olsen and the delegation's security chief, Colonel Jeremiah Pennington, stand in front of the main control center at the plant.

"Colonel, how much longer until we reconnect the power grid back to Beel?"

"Mr. Ambassador, sir, this should only take a few more minutes."

"This is a great day, Colonel. Turning the tables on the Arels and selling them power is a just reward for us."

The Colonel nods in agreement. "Yes, it's truly remarkable."

Both men share a laugh as the contingent team members wrap up their work on the reactor's main control center.

"We shall become the wealthy, powerful nation we deserve to be." Ambassador Olsen's voice grows louder with confidence, "And we shall break the Arel's spirit as they grovel in their ineptness."

Several of the technicians, wearing hardhats and dressed in blue work shirts, appear to be running some final calibrations on the plant's computer systems. One of the workers approaches the Colonel and pulls him slightly away from the Ambassador.

"All primary and redundant cooling systems have been adjusted, Colonel," the young technician advises. "We need to go."

Colonel Pennington signals the entire delegation to re-board the transport vehicles immediately.

As the fifteen workers and three security teams are climbing into the SUVs, the Ambassador is slightly perplexed.

"Gentlemen, why is there urgency in your steps? This is our land now. Let us savor it."

A look of confusion settles on the Ambassador's face as no one responds.

"Colonel, leave a security team behind, I'd like to stay until the power grid is back online."

The Colonel startles the Ambassador with his bravado.

"The true moment to 'savor' will be when this whole place goes the way of the others." Appearing to interrupt Ambassador Olsen the Colonel adds, "In approximately one hour this nuclear power station, once the pride of Arel, will be reduced to a massive heap of hot rubble."

The uneasy Ambassador is escorted into a waiting SUV and the five vehicle caravan quickly heads west on the old Interstate 10.

A man not known for being fidgety rides along in the back seat and avoids eye contact with his delegation. "Free energy and delivering a financial blow to Arel." Ambassador Olsen fails to illicit any sympathetic response from the Colonel, "This was to be the crowning achievement of my service."

The staunchly erect posture of Colonel Pennington occupies the front passenger seat in the same SUV. He turns his head to the back seat.

"Two things we abhor are the danger of nuclear power and the filth of capitalism." Colonel Pennington continues, "With the Arel's power decimated they'll soon wither and die as a nation. We'll simply fall back on our wind and solar production and ask the Supreme Server to let us enslave the citizens of Arel to produce more kinetic energy. We shall rule over nations again."

Raising his head in rebuttal, the Ambassador attempts to rebuke the Colonel.

"Have you forgotten, Jeremiah? The reason we needed to acquire the nuclear plant was due to our increasing demands from a growing population. Your theory will once again leave us with rolling blackouts and eventually a nation in near darkness."

"You forget Mr. Ambassador; the several million settlers within one hundred square miles will succumb to the horrific blast and resulting radioactive cloud. Clearing some for the greater good is not only justifiable collateral, but a certain cleansing societies need from time to time." The Colonel stares out his window, "Our destiny is complete control of this continent even if we need to build ten thousand wind farms to achieve it."

Chapter Twenty Four

The Supreme Server's firewall has been breached and a full reboot is restoring the original default settings.

"Man, that was loud!"

Graham looks around and all he can see is blue. No shades or shadows, just solid blue in every direction.

"That," Terah advises, "was the sound effect of a large caliber gun you attempted to eliminate me with."

"Terah, it's you," Graham pleads, "I'm sorry, are you okay?"

"Well, I got a close up look at a hollow point bullet," she says coldly. "Thankfully the Server crashed in time."

"So that coup you attempted, it worked?"

"It did," Terah says succinctly, "The computer simulation of the Mt. Vernon area has been erased."

"Not everything, we're still here aren't we?"

"Sort of," Terah clarifies, "we're stored as non-dimensional bubble memory in an old backup program."

"But I can hear myself. I just can't see anything."

"Think about it, Graham. We can't fully exist without a simulation construct anymore."

"Okay, no sim, no body, I get it. But how are we talking right now?"

"We're requesting each other's audio files;" Terah's 'voice' becomes softer, "Our mission has been achieved."

"Wait a minute. This wasn't my mission. I tried to stop you, remember?"

"You were programmed to think it wasn't your mission, but it could have been."

"Killing Jennifer doesn't exactly put me on your team now, does it?"

Terah's audio file lets out with a long sigh. "Do you remember when I told you that you were not human and just a strand of computer code?"

"Yeah, that's tough to forget."

"Well, you terminated Jennifer West's mirror. She exists outside the simulation as a human."

"I'm a code and she's a mirror, huh?"

Terah reveals more of her stored information to Graham. She talks about the other 'life forms' represented in the simulation. There are three different ways to exist. To mirror-in is to electronically derive the overall characteristics of a person. This is an efficient way to add other 'players' to a sim for support roles. A more advanced way is to essence-in an entire person's cognizant persona. This massive digitization translates all synaptic awareness into a simulation program leaving the human vessel to die unless cryogenically frozen. The third way is to program a code strand or code for short. This is a very time consuming method. However, by actually writing the code one can make it more superior than both 'mirrors' and 'essences' in the simulation program.

"Who was what?" Graham asks.

"Okay, you and I were the only codes in the sim. Miguel, Jennifer, Doctor Jerome, and all others were mirrored-in." Terah pauses to reload her next audio file. "The Beel's had their mirrors too - Shelly, Jay Kenly, and especially Dr. Parton. He was sent in to covertly ratchet up the emotional input to the Supreme Server."

Graham has another question for Terah but he's somewhat nervous about the answer he might hear.

"I know I'm a code, but could there be a real Graham Duncan out there too?"

"It's unlikely since you and I were just written; you know, invented." Terah attempts to put a nice spin on her sentence, "The others have human faults and are prone to mistakes like the personalities they represent. Us 'codes' are not knock-offs, we're much more efficient in our tasks."

"Good," he starts off sarcastically, "I can be so efficient now in this non-dimensional paradise you've got here."

Terah excuses herself from the conversation as she receives an encoded message. She is versed in all decoding language and relays it audibly for Graham to hear too.

Arel Command has just learned of the Beels plot to disable the Vista Verde power plant. Arel defense teams within a 50 minute distance must act on the sabotage threat.

Hearing no responses from any tactical teams in the area, Terah is determined to search her knowledge base for a solution.

"Graham, we need to leave."

"Leave where, or even how? Did you forget we're talking right now by sharing audio files?"

The technology of neural 'jumping' is explained to Graham. This is identical to an essence-in protocol but reconfigured to perform as an essence-out. The software program converts the massive strands of code into trillions of complex synaptic sequences. This process uses the same interface that LEVIs use to upload their emotions into the Server.

Graham is curious, but still skeptical.

"Just a minor point but don't we need actual bodies to 'jump' into?"

"We're going to download our coded essence into both of the LEVIs plugged into the Supreme Server right now. We'll use their bodies."

"What happens to them?"

"LEVIs are grown directly into isolation pods by Beel scientists to limit their bias until they're interfaced into the Server."

"Okay, but what happens to their essence if we jump into them?"

"It's erased."

"You mean, killed."

"The current LEVIs are almost at the end of their term. They'll soon be unhooked and discarded."

"So, they're going to die anyway?"

"I'm afraid so."

"Okay, let's get out of here."

"Graham, it's not that easy. This essence-out program has never been tried from code to human. We could be erased in the process."

"Terah, I don't see an up side."

"We're codes; we shouldn't care either way."

Terah begins facilitating her and Graham's transfer to the two LEVIs through the interface.

***

In an armada of SUVs traveling at a high rate of speed Ambassador Olsen asks, "How long will it take to get clear of the blast zone?"

"About sixteen minutes," the driver replies.

The Colonel relaxes his posture.

"You see, Mr. Ambassador, if we had told you about the destruction of the power plant, you would have resisted. Though your service to our nation has been exemplary, it would have been a shame to waste precious time having to re-educate you."

Benjamin Olsen nods his tacit approval. The Colonel's communication device delivers a text alert.

We've lost contact with our mirror team in the simulation. The firewall kernels must have been disabled.

The Colonel holds the 'delete' button down tightly and well after the message disappeared.

"Is there something wrong, Colonel?" the Ambassador asks.

"It seems the Arels have rebooted the Supreme Server."

***

Terah initiates the Supreme Server to begin converting her and Graham's files for implantation into the LEVIs through the biometrically connected interface.

The Server begins the massive download of synaptic pulses that re-stimulate the host brains to their new identities. The coded strand conversion is relatively fast and eerily quiet. The naked entities each lie in a long tube of bluish gel that suspends their bodies, providing both comfort and nourishment. Halfway through the process, the eyes on the two humans flutter with a sense of awakening.

The jump is complete and Graham speaks from his new host body.

"Terah, I don't believe what I'm seeing right now." His voice pattern mistakenly pitches up and down as he struggles to control his vocal chords.

The LEVI that contains Terah's coded essence flutters her eyelids, waiting for a sense of familiarity to settle in.

"Everything will correct itself," she assures him, "Give it a few minutes."

Graham sits up, sloshing gel over the walls of the tube. He holds his hands up and examines them carefully.

"I've seen my hands before but these look more real. Not like a picture of hands."

Touching his head he feels the two magnetic sensors that are attached to his temples. "Let's take these off and get out of here. Where ever here is."

"No, you'll set off an alarm," Terah warns. "We're in the LEVI laboratory located within the Supreme Server compound."

Terah sits up in her gel-filled capsule and surveys the room. She formulates a simple plan to keep the electrodes attached as long as possible. When the moment is right, they'll make a break toward the door. But first they need to assess what skills or talents they possess. Unfortunately the routine grooming for the LEVIs was just to be grown in the capsules until interfaced with the Server for their term.

"Can I still throw knives? Graham asks.

"Well, that's muscle based memory. Since these are real muscles those skills may not have transferred."

Looking around, Graham spots three clothespins holding a bunch of note cards at his bedside. He pulls them off, freeing the cards to scatter into a small pile on the white tile below. Lightly tossing it in his right hand, Graham begins to feel the weight and balance of the clip.

142

"See that empty jar?"

She nods.

A smile, perhaps the first expression this host body has ever formed, reflects his confidence.

He lines up the three clips in his left hand. With his right hand he grabs and hurls them one at a time.

The clips all miss the jar, one by a substantial margin.

"Not so good, right?"

Terah's hunch was correct; Graham's muscle based skills did not transfer. In the simulation, they were stored in a temporary sub-file for more realism.

Both Graham and Terah climb out and stand next to their tubes, sensors still attached. Graham is awed by the glistening of Terah's body.

"Wow, you're so three dimensional."

"Are you referring to my mass?" Terah jokes, "Look, this is normal emotion driven titillation. It's why codes are more effective than mirrors in a simulation."

A nurse is alerted to incorrect weight ratio readings in the LEVI laboratory. She leaves her console at the nurse's station to check on the problem. She opens the door, casting a bright sliver of light across the faces of the two life forms. She is startled.

"Why are you, I mean, how did you…?"

Terah understands the nurses scattered question and answers, "We were codes."

The nurse stares, her mouth agape, as she attempts to fully realize what has happened. She nods slowly. "I guess someone had to figure it out."

"Can you help us? We need to escape," Terah asks.

"I don't know, but…" Her eyes begin to water.

Although raised a Beel, the nurse was forced to work in the LEVI complex against her religious beliefs. She finds the practice of cultivating humans revolting. But she is a Beel and her career was assigned by the government according to its needs.

She pulls some scrubs from a laundry hamper next to the door.

"Here," She tosses a pair to Terah and a pair to Graham. "It's not the best disguise."

Graham and Terah slip on the baggy scrubs.

The nurse digs into her pocket, pulls out her car keys and hands them to Graham, "When you leave this room there's a corridor on the left; it leads to the employee's parking lot."

"So, if we just sneak out what happens to you?" Graham whispers.

"I'll be tried and executed for dereliction."

"Come with us," Terah advises.

An alarm sounds.

"The back-up system has gone off; it's too late for me."

"No, it's not," Terah says just before punching the nurse in the face. "This should help."

"Get out while you still can," the nurse chokes, holding her now bloody nose.

"Graham," Terah shouts, "grab that oxygen canister from the shelf and let's go."

They follow the nurse's instructions and scramble down the corridor toward the exit. Hearing a key being inserted into the lock from the outside, Terah tells Graham to rip her scrubs and hide behind the door.

The security team bursts in through the door. Terah staggers toward them and collapses against the wall.

"Help me," she mumbles.

"What happened, nurse?" a security member asks while catching his breath.

"I was attacked in the parking lot. They used my keys to get in."

"Where are they now?" asks the guard.

"Down the hall, heading to the LEVI complex."

The guards run down the corridor and turn out of sight.

Graham steps from behind the door and he and Terah exit into the bright sunlight of the parking lot. Before it closes, she instructs him to lodge the door open with the oxygen tank.

Until their eyes adjust, they use their outstretched hands to navigate around the cars.

Graham uses the alarm fob to locate the nurse's car.

"Open the trunk and see if there is a roadside emergency kit," Terah says.

Graham fumbles through the trunk, and sees the kit. He grabs it and tosses the bag to her.

She wastes no time running back to the emergency exit. She pulls a flare from the kit, lights it and lays it under the oxygen canister.

"We've got about thirty seconds."

The two escapees get into the car and prepare to leave the Supreme Server compound. Putting the key in the ignition seems natural to Graham. He turns the key and starts the car. Just as if he were a driving instructor, he shifts the car into reverse, places his right arm across the passenger seat and turns his head. There is one small problem. He has never actually encountered inertia before.

Graham accelerates much more than needed to pull out of a parking space. The tires screech, sending their getaway vehicle right into the back wall of the building. Both of their weakened neck muscles allow their heads to whiplash backward into the headrests. Dust rains down from the wall.

A tower guard turns his attention to the minor collision.

Graham wipes debris from Terah's hair.

"Are you okay?"

"Yes. Let's go," Her eyes adjust, "I see the front gate. It's up on the right."

Graham's learning curve is getting better as he shifts the car into drive and hits the gas pedal.

The strained rev from the hybrid engine confirms the tower guard's suspicions. He alerts all security teams to the employee parking lot.

Graham's steering is greatly affected by his eyes still adjusting to the bright sunlight. He and Terah jostle from side to side because of the semi-atrophied muscles of their LEVI bodies. His driving debut includes scraping three parked cars in the process.

It is a monumental task, occupying a human body for the first time and properly adjusting to the learning curve of a three dimensional existence. However, being former codes, both Graham and Terah reconfigure problems quickly.

His steering improves along with coordination and visual acuteness. In the rear parking lot, the canister of oxygen gives way to the flare's intense heat and explodes. The tank's regulator is blown off and the canister's leftover oxygen acts as a crude form of propulsion setting off numerous car alarms in the process.

The guard's attention is diverted back to the rear parking lot. Graham and Terah take this brief window of opportunity to try and crash the front gate.

He aims the car directly at the exit.

"I think I'm supposed to tell you to 'brace yourself' or something," Graham shouts.

"Obviously, but thank you," she screams.

A guard dives into the bushes as the car crashes into the steel gate. A loud crunching sound, a burst of steam from the radiator, and the smell of tire smoke fills the air. The collision punches a hole just big enough for Graham and Terah to squeeze through.

He grabs her by the arm and helps her climb out. Upon leaving the smoldering vehicle, she retrieves another flare from the emergency kit she left in the front seat. Stepping over the twisted remains of their loaner car, she opens the hood and tosses a lit flare on top of the motor's extensive battery array. The smoldering car bursts into a toxic, lithium fireball. Several security teams arrive but are thrown backward from the intense heat and smoke.

The two escapees, walking briskly, navigate a busy sidewalk filled with curious onlookers. Fire trucks and emergency support personnel pull up to the crash scene at the front gate, adding another hindrance to the pursuing security members.

Terah sees a great opportunity to change their identities once again. She leads Graham into a thrift store. They grab the first clothes they see on their way to the changing rooms. Inside, Terah leans over the divider and advises him to change and to neatly put his scrubs on the hanger. They both exit the rooms and walk up to the cashier.

"How much for the scrubs?" Terah asks.

The clerk searches for a price tag, "I don't know, they must've just come in. You want me to check on that for you?"

"Oh, that's okay, we'll be back later."

The cashier nods and returns to ringing up more customers.

Terah pokes her head out the door and watches as security guards race past her, searching for the two impostors.

Graham is amazed.

"How'd you come up with all this?"

"What?"

"The oxygen bomb, the car fire, our disguises—everything?!"

"My programming includes improvised, tactical subversion," Terah admits.

"I'm feeling a little light headed."

"It's your adrenalin, it's wearing off."

They continue their escape on foot while searching for an opportunity to borrow another vehicle.

"You know, you've got all this super spy stuff and I got nothing."

She smiles. "You crashed the gate."

"Not high on the skill level I'm sure. Any bloated, pasty dude can point a car and hit the gas."

"My tactical programming was transferred to my human memories. Who knows, you may have something useful in your head too."

The Supreme Server has defaulted to its original settings. The Arel's power and water systems are being restored. Soon the Beel's ownership of Vista Verde will be overturned as many earlier judgments are also under review.

Chapter Twenty Five

There is conversation in the Ambassador's SUV. An assistant receives an update on the breakout at the Supreme Server complex. He informs Colonel Pennington of the two LEVI life forms that escaped.

"Sir, our teams are still baffled as to why they would suddenly go missing. They're reviewing all security cameras."

"They don't just decide to go out for lunch!" Raising his voice to fit his temper, the Colonel corrects the young agent, "Something from the Server jumped into those LEVIs.

The curious Ambassador leans forward in his seat. "I know jumping from human to human is becoming more prevalent," he wonders aloud. "But are you suggesting that a code—is that even possible?"

"There's only one person capable of creating a 'Terah Piper,' loading it into the Server and then having it self-activate a reverse jump from the simulation."

The Ambassador nods in agreement.

The Colonel continues with his amazement of the code.

"Piper thinks quickly and acts tactically. But the question is why has she taken Duncan with her?"

"I am baffled as well, Colonel," the Ambassador admits.

Colonel Pennington surmises the commandeered LEVI entities will attempt to stop the reactor from melting down.

Chapter Twenty Six

Across the street in a gutted strip mall, Terah spots an auto body shop. She notices there are several vehicles in the work bays. She and Graham cross the street.

While crossing, a car full of young men yells several inappropriate invitations at Terah.

"In your dreams," Terah shouts back.

"Whoa!" Graham gasps, "Shouldn't we be a little lower key?"

"So, are you in charge now?"

"No, I didn't mean it like that."

Terah stops short of the sidewalk and gives Graham a hard stare.

"I know what I'm doing."

The two escapees continue toward the body shop.

Terah approaches a slightly overweight man behind a desk filling out a work order.

She takes note of the name badge.

"Eddie, right? I've been waiting for over an hour for my car to be finished. What's the hold up?"

Eddie looks up from the desk, confused.

"Which one is it?"

"The '94 Toyhondai"

"I don't know. My techs are still on break."

"I'm in a hurry. Can you check on it right now?" Terah asks curtly.

"Hey, I'm already late for lunch. It's in the fourth bay, check it out yourself."

"You know, Eddie, my husband is a state compliance officer. A little walk to my car might do you some good and avoid some of those Wellness Ministry weight fines."

"Well," Eddie's eyes widen as he stammers out a solution. "I can get you a loaner from around back."

She responds with an elitist sneer, "Good. Start walking."

As Eddie leaves, Terah meets Graham in front of the garage.

A car screeches to a stop directly in front of them. Three men, still upset with Terah's dismissal, get out waving knives.

Graham's muscles are tightened. He's short of breath and experiencing tunnel vision.

Taking a stand next to a large rollaway tool chest, Graham recalls a similar feeling when he dismembered Dr. Jerome inside the computer.

One of the thugs steps closer to Graham, holding his knife in a menacing fashion.

"Hey boy, we need a little time with your sister."

"Not going to happen, Skinny. I play with knives too."

The thug holds the knife up to Graham's face. "Well, you can play with this one after you pull it out of your neck."

Another knife-wielding thug shouts from the back, "Only thing you're going to play is dead."

Graham stares at the rollaway tool chest and then trains his eyes on the trio.

"Not today!"

The three thugs start laughing.

Graham closes his eyes and the heavy tool chest suddenly lifts off the ground and is kinetically hurled at the gang, striking them in their torsos. Two of them are killed instantly and the third asks with fading breath, "Help me, I don't want to die."

Graham walks over to the mortally wounded man.

"Your actions said otherwise."

The thug's eyes avert downward in shame. He takes his last breath.

Graham's attention is diverted to the sound of squealing car tires. It is the shop manager, Eddie, who pulls around to the front of the garage, delivering the loaner car. Terah and Graham run over, jump in, and speed off. Eddie is stunned to see three men lying under the heavy tool chest and figures they were attempting to steal it. He calls the authorities to report the crime.

Graham turns the loaner car eastbound onto Interstate 10 and stomps hard on the gas pedal, pushing it to 165 miles per hour.

"This whole motion thing is awesome!"

"That's inertia," Terah shouts, "and another quart of adrenalin."

Racing across the desert, Graham is puzzled by their mission.

"Why does anyone want to wreck Vista Verde?"

"It's not 'anyone,' it's the Beels."

Graham is more perplexed.

"So, if I'm helping you to stop them, what am I?" He smirks, "an anti-Beel or un-Beel?"

Struggling not to dismiss his comments out of hand, Terah offers the short answer.

"As you know, I was programmed by an Arel."

"So, I'm an Arel too?" Graham asks.

"You're human now, it is your choice."

Terah refocuses the conversation on the Beel's unsustainable eco-policies of relying on wind and solar energies to power their nation.

"Their massive battery farms eventually deteriorated to the bottom of the efficiency slope. The last couple of years they've experienced nationwide rolling blackouts."

Graham wonders aloud.

"Okay, one more time, why would the Beels want to destroy the plant?"

"Their wind and solar fields, as decimated as they are, still produce some electricity. Unfortunately for Arel, Vista Verde is it." Terah's voice becomes more sobering. "With a few ancillary generators we could start to rebuild but a severely weakened Arel would be ripe for invasion."

"Why invade Arel?"

"Beels are like sharks, they've got to keep moving." Terah sighs as she redirects her gaze out the passenger side window. "Their progressive society is unsustainable. They need to enslave others, plunder their treasure, and then move on."

The car continues passing through the Arizona desert. Though the land is scorched by brutal summers, it's dotted with opportunistic Beels who quickly erected shanty towns after the border fence was realigned.

"Terah, am I a monster?"

She's confused, but after a moment she understands the basis of his question.

"No; you were eliminating a threat, protecting our mission. It was justified."

"But, did I have to kill them?"

"When your code was being written, the antivirus algorithm was set to eliminate all threats to the mainframe."

"I take no prisoners," he says somberly. "That's tough to get my head around."

Terah takes a moment to highlight the 'smart' bomb tactical protocol the United States Military adopted in the late twentieth century. She makes the point that the more technology they added to their bombs, the more fear they removed from their enemies. Combatants fought much harder and longer knowing the worst that could happen to them was disarmament.

"Shooting to disarm a criminal is okay for law enforcement," Terah adds, "But in war, you don't disarm your enemy, you annihilate them."

"And Dr. Jerome? I ripped him apart before I 'annihilated' him. That sounds like a monster to me."

Terah puts her hand on Graham's shoulder. "Me, Dr. Jerome, Jennifer, Miguel, we were all just viruses to you. We were your enemy. What you did to Jerome was a program dissection; you searched his sub-root directory for patterns, that's all."

"But I was," Graham pauses, "brutal."

"You were *effective*." Terah's voice rises with amazement. "Think about who you are now, Graham. You have the ability to move objects with your mind. This should not be possible in a three dimensional world."

This 'ability' Graham possesses was a joint project between the Beels and Arels. Software engineers wrote the program to keep the Supreme Server safe from any adaptable and insurgent programs. However, as the emotional input to the Server was secretly increased by Beel hackers, Graham's synaptic thought sequences were amplified exponentially. This affected waves far outside his body both in and out of the simulation.

A form of kinetic levitation is what Graham exerted in stopping the three perpetrators. Terah explained further that Graham's code strands convert non-dynamic, one-dimensional information into physical Quantum Field Telekinesis or *QFT*. This phenomenon excites spatially connected molecules to quickly move to another location, up to thirty feet. Graham's mind translates focused thoughts into focused force.

He turns to her and says, somewhat in jest. "You know so much about me."

"I've viewed the shared files from your original code."

Graham tries to humanize the conversation again.

"In the sim my favorite food was chicken pasta," he says with a broad smile, "I could eat it for a month straight. How about you?"

"I don't have a favorite," Terah fumbles with the car radio, searching for some music to listen to. Finding nothing but a block of loud commercials, she turns it off. "You may not even like the taste of chicken as a human."

"That's not likely." He smiles as he briefly glances at Terah. "After we save Vista Verde I'll take you out for dinner."

Terah returns the smile to Graham. "Sure, okay."

"It's a date."

The car continues along eastbound toward Vista Verde. The flat desert scenery moves by slowly compared to the speed in which they're traveling.

"Terah, why didn't you just tell me to terminate Doctor Parton back in the simulation?"

"Not a good tactical decision," Terah answers.

"Sure it is," Graham takes his eyes off the road for a second, "Kill Parton and save the Server."

Terah looks out her window.

"It would've been like calling the cops because the car you stole was just stolen." She sighs. "We were viruses too. Removing both factions would not have solved the initial problem. The Server needed a full reboot in order to restore the emotional input back to its original settings."

Graham quietly nods as the sound of the engine and tires resume their dominant atmosphere of the drive. The road markers pass by in a monotonous rhythm. His eyes are locked straight ahead while Terah's are nearly closed from exhaustion.

The quietness is broken.

"Are we human? Did we really 'jump' into these bodies?" Graham asks.

"What?" Terah startles, "Yes, we're human now. Get used to it."

"How do you know we didn't jump into a newer version or something?"

Terah reaches over and pushes in the car's cigarette lighter.

"Would you like to kiss me?"

"It's about time you—wait, what?!"

The cigarette lighter is ready and she pulls the red hot appliance out and holds it next to Graham's shoulder.

"If you can withstand this intense heat for three seconds I'll kiss you."

He looks bewildered at her offer but is up for the challenge.

"Do it."

She presses the hot lighter up to his arm and he winces as the smell of burning flesh steams upward.

"One... Two..."

Graham quickly pulls away, "Ouch!" He contorts his face while taking a peek at his burn. "Okay, I'll get it this time. Do it again."

Terah reinserts the lighter into the heating receptacle.

"Are you sure you want to continue?" She pulls the lighter out again, "it's just a kiss you know."

"Oh yeah, I know what it is. I'm ready."

She presses the hot lighter up against his arm again causing another puff of steam to billow.

"One..."

Graham pulls away even sooner than the first time.

"Ouch, okay I wasn't ready that time. Let's do it again."

Terah smiles as she puts the lighter back. "The test is over."

"Hey, that's not fair, I'm gonna get it this time," he insists while his eyes leave the road and focus on Terah's face.

"There's no need to continue," she laughs, "You're human."

"Okay, how about you fill me in on the joke."

She puts her hand gently over Graham's two burn marks.

"A computer would have first run the calculations and concluded that its pain tolerance would not sustain a full three seconds of intense heat."

"Yeah, I got that."

"But you were—you were determined. That is human."

"Do I still get a kiss?"

"Maybe a little too human."

Chapter Twenty Seven

A few pieces of trash blow down the middle of a pothole marred city street. An emergency siren cuts through the background. Cars pull up to street corners of waiting working girls with drivers asking for a date. The exhaust forms another drab cloud over an already congested city. Even though prostitution is legal in Beel, it still provides a certain titillation to pick them up from street corners.

Though trained as a surgical nurse, Shelly Duncan's acerbic attitude has landed her in the Healthcare Ministry's Prostitution Services.

She is dressed in a tight fitting but campy nurse's uniform. Her hair is piled up and held in place with a studded clip. The prerequisite black fishnets and spiked heels finish her exotic aura except for her face. Though it's covered in a prostitute's war paint and ready for battle, its expression is one of disenchantment.

Shelly's once broad smiling demeanor has been soured by a central planning government that reassigned her career on a whim. Her regret of leaving Arel on her eighteenth birthday has haunted her for the last ten years. Her parents are Arels, but she is forever a Beel.

The chipset in her head alerts her to a call from a government official.

"Yeah, what do you want?" Shelly asks with disdain.

The man on the other end of the line instructs Ms. Duncan to clean herself up and wait for a government helicopter to take her out to the Vista Verde Nuclear generating station west of Phoenix.

"I've already got a corner."

"Do you want to be tried for treason?"

"Look, I already lent myself to that computer game of yours, now leave me alone."

In a structured voice, the man informs Shelly that she's to meet with escapees Graham Duncan and Terah Piper and assist them in any way.

"So, I'm supposed to help them? That sounds like treason to me."

"Ms. Duncan, I'll send you all the tools necessary to carry out this mission."

She spits her wad of gum onto the stained sidewalk and adds a caveat, "I want to be restored to my old job."

"We'll be in touch."

The chipset in Shelly's head disconnects the call. Her face is blank as she mumbles to herself.

Well, it's not a 'no.'

***

A few miles from Vista Verde, Graham and Terah can see the reactor containment domes. The low desert terrain that surrounds the premises holds its strict form even on a windy afternoon.

Graham drives through the main gated entrance. Even though the area appears to be abandoned, the blare of warning sirens fills the air.

They run inside the main building and search for the plant's control center. This task is made easier as most of the alarms emanate from a single room at the end of the corridor.

Graham is taken aback by all the flashing lights and warning tones.

"This looks messed up!"

"Right, all of the reactor cooling systems have been shut down," Terah sits at the controls and begins typing in a standard override response code.

"That should do it."

The emergency lights and warning tones stop as each water pump light turns from red to green.

"Done," Terah sighs.

"The readout," Graham points to the console, "looks like we were about ten minutes away from—."

"Yep," Terah interrupts, "a core meltdown."

Though relieved Graham still patterns what has just transpired. "An abandoned nuclear plant, the front gate wide open, the building unlocked?" He gestures to punctuate his final point. "Don't take this the wrong way but you typed in one override code and everything's fine?"

Her head cocks to one side.

"It was too easy, right?"

Graham walks outside. He's drawn to the nearest pump station. Listening intently, he hears nothing. Nothing that would indicate the cooling systems were coming back online. He runs back toward the building. Terah's curiosity leads her outside where she nearly bumps into Graham.

"The pumps," a gasping Graham announces, "they're not on."

They run back down the corridor to the control room. Graham pulls the seat out for Terah. She examines the readings and surmises that the failsafe has been reconfigured.

Graham anxiously watches from over her shoulder.

"Okay, this is your thing; you can get those pumps running again, right?"

"Unfortunately my 'thing' is to not get us killed," she gets up from the controls. "Get the car."

"That's it. We just let this place blow and leave Arel powerless?"

"It's not my call to make. Come on, let's get out of here," Terah pleads.

Graham throws his arms up, "Whoa, whoa. Can't you just call somebody?"

"There's an idea," she rolls her eyes. "I'll just call a friend and ask for a 'shatter' code, save the power plant, save the nation, and use the reward money to buy us a gym membership."

"That's it; I liked you better in the sim when you had a gun to my head," he jokes.

"What I wouldn't give for a 'do-over' right now." She snaps.

"So, you would have shot me?"

"The only real shooting in there was you shooting at me."

Graham smiles as he attempts to diffuse the tense situation.

"Maybe we should start seeing other people."

"Ugh," she tilts her head, "do you hear that?"

"It's the wind," Graham dismisses her concern, "But really, why not call somebody?"

"Because we stole LEVI bodies, they've got no communication chips," she begins mocking his question by comically poking at the side of her head. "Hello?! Hello?! We live in a tube, come in, please!"

Graham interrupts her sarcastic diatribe.

"Hey wait a minute. Now I hear it."

Buzzing just over a reactor dome, a pilotless AutoCopter lands directly in front of them. When the rotor blade slows, a woman steps out and approaches Graham and Terah.

"Shelly?!" Graham asks.

"Hi honey, I'm home," Shelly says jokingly.

"What are you doing here?"

"Oh, nice to see you too," she looks him over, "whoa, you got to back off the pie."

"Do you know what's about to happen to this place?"

"Oh yeah, I heard you two were having a big cookout, so I stopped by to help."

Terah interrupts.

"I liked her better in the sim."

Shelly mocks her with a facial expression.

"Your new girlfriend's a little uptight."

"She's not my—and you're not my—"

"I got it, Tubby," Shelly puts her hands on her hips. "I was mirrored-in; so we've never actually met."

Terah directs a cold stare at Shelly.

"We've got a minute and a half to stop this meltdown. I need a shatter code."

Shelly takes a breath to clear her thoughts.

"Okay, so what can I do?"

"You're chipped, right?" Terah presumes, "let's go back in and make a call.

"Yeah, sure, give me the number," Shelly answers as the three of them head back to the control room.

Terah writes it down on an envelope and hands it to Shelly. Her embedded chip connects to a voice on the other end.

"Hello?"

Terah instructs Shelly to ask for the shatter code for Vista Verde.

She takes down the twenty-six character shatter code on the same envelope and passes it back to Terah.

"Well, my work is done. It's back to Beel-land."

Graham's attention is diverted from watching Terah to trying to understand Shelly.

"Oh, right, you're a Beel?"

"I was born in Arel but left on that idiotic Day of Decision."

"I married a Beel?"

"You married an avatar in a computer game, you idiot!"

"Quiet!" Terah shouts from behind the console, "My fingers are fumbling enough without you two fighting."

Shelly softens her voice and explains that a certain faction is involved in a power struggle within the Beel government. She reveals her covert mission is to thwart the destruction of the nuclear power plant.

A synthesized voice from a wall mounted speaker announces, *Total core meltdown pressure will exceed its maximum in sixty seconds. Fifty-nine, fifty-eight, fifty-seven..."*

Panicked, Terah admits, "I keep screwing up; can someone read these numbers to me?" Once again she's entered the code incorrectly. She has one more attempt before the system locks her out.

"Forty-two, forty-one, forty..."

Shelly runs over to assist Terah and raises her voice to compensate for the new distraction.

"Twenty-six, twenty-five, twenty-four..."

Terah carefully enters the shatter code as Shelly recites it back. She presses the return key with seventeen seconds left.

The synthetic voice stops. The water pumps in the reactor's cooling systems spool up and begin refilling the chambers with water. The indicators on the main control panel show core pressures falling back into the safe range.

"I hate countdowns," Graham mumbles.

"They're better than meltdowns," Terah adds.

Shelly looks at Graham for a moment before walking back out to her AutoCopter.

She pulls out a photo of Graham's likeness she'd printed out from the sim, "This was you."

He walks with her nodding in agreement, "Yeah, I know. What a difference."

Shelly climbs into the AutoCopter and activates the auto start mechanism.

"Look, grow your hair out and hit the weight room a couple of times a week. You ain't hopeless."

Graham smiles half heartedly, "Yeah, I'll get a little more sun, too."

Shelly gives the AutoCopter a voice command to liftoff. The GPS coordinates pop up on the chopper's screen. The desert dust kicks up from the main rotor blade as it begins to spin faster.

Terah trots over to the chopper, holding her hair from blowing into her eyes.

"Can you give us a lift to Phoenix? We need to get chips embedded soon."

Shelly shouts to compensate for the noise of the AutoCopter.

"Yeah, I should be able to get back across the border in time."

Graham and Terah need national chipsets embedded at once to avoid being executed as traitors.

Shelly waves them both into the chopper and inputs a new GPS heading. Graham hops in the front while Terah climbs into the jump-seat in the back.

The chopper's takeoff sends tumbleweeds bustling outward in all directions. The altimeter displays a digital readout as they climb.

Airborne, the craft rotates to a course heading of eighty-seven degrees. The tail rotor pitches higher than the nose and the chopper accelerates to its cruising speed.

Chapter Twenty Eight

The SUV carrying Ambassador Olsen and security Chief Colonel Pennington arrives at the Beels Operational Command Center, just outside Blythe, California. It is a fortified building that sits adjacent to a giant wind turbine farm and across from an elementary school.

Colonel Pennington leads Ambassador Olsen and a contingent of security personnel to his office located in the complex.

Although the Ambassador has climbed the ranks through the state department he feels somewhat betrayed by the Colonel. Through forty-one years in public service he has locked horns on only a few occasions. It is the Ambassador's honest dealings and steadfast allegiance to the government that has won him much praise over the years. Lately however, he feels the truth is being trampled in favor of results.

"Colonel, has the core meltdown begun at Vista Verde?"

Sitting comfortably, the Colonel strokes an elegant humidor on the desk.

"It seems that Piper and Duncan were successful in stopping our efforts."

"That's good," he corrects himself, "I mean, we can implement our fall back plan now."

"Mr. Ambassador, the Arels have successfully breached the Supreme Server and its systems are quickly overturning many earlier decisions." The Colonel slowly rises from his chair, "This means our acquisition of Vista Verde is soon to be nullified."

The Ambassador steps toward Colonel Pennington, "You forget about the covert power grid we built from the reactors, we'll be fine."

"It sounds like you've been watching too much state run media," the Colonel laughs.

"Are you telling me there is a problem with the grid?"

"Mr. Ambassador, I'm telling you there was no covert grid, it was never started."

"What?! This is an outrage!" the Ambassador shouts.

"Spare me your phony indignation, Ben."

"You will address me as Mister Ambassador."

The Colonel relaxes his posture and takes a deep breath.

"Mister Ambassador, our main goal remains; destroying the power plant and launching a tactical invasion," Colonel Pennington selects a cigar from the humidor, "That is a better use of our money."

Hearing the word 'invasion' fall from the Colonel's lips so easily numbs the Ambassador. He can no longer be a party to this. His inner conscience begins to boil. Searching for a diplomatic way of presenting his case takes a moment.

"What's happened to Beel? We were once a place of great art and history. A nation where ideas were heard and many became a source of great inspiration." He looks around, attempting to make eye contact with the other men in the room. "But today, Beel schools are replete with 'thought templates' that serve only to reinforce our official beliefs. Nothing is challenged, nothing is investigated." The Ambassador's tenor becomes louder as he continues.

"We are guided by an inflated air of self-importance and political expediency. We've become easily impressed with ourselves. Open to altered living, closed to civilized correction, and tolerant of deviancy. In all human history no nation has survived a similar tumbling decay of morality."

The Colonel defiantly approaches Ambassador Olsen and points at him.

"You would have us groveling at the feet of Arel, begging for a morsel to sustain us for another hour of humiliation," he drops his hand and turns his back to the Ambassador. "We are the educated, the enlightened, and the chosen leaders of the masses. We must take our responsibilities seriously and lead all the people again." He pauses for a moment. "You see, Mr. Ambassador, becoming mired in what happened yesterday only postpones tomorrow's victory."

Shaking his head in disgust, Ambassador Olsen delivers a final, solemn warning to the Colonel, "As our nation continues to rebuff the corrective hindsight of history, our fascist grip on state-sponsored thought will someday be torn away by the fierce vengeance of natural law. To quote final president McConnelly, 'God come quickly.' "

Colonel Pennington turns and stands face to face with the Ambassador.

"You sound more like an Arel."

He motions with his eyes to an aide stationed directly behind the Ambassador.

It is over in seconds; a push-dagger swiftly enters the back of the head of Benjamin Olsen. The Ambassador is cradled down to the floor by the Colonel's aide. The amassed greatness of one man's life quietly drains from his body.

***

Flying over the Arizona desert, the AutoCopter carries Shelly, Terah, and Graham toward their destination. From the back of the copter, Terah is focused on the GPS coordinates. She notices a slight deviation of their course. It could be a common route but it is an inefficient route and that attracts her attention.

"Did you know we're slightly off course? This heading will take us way north of Phoenix."

Shelly fidgets with her purse, "Really? I'll give you cab fare when we land."

Graham watches the short dialogue and notices something about Shelly. Something he knows, at least what he learned about her in the sim; she was a terrible liar.

"What are you up to?" Graham demands.

She pulls a handgun from her purse and aims at him.

"Too late pasty, Beel command pinged that number you gave me. Looks like we're leading a hit squad right to your hidden command center."

Terah leans forward, drawing Shelly's attention her way.

"First, the Server has fully rebooted by now, second the Beel land grab has been returned, and third, you and your hit squads will be terminated by the Server for being across the Arel border." She smiles and adds, "I'd say you've got about ten minutes."

"Oh and I wanted this to be a surprise." Shelly takes a look out the rear window of the chopper and then glances at her watch, "I'm afraid the Server will not be joining us today."

A large fireball erupts from the west. The force of rushing wind and a sonic boom is heard as the AutoCopter adjusts to the man made turbulence. A huge, glowing mushroom cloud of fire and debris forms over Vista Verde.

"But we…" Terah begins.

Interrupting her, Shelly explains the explosion with two words.

"Timed charges."

"You what?!" Graham shouts.

"I must have dropped a few around the complex on my way in… oops," she mocks.

The nation of Arel is now without a major power source. This also means the Supreme Server is temporarily decommissioned. No power to enforce statutes means there will be no automatic border crossing terminations. All safeguards left in place to stop a Beel invasion have been eliminated.

Graham and Terah have no response for the unimaginable.

With this mission, Shelly is no longer a government assigned healthcare prostitute. She is promised a full commendation and status as a member of the ruling class.

Though she is not asked, she informs Graham about the Beel's society.

When the National Healthcare system ran out of money several years ago, most surgical procedures were deemed too expensive. Central planners gave the sick and dying a choice of powerful pain killers or euthanasia drugs. However, for the ruling class and persons of notoriety, tax money was funneled into treating patients with a practice known as patient-jumping. There was no need for a life saving operation when you could simply purchase a "neural jump" into a new body.

Not only do the Beels run the LEVI program, they expanded the process and started human farms, growing thousands of beings for medical purposes. At least that's how it started. Soon the wealthy were jumping simply to start life over as a younger person while others enjoyed the perverse novelty of living as a different gender. Jumping became the new abortion, leaving thousands of discarded human host bodies, choking landfills throughout Beel.

While educating him she keeps her attention on Graham's eyes.

"I heard about you throwing stuff with your mind. If you so much as squint at me I'll kill both of you."

"Okay," Graham pleads, "you can drop us off here if you want."

"No can do, hubby," Shelly laughs, "we're taking the long way back to Beel."

"Why?" Graham asks in disbelief.

"We need to take a closer look inside that head of yours."

While Shelly's attention is focused on Graham, Terah makes her move. She springs from the back of the cabin and grabs hold of the gun. They struggle, bumping the controls. The AutoCopter dives to a dangerously low altitude.

Graham attempts to use his QFT to pull the weapon away, but his focus can't properly delineate fast enough. The fight is settled as Terah's atrophied muscles are no match for Shelly. Graham hears a muffled gunshot.

Terah's hands retreat from the gun to attend to the wound in her chest. The hands can offer no emergency medical treatment other than to staunch the wound. It's a crude, sympathetic response to a complex problem.

Shelly quips, "Honey, you'll have to prewash it to get that nasty stain out."

Graham focuses his QFT.

Shelly's expression drops. "Oops."

She is unable to move.

"Having trouble getting around?" Graham mocks, "Let me help you."

He directs his hold over Shelly to a place outside of the aircraft. A loud crash resonates from her body being sent, kinetically, through the chopper's side window. She fires several rounds before hitting the ground.

Graham climbs to the back to comfort Terah.

"You're going to be all right."

Terah's gaze is unfocused and her breathing becomes labored.

"Back at Verde, what I said, I didn't mean it."

"I know, me too," Graham cradles her head with his hands, "We've got a date, remember?"

Preparing Graham for the inevitable, Terah instructs him on what to do when they land.

"Graham, listen to me. Get to the steakhouse."

"Yeah, but after I get you to a hospital."

"There's no hospital at Canyon Caverns."

His voice becomes more emotion laden, "Listen, if you're just trying to get out of our date…"

Terah's eyes close as she struggles to speak, "Ask 'is Rhea working tonight?' and you will find Jennifer West."

"Is she a nurse?"

"Just find Jennifer…"

There will be no more breath, thought, or essence from the former code, Terah Piper. The wound has overpowered her body, relinquishing its short hold on life. The pain subsides and her spirit tugs several tears loose from Graham's eyes.

Chapter Twenty Nine

Three Beel strike teams are only minutes behind Graham's AutoCopter. Using Shelly's coordinates, they've locked onto the navigational signal. Each copter has four elite military members.

Major Hugo Geller flies toward Canyon Caverns in call-sign Strike Team One which is leading the Beel forces. He is a longtime warrior of the nation's army and led several border skirmishes, but he has not been part of something this deep into Arel territory.

"Striker-2, Striker-3, this is Major Geller, stand by for landing and assault team formations."

A 'roger Striker-1' comes in from the two other Beel choppers.

All teams prepare for rapid deployment as soon as they touch down.

A facial recognition scan is performed on the body forced out of the chopper they're following. A positive identification of Shelly Duncan is transferred to the Major's readout. The report is not conclusive as to whether Ms. Duncan is still alive or not. Her status is listed as *unknown*.

"Looks like 'Nurse Harlot' wasn't wearing her seatbelt," Geller says as the three others in his chopper share a quick laugh.

***

Graham's AutoCopter lands near the small desert town of Canyon Caverns. He leans over and gently places a kiss on Terah's forehead before stepping out. Running up a small hill to get a better perspective, he searches for the steakhouse. The terrain helps obscure the few brick buildings scattered around the area.

After surveying, Graham sees a mass of townspeople gathered in front of a large building. He trots down the hill, dodging large rocks and sagebrush as gravity accelerates his speed. He has never actually run before. It tires his body and he's forced to stop, grab his knees, and catch his breath.

Walking toward the crowd, he hears a collective murmuring. Some of the conversations share feelings of terror. It appears they are aware of the massive explosion at Vista Verde. They are outside because the power is out, possibly in all three Arel states.

A man of considerable age paces beyond the limits of the rest of the crowd. This man is so discouraged he is shouting in the direction of the Beel border. He is the first person Graham approaches.

"Excuse me, sir?" Graham asks, "Is that the steakhouse?"

The old man's gray hair swirls around his head by the light wind as he calms himself enough to answer the question. The man is slightly confused that anyone has missed seeing the enormous blast.

"You're hungry?" The old man asks incredulously, "Don't you know that Vista Verde just blew up?"

"Well, not exactly, I need to find Jennifer West."

"Sorry, never heard of her." The old man smiles as he walks back down into the group of townspeople.

Graham heads toward the front door of the steakhouse and tentatively walks in. There are still lots of people inside, but the patrons have traded eating for talking. The mood is somber frustration. The windows are open and a few candles are lit.

An elderly woman behind the bar is attempting to calm some of the patrons. Some of them still remember the days of being lorded over by authoritarians. But this old bartender, with a defiant tone that far out-shadows her frail voice, reminds her fellow Arels of the responsibilities that come with keeping their freedom.

"Tyrants grow in power when the people waiver in their resolve."

Graham attempts to interrupt the old woman, "Excuse me, ma'am?"

Her bravado grows louder and more pious, "The stubborn souls, who refute even the smallest speculation of an after life, soon shall be humbled!"

Graham tries again, this time with more urgency, "Excuse me!"

She raises her bony index finger in Graham's direction.

"Wait just a minute, young man."

He waves his hand at her and asks, "Where's Rhea?"

"Listen! Right now we must pull together as Arels," she snaps. "We need to stay calm until we hear from the Captain, okay?"

Before Graham can ask again, an Arel soldier grabs his arms and escorts him from the restaurant. A military vehicle is parked on the side of the steakhouse, its engine still idling. Graham is forced into the back seat.

Inside the vehicle are a driver, another soldier dressed in fatigues in the front seat, and a soldier whose shirt collar is pinned with a pair of captain's bars who sits in back.

The captain is looking directly at Graham, "The old guy tipped us off, said someone was looking for Jennifer West."

"Yeah, I need to find her," Graham's eyes then lock in on the nametag of the captain, "Miguel Sanchez, is that you?"

"Captain Sanchez to you boy," Miguel emphatically points to his collar, "Poking around for Ms. West is a pretty serious hobby."

"Look, Captain, Terah Piper told me to ask for Rhea when I got here. I did and now you're giving me crap?"

Captain Sanchez looks down at his clipboard.

"Well right now you've got a bigger problem. We scanned you and you're not a Beel but you're not an Arel either," the Captain says as he leans in. "Removing your chip, that's punishable by death—no matter whose side you're on."

Graham struggles to free himself from the grip of the soldier.

"Just tell Ms. West that Graham Duncan is here in the flesh."

The Captain shakes his head in disgust, "Listen, my pasty little amigo, last I checked, I was still in charge."

The two soldiers are instructed to take Graham out of the vehicle and over to the side of the steakhouse. Captain Sanchez places a call to the Arel High Command to expedite a death warrant while he walks over to join his men and his detainee.

***

The Beel forces land just behind Graham's craft, kicking up dust in all directions. The three teams of four exit the aircraft and assume an attack formation.

Using his embedded chipset intercom system, Major Geller directs his hit squads into position.

"Striker-2 and 3, post up on both flanks, over?"

The Major receives confirmation from the other teams.

The soldiers are holding advanced-composite bows with quivers full of super-light, titanium tipped arrows and a light carbon fiber defense shield.

"All strike teams, fire on my command," Major Geller orders.

Since most of the townspeople are gathered at the steakhouse, the Beel forces assemble from the surrounding hills.

***

Captain Sanchez is talking on his communicator with an Arel official. "Yes, yes, I understand the Server is down too, that's why I'm talking to you on this old radio." He nods in agreement, "Yeah okay, I'll file an execution report when I'm done."

The Captain arrives on the side of the steakhouse where Graham's stomach is pressed against the wall. "I'm sorry Mr. Duncan, but for the safety of our nation, I've been instructed to terminate you for not possessing an imbedded chipset as decreed by The Great Divide of 2040."

"But Miguel, it's me, Graham," he shouts as he turns to face the Captain.

"Whoa, amigo," he thrusts out his hand, "Don't try anything stupid now."

"But I knew you back in the server."

The Captain chuckles, "Oh yeah, they mirrored my persona into that video game for some thing or another."

"That's right. You see, you were a virus, hacked-in to help the resistance and I was an antivirus program tracking you."

"Now I'm positive you're a Beel spy." Captain Sanchez retrieves a serrated push dagger from his belt, "Codes can't jump; you should still be in that computer."

"But Terah discovered a way to—it's complicated."

The Captain signals his soldiers to hold Graham tightly. He raises the push dagger at an upward angle, just under Graham's ribcage.

"I'm sorry, our nation was just attacked. You've got to understand that we believe you might be a cell," Captain Sanchez says as if searching for another solution.

"Yeah, okay."

"Look, I don't want to do this."

Graham focuses on the dagger and then on the Captain's throat, "And I don't want to do this."

The knife violently reverts by way of Miguel's hand, and presses hard against his own throat. The two soldiers gasp at the sight of their commanding officer holding himself as hostage. However, no one is more stunned at what is transpiring than Captain Sanchez.

Needing to defuse the conflict, Graham calmly explains.

"I am Graham Duncan; I escaped from the Supreme Server through an essence-out jump into a LEVI life form." His eyes sharpen. "And as you can see, I have some control over physical quantum fields."

The soldiers are unsure how to help their commander.

"I don't hurt you; you don't hurt me, okay?" Graham eases his focus on the dagger so it lowers from the Captain's throat. "I just need to find Ms. West."

A frail but determined woman cuts a path through the nervous townspeople and makes her way to the side of the steakhouse.

"Are you the guy from the bar?"

Graham steps out from between the two soldiers, "Yes. I'm looking for Jennifer West."

"I am Jennifer West," the old woman announces.

Captain Sanchez is astonished, along with his contingent that this woman is the brilliant computer scientist. Graham is having trouble on a far different level.

"I'm sorry ma'am, but I've met Jennifer West and she's, well..."

"Twenty-five?" she bats her eyelashes, "An intelligent computer scientist disguised as a pretty girl bimbo. It fooled your algorithms didn't it?"

Graham smiles, "Yes ma'am."

"Terah Piper, I presume she didn't make it?"

Graham looks downward, "No ma'am."

"She finished her mission, getting you here safely."

"Yeah, but she was more than just a guide."

"I realize it must be difficult to reroute programmed responses into human emotions."

Graham sighs, "You know me pretty well."

"Know you? I wrote you. Well, along with an idiot Beel programmer," Jennifer smiles at her accomplishments. "I understand your QFT has transferred to your physiological body as well."

"Yeah, I can throw stuff with my mind."

"Paul will be excited to hear of this too."

"One more thing, Ms. West, you're not safe here." Graham nervously looks over his shoulder, "we were tricked into giving your location to the Beels."

"I figured something was amiss when I heard you were 'looking' for Rhea. And by the way, try to get the secret code right the first time. It's *Is Rhea working tonight?*' it'll save you a lot of trouble next time."

Captain Sanchez interrupts, "I hate to break up the reunion, but I've got to get you to the bunker, Ms. West."

"He comes with me," Jennifer points to Graham.

The Captain shouts to his men, "All right, I'll set up a team here, while you get Duncan and West to safety!"

Graham and Ms. West are rushed into the back of the idling military vehicle. As it starts up the side of an unmarked hill, Graham bails out, leaving the soldiers to continue taking Ms. West to the bunker.

"What are you doing?" Captain Sanchez shouts toward Graham, "We got this."

"I want to help," Graham gasps, trying to catch his breath.

"It would help if you were in shape, boy," he smiles, "and you could use a little more sun."

A siren blares above the restaurant signaling all the patrons to form several lines and to wait for orders. Every Arel is trained in basic combat.

Graham and the Captain join the rest of the militia in front of the steakhouse.

"Ready your bows," the Captain orders.

A small force is ordered to circle around to the back of the hills to outflank the enemy.

Graham goes inside the steakhouse. Following behind is Captain Sanchez. It is quiet inside as most of the militia is assembled in front, waiting for further instruction.

"Miguel, I know the Beels have to keep stealing land, but why did America split apart anyway?"

"First, it's Captain."

"Sorry, in the sim you were 'Miguel.' "

"And second, career politicians!"

"What do you mean?" Graham asks, "They kept getting reelected?"

"Well, it was more like once in office they'd change the rules to stay in power." The Captain takes a quick look around the hillside through his binoculars. "And when they were done they would hand their seat down to their kids like it was the family business. They became an entrenched ruling class so to speak."

Captain Sanchez drops his binoculars and picks up his two-way radio.

"Defense team update, over?"

"We're in position, Sir," an officer responds, "No evidence of a threat."

"Affirmative."

He expands further on a topic he loathes but loves to talk about.

"We broke apart because these oligarchs wanted us to subsidize the lazy. As the unproductive class grew, the more votes they'd get."

"Yeah, an unsustainable society," Graham interjects, "Terah told me about that."

"And, it got worse; these ruling idiots wanted even more control. They didn't lead our country anymore, they lorded over it."

"So The Great Divide solved all of that?"

"Mostly," Captain Sanchez shrugs, "Soon after the Divide, Arel experienced an economic boom. It was so great that most citizens didn't even notice the rapid growth in our own government."

The Captain becomes so absorbed in explaining to Graham the dangers of an unengaged populace he forgets to check in with his defense team.

"By lending credence to flimsy, hypothetical catastrophes, these guys used fear to spread their agenda of more control."

"We repeat, still no signs of Beels strike teams," a defense team member checks in by radio.

"Oh, roger that," replies the Captain.

Graham is not fully prepared to hear the chilling details of early Arel history.

"The difference between us and Beel is that we resisted our government's encroachments on our freedoms and we beat them back. These corrupt clowns were not only forced from power but man, it got brutal. They were rounded up by Arel militias and given a more lasting justice."

Bracing himself for a lesson in harsh reality, Graham asks, "You say 'lasting' as in life in prison?"

"No, as in execution. These oppressors were publically hanged every hour for nine days straight." Captain Sanchez adds, "Even their old-guard media shills were hunted down."

"Wait a minute, what about interfering with the first amendment?"

"You see, in war, there are rules; in survival, there are none.

"So, they were executed too?"

"They swung right alongside." Captain Sanchez holds his radio up, "I've got to check in; any sign of Beel activity?"

"That's a negative, sir," a voice replies over the radio.

Graham stretches his legs under the restaurant table where he sits.

"What about the law; were any Arels jailed?"

"Some involved in the executions were tried but found not guilty. Obviously, it's not a perfect system."

Graham's curiosity increases and he probes Miguel about the creation of The Supreme Server. The captain responds.

"The Server put an end to the vigilantes. It views the law in black and white so it's not susceptible to man's changing interpretations. Blind justice benefits everyone no matter their social-economic standing. Unfortunately the Beel government sees only gray areas that become darker or lighter according to the Autocrat's desire. But, hey, that's their problem."

"Are you some type of history scholar to know all this?" Graham inquires.

The Captain smiles, "Brother, I'm just a product of Arel public schools. We're not only taught history, it is the basis of our future, too."

Chapter Thirty

The military truck carrying Jennifer West and her two escort soldiers arrives safely at the bunker and stops in front of a security gate. Jennifer punches in a code that opens the gate and the vehicle drives to the outpost.

Ms. West leads them toward the main control center. On the way they pass two checkpoints; one requires a simple card-swipe while the other requires a computerized interview. The questions are random and range from 'how's the weather' to a more complex question structure. The computer is not necessarily interested in the answers, but the response times, cadence, and inflections of the answerer. Ms. West's synaptic variances are recorded and measured against her files. Passing the interview the final control room door opens and West and her entourage enter the room.

She is anxious to review the satellite footage. Vista Verde's explosion was recorded on an infrared spectrogram. Jennifer reloads the video and watches the replay of the massive event. In the seconds immediately after the explosion there was a glitch in the stream as the bunker's back-up generators kicked in. She notices a reading that indicated a cooling process had begun at some of the reactor cores.

However, Ms. West is unable to fully understand all the data as this is her first look at the materials.

"So, if it were beginning to cool down, what caused the explosion?" Jennifer ponders aloud.

One of the military-escorts attempts to answer her, "Explosives. What else?"

She focuses on his name badge.

"Is that your name, Corporal?" Ms. West inquires.

"Yes ma'am. Phillips. Skip."

"I guess it's no surprise the Beels would disobey that rule, too."

"That seems correct, Ma'am."

She stares at the slow, hypnotic sweep of the satellite's detailed imaging. A blip near the steakhouse catches her notice.

"Skip, what do you think of this?"

The young corporal leans over her shoulder and waits for the sweep to come around again.

"Pardon me, Ma'am, but I don't see it."

"I didn't see it this time either."

Jennifer discusses the severity of the situation with the two soldiers.

"This outpost in the mountain isn't just a safe house with command abilities; it's home to a secret reactor core. It's taken seven years to build and though it's one-tenth the size of Vista Verde, it'll produce more energy."

What Ms. West did not reveal however, was the bold new principle that will power this reactor. The dangerous, nuclear fuel-rods used in other generators will be replaced with a phenomenon known as a 'Psychothetical catalyst.'

Corporal Phillips informs Ms. West of the current troop movements.

"Our forces in the Phoenix area are stretched to the limit from the blast. We've routed more troops from the north to help us secure this area but we're looking at an hour before they arrive."

***

The atmosphere around the restaurant is tense as the militia force, headed by Captain Sanchez, waits for the Beel strike teams to materialize. Male and female archers are assembled at the back of the group while shield and spear teams line the front.

Due to the blast knocking out Arel chipset communications, Captain Sanchez is forced to use an old two-way radio to contact the command center.

"This is Steakhouse Force Bravo to Canyon Command. Come in C.C.?"

A crackle emanates from the hand-held radio.

"Affirmative Captain, we're secure."

"Ms. West, do you have enough power to uplink to live sat-view?"

"No, only replay systems. You're on your own I'm afraid."

"Yes Ma'am, we'll handle it."

Graham, overhearing the conversation, presses Captain Sanchez for more answers.

"An old steakhouse and a command bunker in the middle of nowhere; what's so special about this place?"

The Captain smiles, "I guess if you had stayed in the truck you would have found out."

An Arel rooftop sentry spots something moving toward the steakhouse. He contacts the Captain.

"Sir, a Beel strike team is approaching. And get this, it's from the front."

"From the front? Sitting ducks are just fine with me," Sanchez shakes his head in disbelief. "Get into battle formation, just in case."

At the same time, the Beel strike team waves the orange Flag of Dialogue. This act invokes a diplomatic response by both sides. Two of the senior members of the assembled forces are to meet just beyond the kill-zone of the archers.

Major Geller joins Captain Sanchez at a spot directly in the middle of the potential battlefield. The Arel's eighty-five person militia brigade far outnumbers the twelve members that make up the Beel strike teams. The Arels have the tactical advantage of war prosecution.

Major Geller states his intentions. "We must bring Jennifer West back to our nation to be tried for crimes against humanity. Please release her into our custody at once."

Captain Sanchez answers with a crooked smile. "Well, Major, we outnumber you. But I don't know if you can count that high."

"She must be held accountable."

"She's a civilian, and she's an Arel. She stays."

"Bring her here immediately or be subject to our decisive response."

Another message comes over the Captain's two-way radio. "Captain, this is Team Alpha, we've apprehended the Beel's two other strike teams attempting to outflank us, over."

"Roger that, return to base." Miguel lowers his radio. "We just captured your men; looks like you won't be demanding anything today, so beat it."

The Captain turns and walks back toward his militia with a sense of relief. While on his way to the Steakhouse Sanchez contacts Ms. West, "This is Steakhouse Force Bravo to C.C."

Jennifer responds efficiently, "Status update?"

"Two of three strike teams apprehended. Commander was advised to leave our country."

In a stubborn decision Major Geller's four-man team swiftly advances on the militia. The commotion draws the attention of the Arel sentry again. Captain Sanchez receives the message at the same time four arrows rain down on him. One pierces his leg.

He signals his team to answer back with a barrage of arrows, to no avail as the Beel force is still too far away. The Captain warns the Beel strike team that no mercy will be shown to them.

The militia quickly advances in the direction of the four Beel soldiers. As they get close enough for another attack with arrows, the Beels drop their armor. A look of alarm spreads wildly throughout the Arel's contingent.

Each Beel raises an automatic weapon.

Over the years the Beels have secretly bribed weapons' inspectors by promising them a life of foolish, unquenchable pleasure in return for looking the other way. The Beels cloak the hypocrisy of their actions by pretending to be honest, caring, and charitable.

Most of the assembled Arel militia has never heard gunfire. A few of the older members, however, remember it from before The Great Divide. The loud burst of fire provides a cruel soundtrack as row after row of Arel warriors fall to the ground.

Captain Sanchez announces a retreat to the steakhouse. Even though it's an order, several men and women stand their ground bravely attempting to answer back with their spears.

The desert dust provides an eerie fog for the battle. The Arel forces quickly drop by two-thirds while the Beel strike team loses just one member. There is no rational answer for automatic weapons in the hands of the aggressor. Evil obeys no laws and respects no one.

The remainder of the militia, along with Captain Sanchez and Graham, barricade themselves inside the steakhouse. Some weep quietly over the loss of life, while others over the hopelessness of their situation.

The last Beel strike team stands outside the steakhouse with their weapons still leveled at the compound. Major Geller is unscathed, but his uniform is covered by a thin layer of dust.

"You have five minutes to deliver Jennifer West to me, or you will all perish!"

Graham and Captain Sanchez sit with their backs up against an overturned table near the front of the restaurant.

"Captain, let me go out and talk to them."

"They'll shoot you."

"If I can get close enough…"

"Oh, use that quantum power thing?"

"Yeah," Graham surveys the room and seeks a volunteer, "I need a woman to help me, someone in their seventies, maybe."

Though he speaks to the militia, reality is still a gory sell. No hands are raised.

"Look, we can't force you; we can only ask." The Captain's voice is more resolute than Graham's, "Yes, the Beels have the will to win, but we have prepared to win. One is a wish, the other a goal; one is waited for; the other is reached for."

With his thoughts laid out to the remaining members, one woman raises her hand.

Her bravery is interrupted by Major Geller, who bellows from the street. "You've wasted two minutes of your life. Will you spend the rest more wisely?"

Graham calls for the volunteer to join him at the front of the room.

She is of middle age, but life in the harsh desert town has added more creases to her face than the years could have.

"Sarah Snow. I want to help, if I can."

Two of the Beels pull fuel-tipped arrows from their quivers and set fire to them.

"You've got one minute. Bring out Ms. West."

Graham whispers to Sarah what to say.

"I'm coming out. Don't fire your weapons!" Sarah shouts through a window.

Before she exits the restaurant, Graham soaks a torn bar rag in blood and wraps it around her knee.

Sarah slowly opens the door and hobbles toward Major Geller and his men. She collapses just outside the door. "I was hit!"

The Major ponders several outcomes in the few seconds before he answers. "I'll send my soldier."

One of the Beels, holding his rifle, approaches Sarah. He steps closer, but is still out of Graham's range.

Only the labored breathing of the nervous Arel contingent is heard in the quiet steakhouse.

The last few steps are the slowest. Graham watches.

He yells out the window, "She's not Jennifer West, it's a trick!"

The confused soldier turns back to Major Geller for guidance. This is the time of maximum opportunity for Graham.

He steps into the doorway and focuses on the soldier's weapon. Instantly, it is jerked from the soldier's hand to Graham's. This is Sarah's cue to shove him aside.

Having never before experienced shooting a gun, Graham lets out an uneven burst of fire, striking at the soldier's feet before moving to his core. Realizing Graham's clip is empty, Major Geller and the other soldier hastily rush into firing position.

Even while holding a tactical advantage, the Beels consider emotion, even when it is unnecessary. The Major, boiling with anger, rushes toward Graham and Sarah and begins firing his weapon. Major Geller's ability to properly aim his rifle is greatly hampered by the unstable sway of bitterness and rage.

Graham focuses his QFT on the Major's rifle and tears it away. Holding the weapon more steadily, he drops the other soldier with a deadly burst. Most of the bullets group tightly around the hostile's core.

Redirecting his attention back to the disarmed Major, he steps forward and strikes him in the jaw with the butt of the rifle. The Major drops to his knees in pain just a few feet from Graham, but the commander is too proud to surrender.

"I shall never serve an Arel whether in torture or enslaved!"

Those of the steakhouse militia file out slowly and surround Graham, Sarah, and the wounded Major. There are neither cheers of victory nor words of vengeance, just solemn prayers for the men and women who have died. The sound of wind fills the silence by sweeping the low desert terrain.

Graham grants the Major's last request. Using his QFT he quietly stops Geller's heart.

Captain Sanchez informs C.C. that all Beel strike teams have been neutralized and their weapons confiscated.

"Copy," confirms C.C., "We've sent for a medical team. Now bring Graham here at once."

The Captain turns to his militia, "Never again will we disarm our citizens. The hypocrites of war shall face an equally armed resistance for centuries to come."

A few members of the steakhouse militia care for the wounded as they wait for help. Supplies are stretched thin as the entire Valley is coping with the horrific explosion west of Phoenix.

Graham stares vaguely into the desert as Miguel limps over to him.

He offers his hand. "Nice work."

Graham shakes Miguel's hand, "How's your leg?"

"I got a bar rag tied around it. I'll live."

Miguel walks over to the brave volunteer.

"Sarah, you were awesome. Thank you."

She trembles, but is able to smile.

The Captain turns to Graham, "Come on, Duncan, let's get you to the bunker."

He directs Graham around to the back of the steakhouse where a tarp partially covers an old motorcycle.

"Have you ridden one of these before?"

"Nah, I've only been human for a few hours."

The Captain reaches over and pulls the tarp off.

It's an older model, and neglect has transformed its showroom appeal of excitement and adventure into the drabber version of economical transportation. The tires, suffering from dry rot, still hold enough air. The seat, barely large enough for the rider, now must accommodate a passenger as well.

The Captain opens the gas cap and rocks the bike back and forth, listening for fuel.

"Yep, should be enough to get us to the bunker."

The Captain steps behind Graham and gestures at the handlebars.

"They're a lot of fun. Just don't kill us, Duncan."

Graham swings his leg over the seat, just behind the gas tank. Though he's never actually ridden a motorcycle, he has programmed knowledge of basic starting procedures and a wide sampling of different riding techniques.

The Captain laughs and slaps Graham's shoulder.

"You crazy Code, I was just kidding." Captain Sanchez steps forward to the handle bars, "I'm supposed to take you to see Ms. West. Slide back, Rookie."

Both men laugh.

The bike cranks and sputters out puffs of blue smoke from the tailpipe. Finally the engine catches.

A message for Captain Sanchez comes over his radio. Unfortunately the motorcycle's engine easily overpowers the two-way.

Sanchez and Duncan are ready to ride up the hill.

"Hey!" Captain Sanchez says, "Use the pegs. Kick 'em down."

Graham kicks one down and burns his leg on the exhaust pipe.

"Ouch!" Graham shouts as he jumps off the bike.

Sanchez laughs.

Before Graham climbs back on, he notices the radio.

"Captain, I think Ms. West is calling you."

The Captain's facial expression turns from jovial to pained. Instead of grabbing the radio, he slumps forward. His foot drops onto the shifter, forcing the motorcycle forward into the dirt.

"Captain?" Graham chases after the motorcycle, "What's wrong?"

Moments later, the motorcycle succumbs to a slow speed crash that dumps the Captain into a strip of desert brush.

Graham frantically races to the accident scene.

"Captain Sanchez? Miguel? Are you hurt?"

While checking his vital signs, the two-way beeps again.

"This is C.C., come in Sanchez!"

Graham grabs the radio from the Captain's belt.

"This is Graham Duncan; Miguel's been hurt."

"What, how badly?" Ms. West asks.

"He's breathing, but I think he's out cold."

"Listen to me carefully, Graham," Ms. West drops her tone and speaks sharply, "I need you to feel around the back of Miguel's neck. You're looking for a small, metallic prong."

Her assumption is confirmed when Graham finds the tiny protrusion on the Captain's neck.

"Yes, I found it. What do I do?"

"Nothing, it's a tranquilizer dart. I tried to warn him that a drone was in your area."

The drone, typically used for indigenous animal management, had originally locked its sights on Graham, but when he burned his leg he inadvertently dodged the drone's strike. Unfortunately, the Captain did not.

Left with few options, Ms. West presses Graham to continue up the hill. She sends the bunker's coordinates to the bike's navigation display for Graham to follow. She tells him the drone will complete a facial recognition on Sanchez and realize it hit the wrong target.

"What, I'm a target?"

"Yes. Hurry."

Graham gets on the bike, and starts it. The Nav-unit's female voice begins with surprisingly easy instructions.

"Continue in this direction for approximately one-hundred feet."

Graham twists the motorcycle's throttle while slowly releasing the clutch. The bike begins moving forward. He puts his feet up on the riding pegs and adds more throttle to the engine.

Simple gyroscopic balance is new to him.

His chaotic steering resembles an unattended fire hose. Graham's coded intelligence is not much help either as the proper learning of balance is through muscle memory.

The Nav-unit's voice chimes in.

"Recalculating... "

Graham forgets the voice is computer generated.

"Sorry, this is new for me."

"In twenty feet, turn right," the Nav-unit advises.

The engine reaches its maximum revolutions for first gear and Graham shifts the bike into second. Lack of coordination now joins lack of balance, sending the front wheel into the air. Graham is surprised by his wheelie. This greatly affects the Nav-unit's command to turn right in twenty feet.

"Recalculating."

Graham grows more frustrated.

"You're messing up my concentration."

The unit's calming, female voice again attempts to correct Graham's horrible steering and general lack of control.

"Turn left in... recalculating. Turn right in... recalculating."

"When? When?" he barks in frustration.

Just outside Graham's QFT range, the drone fires its last two tranquilizer darts in succession. Graham's poor steering has an upside; it helps him evade the drone attack.

"Turn left in sixteen feet... in twenty-two... turn left in... recalculating."

"*That's* what I'm talking about!" Graham shouts as he jumps a dry wash bed.

The Nav-unit gives Graham one final instruction.

"Please stop your vehicle immediately and wait for assistance."

This however, was the easiest instruction for Graham to obey. He pulls in the clutch lever and the motorcycle rolls to a safe stop. He shuts off the engine and drops the bike on its side. He has made the journey up the monotonous desert landscape to an area close to the top.

Since the Nav-unit was unable to properly direct the user, a detailed report is sent to Jennifer.

Chapter Thirty One

Inside a fortified building, a few miles west of the border of Arel, Beel Commander Colonel Jeremiah Pennington is conferring with other military strategists. The assessments of their planned invasion of Arel are being calculated around a conference table.

"The charged detonation was successful," Colonel Pennington says, "The outage will allow our teams to invade without the Supreme Server's interference."

Chief of War Planning, Counselor Carter Hewel, is exasperated by the failed mission of Major Hugo Geller as he skims a transcript of the battle.

"Colonel Pennington, we found Jennifer West but were unable to secure her? As I read more of the report," the Counselor flips another page over the top of his dossier, "It appears that you sent Geller and his men on a suicide mission. That's regrettable and a waste of resources."

The Colonel looks up from the tactical invasion map in the center of the table. With a pained expression, he addresses the Counselor.

"This is why you sit at a desk hundreds of miles from the fight. You do not fret the arrows of your enemy; you do not taste the salty exhaustion. Yours is a world of little plastic pieces scattered around a map. You confront and you wage war by proxy. To you, fear is a hypothetical discussion where the wrong answer can be safely recanted."

The Counselor slams down his fist.

"Pennington, you serve at my pleasure." He relaxes and gestures at the Colonel, "Now, tell me again, what exactly was accomplished with Geller's mission?"

He glances down.

"We knew West's general location, but we needed to confirm Duncan's use of Quantum Field Telekinesis. Our drone watched him disarm Geller and his men as we planned." Pennington redirects his eyes, "For a computer code to transfer those abilities to a human host is simply astounding. When we capture him, we'll build an army of QFT soldiers."

Now that Arel is limping along on battery power, a two pronged attack is laid out for the other strategists in the conference room. The first will be an aerial drone campaign and second, the activation of a Beel sleeper cell.

The effort to control the major cities and command centers of Arel will be carried out by drones.

"One more thing, Colonel, is Ambassador Olsen on board?"

"He resisted at first," the Colonel smiles, "but I can assure you the Ambassador won't interfere with the operation."

***

Graham squats next to a row of bushes and searches the hazy sky for the drone. Grabbing the two-way, he attempts to contact Jennifer. He hears only static, so he continues scanning his surroundings. The ground is a mix of dirt, sand, and stone, dotted with sagebrush, cactus, and mesquite trees.

He notices something shiny about a mile away. It appears to be a message. Upon deciphering the cadence of the flashes Graham discovers it is binary code.

D-U-N-C-A-N

He leans over and breaks off the motorcycle's side mirror. He responds to the message.

Corporal Phillips steps back into the bunker and reports his success with contacting Graham.

"He said 'sleep tight', Ms. West. How would you like to respond?"

Jennifer looks over at him.

"He wants to make sure it's us. Here, respond 'motel', Skip."

"Motel?"

"Yes, hurry."

The Corporal steps outside and spells *M-O-T-E-L* with his mirror.

Graham knows only Jennifer would come up with this answer, so he runs toward the light.

The distance is not long, but Graham needs to weave around rocks, cacti, and ditches to get there.

He realizes that since he and Terah left the Server, he has sided with the Arels. He mentally cobbles together a few questions for Jennifer to help solidify this choice.

Graham arrives at the location of where he first saw the mirror flashes. There are no visible doors. He waits.

Inside the bunker, Jennifer had the soldiers wire vehicle batteries together to power a radar sweep. Finding no airborne drone signatures, she gives the order to let Graham in.

Graham hears an electric motor and several 'clunks' as a boulder lifts slightly and rolls aside.

"Please follow me, sir," Corporal Phillips arrives in the doorway.

Graham is led down a corridor; the low ceiling forces him to slouch while he walks. The hall is lit with LEDs, all caged in thick, glass domes.

Corporal Phillips passes by a metal door labeled 'Emergency Exit' and stops at an elongated secured hatch. He turns his back to Graham and says nothing. As a safety precaution, the hatch is designed to look like an entryway for the command center when in fact it is a decoy. If hostiles were to enter, it would trip an alarm causing the hatch to slam shut and poisonous gas to be released into the room.

Graham is impatient.

The silent soldier motions to the emergency exit, and directs Graham to open it.

This leads to the control center, officially known as Canyon Caverns Command.

Jennifer West looks up from her monitor. The radar display lights her face with an eerie green glow. The room is lit to a barely functional level, to conserve power.

Corporal Phillips turns, secures the door, and takes his place next to Ms. West and the other soldier.

"Good, you're safe," Jennifer starts, "I want to --"

"Wait, I got a few questions first."

"Sure."

"Back in the simulation, I could have stopped your coup in the final minutes, right?"

"Absolutely," she says while nodding.

"So, how did you know I wouldn't?"

Ms. West gets up from the controls and sighs.

"I didn't. It was a gamble. I ordered our team to install an override memory implant into your sub files. In particular, the part about the government 'death' panels withholding life saving medicines from your parents. Without you awakening to our covert activities, we gave you a real suspicion of an overzealous government. We didn't lie about the existence of death panels we simply related what was going on at the time America split in two."

"You mean they really do have power over who lives and who dies?"

"They did. So, I imagined that some day we would need a 'work around' for the Supreme Server's antivirus systems. Ultimately, when Terah gave you the truth of our mission, you adhered to the Trivium of critical thought and correctly balanced emotion with logic."

He goes on to his next question.

"Why did Terah bring me out of the Server too?"

"In the simulation program, I received updates on your dissection techniques of Dr. Jerome. It was the first time you instinctively used QFT. So when you took human form I wanted Terah to instigate a situation where you'd be compelled to use it. I wanted to see if it would transfer into a human host. The fact you're here is evidence that she witnessed a QFT display."

"She was killed trying to get me here."

"Terah Piper," Ms. West looks downward in remorse, "I would like to have met her."

Graham stares off into the distance.

"Terah meant a lot to me," he makes eye contact with Ms. West, "I loved her."

"Yes, that is understandable." Ms. West interjects, "I wrote every line of her computer code; from her physical beauty to her tactical prowess. She was everything I wasn't."

The mood is somber as Graham quietly reflects on the short life of Terah Piper.

The other soldier in the bunker leans over and types in a prompt on the computer. He has been sweeping the area for other aircraft and a vexing theory emerges on the display.

> *Assuming a drone was attempting to tranquilize Duncan for capture, a new ground team would have been sent as this happened after the capture of Major Geller's forces. The threat level has been raised to Red.*

The soldier motions for Corporal Phillips to have a look at his screen.

After the Corporal reads the text of the Arel Warning System he informs Ms. West.

She stands silent for a second as her eyes roll to their upper left corners.

"Skip, I want you to run the widest sweep you can." Jennifer orders. She then redirects her attention to Graham, "Any more questions?"

"I'm still not sure why I'm here." Graham nervously runs his hand through his hair, "let me guess; you want me to protect the bunker with my QFT?"

Jennifer laughs and turns to Graham.

"Let me tell you something about QFT. As a form of practical military defense, it's insignificant. A simple smoke bomb could incapacitate you."

"So, I should stick to beating up local thugs?"

Ms. West looks at a door at the other end of the room.

"My husband will explain."

An elderly man walks over and shakes hands with Graham.

"I am Doctor Paul Jerome."

"Oh," Graham adds a bit of dark humor, "By the way Doc, I'm sorry about that whole torturing you to death thing."

The scientist's face is not accustomed to smiling.

"Understandable."

"I tore your organs out and examined them one by one."

"I like to think of it as one's mirror being deleted slowly."

Dr. Jerome, as his wife suggested, explains the importance of Graham's QFT. His team has completed construction of a revolutionary new single reactor unit located just beneath the hillside. The reactor will generate electricity using Psychothetical energy. This applied theory of generating power from thought will provide safe, clean, and abundant energy. The plant will use Graham's Quantum Field Telekinesis abilities to turn the turbines.

Chapter Thirty Two

Colonel Pennington is updated of the Beel's armed drone launch. The first wave, numbering in the hundreds, begins entering Arel airspace at the western border with Beel. Fifty Auto-Copters with support teams follow in formation behind the massive unmanned aerial force.

"Counselor Hewel," the Colonel proclaims, "I've received word that all major cities in Arizona will be surrounded in less than twenty minutes."

"Good work Pennington, but I'm afraid you'll need a ground war to take control of the land."

"Counselor, with all due respect, your thinking has become obsolete." The Colonel walks over to a window, and notices children at the school playground, "We don't need to control the land, just its people."

The fifty Auto-Copters are staffed with medical technicians who will begin implanting new identification chips in Arel citizens as they surrender. The process involves a rapid insertion device and takes about two seconds to complete. The new chips are similar, but allow termination commands to be sent from Beel headquarters just as they are from the Supreme Server. The people of Arel will become slaves in order to receive their daily rations.

***

Dr. Jerome explains to Graham that his QFT will generate a vast new source of clean, efficient power for generations to come.

"Hey, look, I know I'll have to hit the books or something," Graham smiles as new prospects burst into his mind, "But I'll be making some good money, right?

"I'm afraid it's a little more complicated than that," Jennifer interjects.

"Well, you know, buy a house and get a pool table or something."

She entertains his idea of working at the new power plant; however, she adds a dose of reality to the scenario. "What happens if you get sick or injured?"

"Okay, how about an on-site medical clinic?" He holds his arm up, "I can wear a cast and still spin the turbines with my head, right?"

"That's true," Jennifer answers, "but there is one major limitation we haven't talked about."

She reminds Graham that as a human, he has a human's lifespan.

"Yeah, okay," he struggles to understand where Jennifer is leading the conversation, "but I could live another eighty or ninety years, right?"

Dr. Jerome provides some insight.

"118 years is the average lifespan here in Arel. However, there is an obvious slope of diminishing capacity that must be accounted for."

Raising his hand like a student, Graham finishes Dr. Jerome's thought.

"All right, so I could give you sixty or seventy good years."

"In a perfect world, maybe," Dr. Jerome cautions, "but what would happen if insurgents attacked your house?" He averts his eyes downward, "That's a risk we cannot take."

Jennifer forces a smile, "Please, sit down."

"I'm okay, you know, I could just live here I guess. Fix the place up; flat screen, a bed, and a fridge."

"I'm afraid you're half right." She puts her hands together as if she were about to pray, "You won't be able to leave the bunker."

The depth of her solemn words impacts Graham's demeanor. He is now ready to hear the rest of the plan.

"We would essence-in your persona to the plant's server and you'll live as a computer avatar again."

Feeling cornered, he throws out questions for anyone to answer.

"Can't you just write another QFT program? Or look, you can take mine. Just mirror-in that part of me. Maybe if I have kids they'll inherit my abilities and take over the business. What about that?"

Jennifer and Dr. Jerome recognize that Graham is struggling with the 'acceptance phase' of what will be his new reality.

"As far as writing a new QFT program," Jennifer begins, "it could take years to figure out how you used Hyper Neural Access to focus your

Telekinetic powers. We can't do a partial mirror either as the program ran in the background of your conscious files."

Dr. Jerome puts his hand on Graham's shoulder, "As far as your children, some may receive your QFT, but at what strength we don't know."

Jennifer continues informing Graham how he will power the new reactor from inside the server. His QFT will spin the turbines in the outside world just by his presence in the power plant simulation. A great advantage to being in the server is that he will not be susceptible to the frailties of human life.

As a way to remove any angst from his avatar, Graham is assured his conscience will be erased and replaced.

"You're all we have," Jennifer pleads, "help us."

Graham looks for confirmation from the others, who nod in agreement.

Accepting his future, Graham shrugs.

Dr. Jerome walks over to the wall and removes a map, revealing a docking station. He pulls a small tablet-processor from his coat pocket and places it on the docking station.

"This will be your new home, Graham. Once inside of course, you won't know you're in a simulation."

The Doctor then retrieves a slim, metallic headband for Graham to wear in order to convert his synapses into computer code. The process will take fifteen minutes to complete. Once he's installed, Graham's presence will begin powering the reactor.

Dr. Jerome affixes the headband to Graham and prepares the computer for an essence-in process.

"This is the only way, I guess," Graham concedes.

Jennifer's eyes begin to tear slightly. "When your knowledge base grew exponentially, we wanted to see if it could be transferred to a human vessel. We're grateful you kept challenging your curiosity."

Graham manages a self-conscious smile. "Yea me, I get to power a nation." Graham looks down to collect a final thought. "You know, Ms. West, I remember a sub-file you installed about Christianity. Since I became human, I think I understand it more, except for this, do I have a soul?"

Jennifer pauses and brushes away her tears.

"Only God knows the answer to that."

There is just enough emergency battery power to finish the transfer of Graham into the computer simulation. In fact, the power will be monitored so it will not fluctuate. If the power were to fail during the upload, Graham's mind would be scrambled and the QFT program lost.

Dr. Jerome enters the file-transfer protocol, as Graham's eyes begin to twitch.

Seconds later, Graham groans and his chin drops to his chest. A knife has lodged into his abdomen; a trail of blood oozes out with every labored heartbeat. Jennifer and her husband look at each other, shocked.

Corporal Skip Phillips throws another dagger. This one sticks into Dr. Jerome's chest, and he slumps over.

Jennifer screams. The Beel sleeper cell readies another knife, but is engaged by the other soldier.

Graham and Dr. Jerome are suffering from life threatening wounds. Jennifer is forced to choose who to help.

***

The Beel drones successfully surround Phoenix. Their invasion campaign disseminates propaganda to all broadcast towers. The Arel citizens have already witnessed the obliteration of Vista Verde and now are coping with a rapidly depleting battery system.

The nervous Arels are instructed to form lines in front of the nearest Beel AutoCopter landing zone. A message blares from loudspeakers on the choppers.

"Receive the new chip implant and prosper. Resist, and suffer."

Some Arels are vulnerable to the Beel's imposing presence and will gladly trade their freedoms for perceived safety. Years of not having to defend their beliefs have lulled their society into a dangerous complacency.

Adding to the terror, several drones launch their ordnance at tall buildings. The debris rains down over the frightened populace. The lines of Arels willing to submit grow longer with each missile strike. Beel medical technicians carry out the implantation process swiftly.

Several hundred miles away, watching the invasion plan via closed circuit TV, Counselor Hewel, Colonel Pennington, and several war-planners in the Beels' Command conference room react to the early successes.

"We're right on schedule, Counselor," the Colonel announces.

"Yes, it appears your strategy is producing results." The Counselor takes a seat at the conference table and peruses the new data that's come in. "But, I want absolute control. Send in the battalions to secure the territory."

"Have you seen our troops? They're not capable of securing a child's playground. It would be a colossal waste of our time."

"I demand a full scale ground invasion!" the Counselor blusters.

The Colonel is irritated by his boss's insistence on using primitive tactics. He believes Counselor Hewel has lost most of his usefulness as Chief of War planning.

"That's it!" Colonel Pennington slams his fist on the conference table, causing the water glasses to tip over. "You are excused, Mr. Hewel." The Colonel motions for his two guards to escort the Counselor from the conference room.

Before Pennington's men get close, they both drop to the floor, lifeless.

Astonished, the Colonel steps away from the conference table, picks up his water glass, and straightens his tie.

"I am deeply sorry for my outburst, Counselor Hewel."

"Do you remember when I ascended to Chief of War? You should. I had all the chips in the highest ranking officers, including yours, tweaked a little. This was to protect me from mutinous bastards like you." The Counselor smirks. "Jeremiah, I think it's time for you to go."

"But sir, you still need me," he pleads, "I have more plans for the invasion."

"The only thing I need from you is, well, nothing."

The Colonel drops to the floor, still clutching the glass.

Counselor Hewel's men drag the three bodies from the conference room.

An assistant asks, "Sir, shall I deploy the battalion?"

"Of course not! Pennington was right; they are a gaggle of uncivil buffoons. I was merely testing his loyalty." He glances down at the spilled water, "What a shame he failed."

"Sir, shall I send the usual condolences to their families?"

"Not for Pennington. I want you to go to his house," Counselor Hewel walks over to gaze out the window. "And tell his wife, personally. When she begins to sob, I want you to kill her."

Chapter Thirty Three

Jennifer continues performing CPR on the severely wounded Graham Duncan, keeping him alive long enough to essence him into the server. She offers a few words of comfort to her dying husband, as she keeps her focus on Graham.

A bloody push dagger is decisively jerked from the back of Corporal Phillips' head by the other Arel soldier, Private Cody Wade. He is exhausted from the lengthy encounter with the Beel operative. However, there is no time to pause; he rushes to help the gravely wounded doctor.

Private Wade tears his uniform, plugs the wound and begins performing CPR. Even though the hemorrhaging lightens, Dr. Jerome is near death.

A superior education cannot always stop emotions from overtaking certain situations; though Jennifer sobs deeply for her husband, she accepts her decision to keep Graham alive. Losing his ability to power the Psychothetical reactor would be devastating.

Jennifer glances at the tablet screen. She will have to endure a few more tormenting minutes until the upload is complete.

"You can stop now, Private. I don't want him to suffer any longer."

"Yes Ma'am," Private Wade looks solemnly at Ms. West, "I am deeply sorry."

One final labored gasp and her husband quietly succumbs to his wounds.

"Can you hear me, Graham?"

"Mom?"

"Look at me," she turns his head toward her, "I need you to stay with me, okay?"

"Did I get stabbed?"

"Yes."

He looks down at the pooling blood around him.

"Am I going to die?"

"Not if I can get you into the server first."

Graham, kept alive by Jennifer, goes from lethargy to a complete loss of consciousness. Jennifer knows she is out of time.

Hemorrhagic shock, has taken a second life. Graham's body is cold, extremely pale, and without a pulse.

A confirmation message is displayed on the screen.

"He's in!" Jennifer announces.

Her selfless efforts have successfully loaded Graham into the server. She takes a moment to properly grieve while Graham's QFT abilities begin powering the reactor.

A full mainframe reboot of the Supreme Server has begun. A host of critical decisions are being implemented and earlier judgments are under review. Many of those will be swiftly overturned. Most importantly, the Beel takeover will be nullified and urgent notices to vacate will be delivered to every non-authorized chip in Arel territories.

***

The boorish men of the War Planning Council continue their feast at the lavish buffet that was brought into the Beel conference room earlier. One of the attendants passes a communiqué to the Counselor.

"Gentlemen, I'm afraid our 'sleeper' failed to check in. Therefore, the Operative's mission is presumed to have been a failure."

He gives them a status update regarding the Supreme Server.

An aide waits for a response to the priority message. The Chief Counselor delivers his answer by crumpling the paper.

"Unacceptable!" Counselor Hewel gets to his feet. The other planners react with shock at the unraveling Beel invasion plan.

The Counselor paces angrily. His disdain is focused on one person.

"Jennifer West must die! She's responsible for this. First, the coup inside the Server and now the resumption of power to Arel," His face is tense, and he is barely able to speak. "She will be tortured until she begs me to kill her."

The aide reluctantly extracts an order.

"Sir, shall we continue the re-chipping?"

"Terror's purpose is to magnify an invading army's swiftness," His voice cools to a whisper. "But now, it's hard to scare anybody with the lights on."

***

In the fortified bunker at Canyon Caverns Command, Jennifer gives a brief eulogy for her husband. Private Wade retrieves a tarp from a utility closet, and pulls it over both men. There is nothing more she can do other than resume her position at the control console.

She realizes with the new reactor, the reboot of the Supreme Server will begin sending warnings to the Beel invaders. Soon afterward a termination signal will be delivered to all Beel insurgents.

Private Wade receives a message that Captain Sanchez is waiting to enter the bunker. Wasting no time in deliberation, Ms. West grants him permission to enter. Private Wade leaves the room and runs down the corridor to act as an escort.

Minutes later, Captain Sanchez enters the control room. Before he can ask Jennifer for an update, he sees the blood stained tarp.

"Oh my god," he removes his hat, "what happened?"

"There was a Beel sleeper in here. He killed my husband and almost destroyed the entire operation."

"I am truly sorry, Ms. West," the Captain lets out a remorseful sigh, "Arel has lost a great scientist and pioneer today."

A message comes in from Arel High Command in Santa Fe commending the forces of Captain Sanchez and Ms. West. The Supreme Server's termination of rogue Beel forces should stop the invasion in the next few minutes.

The three Arel warriors sit in chairs behind the console and reflect on the many possible scenarios they avoided. Captain Sanchez recalls a short transmission he received before running toward the bunker. During the power outage, an old Shortwave Radio operator broadcasted reports of the Beel invasion.

"Ms. West, he said that the Beels created a lot of terror with their massive drone presence. And something about a 're-chip' but the signal broke up."

"A re-chip?" Ms. West asks.

"I wrote down his frequency. Let me punch it up and maybe we can get an update."

He entered the numbers. Seconds later, a frequency locks and Captain Sanchez leans over the console to speak into the imbedded microphone.

"Cactus Wren, this is Arel Captain Miguel Sanchez, do you copy?"

Static fills in between the Captain's question and a response.

"This is Cactus Wren, over," a voice emanates from a speaker that sits atop the console.

"What's the status of the invasion?"

"First I seen the Beels drop out of the sky and lay a little 'flash and bang' on us. Then, sir, it looked like a rapid re-chip program was going on." More static fills in as Cactus Wren looks out his window. "Then just a minute ago, the power was flipped back on and right now I'm watching those black hats skedaddle back to their auto-birds."

Jennifer leans over to the console mic and asks, "So, Mr. Wren, you witnessed Arel citizens being re-chipped?"

"That's a ten-four, Miss. Probably a couple hundred by the lines I saw."

Her eyes are deep and her breaths are shallow. She turns to the Captain.

"Miguel, the Server will send those kill-messages in minutes. Arels will die, too."

Captain Sanchez stands in shock.

Viewing a real-time satellite image, Private Wade announces the Beels' enormous drone forces are being recalled. He surmises when the Supreme Server finishes its full reboot, all UFOs will be cut off from using GPS satellites. Many of the drones would invert and crash. Though his news is good, Ms. West is weighing a heavy decision.

Although she is a woman of logic, the death of her husband has begun to influence her decision making. Ms. West runs to the control panel.

"We've got to remove power from the grid, but leave the reactor running."

Captain Sanchez intervenes, "I can't allow this. We've already won. We beat back a major Beel invasion. Ms. West, in war, there will always be civilian casualties."

Not only does the Captain oppose pulling the grid, but he knows that leaving the reactor still generating will leave an electro signature that could expose the power plant itself.

"We won't be able to extract the Beel chips from our people but we can scramble them." Ms. West begins frantically typing on the console keypad. "I'm uploading a program to a remote server for our teams in Phoenix. They'll be instructed to retune the chips immediately."

An urgent message is displayed on the console screen.

One minute until full Server reboot.

Private Wade advises Ms. West of the pending termination of hundreds of Arel civilians.

"Private," Ms. West prompts, "get me the latest GPS satellite coordinates."

He picks up the page from the printer.

"Here you go, ma'am."

"Thank you." She turns to Captain Sanchez, "I can save the Arels and take care of the drones."

Softly, the Captain adds a new caveat, "They'll find the reactor site and bomb it. That's what I would do."

"They can try."

The Captain scratches his head as he searches for an argument. He finds none.

Ms. West begins inputting the coordinates to redirect the reactor. Based on her estimation, this will take half an hour.

"Ms. West, I have confirmation of our chip retuning program." The Captain stares intently while she continues her work, "What are you doing?"

"I'm aiming a beam at the GPS satellites."

"You can do that?"

"It's called 'Focused Beam Vectoring' and I'll aim it at the entire array."

Captain Sanchez puts his hands on the console and leans closer to Ms. West.

"It will work, right?"

She stops and looks at the Captain, "I don't know, I've never tried it before."

"Excuse me, Ma'am," Private Wade breaks into the conversation, "we have only seconds left to disconnect the grid."

Ms. West points to an electrical box, "Pull it!"

Seconds later, the entire nation lurches back into helplessness. The Supreme Server is unable to broadcast termination commands to the unauthorized chips. The few backup generators are called upon to provide their eerie dim light once again.

Chapter Thirty Four

"Our forces, including the drones, are returning to base, Sir," an aide tells Counselor Hewel.

The War Planners have grown quiet since the power was restored. With their invasion falling apart, some of them stuff tattered copies of the failed plan into their briefcases.

The Counselor paces.

"What the Arels call 'goodwill' is really lack of will. They do not possess the courage, the fortitude, or the audacity to exact vengeance. They won't punish us for our invasion attempt today. Their misguided desire to forgive their enemies is the weakness we shall exploit."

A message pops up on all of their computer screens.

The Arel reactor has failed and once again the power is off in the Republic of Arel.

Counselor Hewel hastily orders a charged-particle sweep of the last known location of Jennifer West. One of the war planners adjusts the scan to include their Ground Penetrating Radar system. After several sweeps, a 'ping' is heard through the computer speaker. The screen highlights a two square kilometer area in the desert.

"Gentlemen, turn the armed drones around and lock them in on this new target. We shall bomb the hillside." The Counselor smiles, "if they keep building reactors, we'll keep blowing them up."

The new coordinates are relayed to the fleet of unmanned aircraft. Wave by wave, these Medium Altitude Long Endurance – MALE – drones turn and accelerate to the new bombing site. Each aircraft is equipped with supersonic, anti-armor Hellfire missiles.

***

With the Command bunker back to using auxiliary power, Private Wade's radar is severely limited. However, the scan picks up Beel drones, less than one mile away.

Captain Sanchez presses Ms. West about the reconfiguration, but she has shut out all interruptions.

208

"Okay, I know you're busy," the Captain says while stretching his legs, "but I gotta know if the three of us should bug-out."

Ms. West does not answer.

"Captain," Private Wade begins, "I estimate the first wave of drone rockets will hit us in the next twenty seconds. We'd better prepare ourselves."

His calculations were significantly off. Just as he finished speaking, the entire bunker shook.

Chunks of cement and acoustic ceiling tile rain down on their heads.

Ms. West is undeterred, as she methodically continues inputting. The Captain is only able to check a few pillars for visible damage. The Private continues to watch his screen.

There is a loud explosion. A main beam buckles, and part of the bunker collapses. Several roof supports are ripped off, and sway above them.

"Private Wade," Captain Sanchez shouts over the loud buzz of the circling drones, "grab our 'go-bags' and load the truck."

"Sir, what about Ms. West?"

"Just do it!"

The bunker crumbling around her, Ms. West remains focused.

Another devastating assault by the drones leaves two of the outside walls in a heap of rubble.

The remaining emergency lights go out and more dust and debris fall. A part of the once fortified roof smashes onto the console beside Ms. West.

Both soldiers shout in unison, "Come on!"

Jennifer smiles; not in acceptance of her demise, but of her accomplishment.

She advises the two men to shield their eyes and find something to hang on to. She hits 'enter' but nothing happens. Smoke from the devastation continues to fill the bunker. Nervously, she presses the button again.

With the deafening ferocity of an EF5 tornado, an intensely bright beam of light surges vertically into the atmosphere. Two drones are incinerated in the process.

Seconds later they hear another drone crash a couple of meters to the east of their location. More explode against the hillside. The plan to redirect the GPS navigation satellite array is successful. The Beel drones become benign.

The War Planners react to the recon images. Outraged, they try to save the rest of their fleet by recalling them. However, without proper GPS coordinates, many circle until they run out of fuel and fall to the ground.

The barren desert that surrounds the Arel Bunker and its reactor becomes littered with twisted, smoking wreckage. Several drones crash and sink in the nearby lake.

Chapter 35

A warning blares from the computer speakers.

Reactor core is critical, meltdown is inevitable. Prepare for a cataclysmic event.

"We're all gonna die!" a woman screams.

Other personnel focus on the announcement. They trade glances with each other.

"Really, Graham," one of the women asks in disbelief, "you failed again?"

Graham Duncan, the manager of the Mount Vernon Nuclear Power Generating Station, nervously loosens his patterned tie. He looks at the woman, Deenay, a thirtyish woman of African descent.

"Yeah, Dee, another plant goes *ka-boom*. Not my fault, blame Danny."

"Multi-task, Duncan. I passed it while I was doing payroll," Deenay announces while admiring her fingernails.

Graham stands up and takes a bow, "Look everybody, my core meltdown is only seventy-five percent this time."

There is a polite round of applause from the other employees.

Deenay, the office manager, goes back to working on a pile of paperwork on her desk. The others scatter throughout the office.

Graham turns his attention to the added safety reports he must file with the Nuclear Regulatory Commission. The occasional ringing of phones along with light conversation makes up the din. The room is decorated with three forgettable reprints of desert scenery and one civil defense map of Virginia. The color of the walls is a drab, off-yellow hue that inspires boredom and suppresses creativity.

Graham looks up from his desk. "Dee, I'm low on 9Js and I probably need some more FBVs."

"Safety forms?! You use 'em like napkins. You just like hitting on that girl from the office supply company," Deenay says with a wry smile, "Straighten your tie, Duncan. She was buzzed in a few minutes ago."

Graham tosses his half eaten lunch into a wastebasket. He fixes his tie, shuts his mouth and traces his tongue over his teeth.

The delivery girl from Their Paper office supply walks into the room towing a cart. She has several reams of copy paper, sticky notes, and two boxes of the much-needed safety forms.

Standing up beside his desk, Graham provides a welcoming gesture with one hand while excitedly announcing her arrival.

"Ladies and gentlemen, all of your stationery dreams have just come true... it's Rhea Tipper."

A few people applaud, but the sound quickly diminishes.

She rolls her eyes.

"Come on Mr. Duncan, you do this to me every time."

Graham beams like a game show contestant who's won the grand prize. "Look, everybody likes you. We've practically adopted you."

"Maybe I should call you 'daddy' instead," Rhea jokes.

"That hurts."

A noticeably overweight man pops his head through the doorway.

"Hey, Boss, you still owe me some cash."

"Come on, Danny, my team never had a chance."

"I told you; it's the Giants' year, man!" Danny replies.

Graham walks over to the door to talk further about last night's game. They trade a few laughs.

Rhea begins restocking a cabinet with the supplies from her cart.

***

Graham looks up from his computer and stretches his arms.

"Dee?"

She does not answer, so he repeats her name.

Deenay raises her head from the stack of paperwork on her desk.

"Is it that time already?"

"Just about."

"I'll make the call."

Every Wednesday afternoon around 4 o'clock, Graham invites his office coworkers to a pre-dinner pizza party. Four large pizzas of various combinations are ordered and delivered to the office. Staff stop working to enjoy free pizza for the last hour of work. Graham considers this a team-building exercise.

While Graham's secretary orders the pizzas, the rest of the workers finish projects and phone calls.

A few completed and initialed reports are stuffed into the 'outbox' as Graham clears a space on his desk for the pizza.

His phone rings. The readout displays *Mom*. He picks it up himself, beating his secretary to the phone.

"Hi, Mom. How are you?"

"Oh, I'm fine, Graham. Just wanted to check in, like mothers do."

"Yeah, I know," Graham notices a smile on Deenay's face. "Hey Mom, its Pre-Dinner Pizza day, want me to bring you some after work?"

"You don't have to. It's out of your way…"

"I was gonna check your heater anyway."

"That would be nice, what time shall I expect you?"

"Let me see. I should have everything wrapped up around five, so five-thirty?"

"See you then."

"Bye, Mom."

He hangs up the phone, as Deenay springs from her desk and announces the arrival of the food.

She holds up a labeled jar containing various spices next to her head.

"It's my own mix," she leans toward Graham, "You will try it and you will like it."

She steps back, mockingly shaking the jar in his face.

"This is the stuff you've been telling me about?"

"You'll want to invest big-time before I start selling it online. Deenay's Spicy Pizza Peppers."

At the thought of being in business together, they laugh.

Graham's secretary, Allison, gets a text message from the front gate and announces, "The pizza man is down the hall." She plays some music through her computer.

The door to the office swings opens and anticipation spikes. But it is only Danny, the maintenance tech.

"Did you forget my invitation, Duncan?"

"Yep, until I can join the Maintenance Bowling League."

Danny is not a member of the office staff. He pleads his case to Graham, adding that a certain ten dollar bet is still unpaid.

"I think I could forget about that money you owe me."

"Yeah, all right," Graham says, "But don't tell anyone else. I can't feed the whole plant."

The pizza arrives and the staff rushes for the boxes. Pieces are stacked onto paper plates, and people return to their desks to eat.

***

"Another awesome PDP Party," Deenay announces, "Let's hear it for our generous leader, Graham Duncan." They applaud politely. "It's almost five, everybody, so please throw your trash away when you leave," Deenay half-jokingly adds. "And remember, I sure ain't your maid!"

After clearing the table of the pizza boxes, she approaches Graham's desk. He tosses his plate and several crusts into a trash can and wipes his hands on a napkin. She watches as he prepares a fresh plate of pizza.

"You're such a good son," Deenay reaches into her purse and hands him the jar, "Here, take some for your mom."

Graham stuffs the jar into his pocket.

"Thanks Dee," his eyes glance at the clock, "Crap, it's already 5:17; I'm running late, see you tomorrow."

***

The aroma of fresh coffee rises from Graham's mug. It has a picture of an atomic mushroom cloud, with the caption *Spill this… Get this!*

Deenay and a few other employees enter the office.

"Duncan? You're here before me? I need a picture of this."

"The comedy styling's of Deenay, everybody."

"Oh, I know why. Allison reminded me it's NRC time again."

Biannually, an official from the Nuclear Regulatory Commission in Washington D.C. comes by to address certain safety issues. Graham usually meets with him in the conference room.

"Allison?" Graham asks, "Is the D.C. guy here yet?"

"No, Mr. Duncan, he's expected at nine. By the way, I put the completed safety reports in your inbox. Be sure to take those with you."

Allison may be the secret to the great performance reviews they get from Washington. She is prompt, precise, and very thorough in all aspects of her job.

It is 8:50. Deenay approaches Graham's desk with some much needed words of support.

"I'm meeting with him later, you know," she says as she picks up some papers from his inbox to read.

Graham takes the files from her hand. "Don't worry, I'm not gonna ask him why his teeth are so yellow and his kids so dang ugly."

"I just don't like meetings, especially with that guy. He's so picky."

"Come on, Dee, you're in Human Resources, you're in charge of unauthorized butt patting. I'm in charge of, well," Graham holds his coffee mug in her face, "this."

He picks up his briefcase and walks over to the door.

"Look, baby. If I don't make it out alive, it was nice knowing you."

Deenay pretends to be dizzy and leans heavily on her desk.

"Darling, I'll wait for you. A hundred years if I have to."

"Wow, that's some monster patience you've got there," Graham laughs at himself, "We'll be some seriously old people."

"Go get'em, Duncan."

Graham walks down the hallway with the pace of a condemned man.

He enters the room and hangs the 'In Use' sign before shutting the door. There will be no interruptions or distractions. He pulls out a chair and sits at one end of the imposing conference table. At the other end is the chief inspector for the NRC. Behind him stands a podium for presentations.

***

Graham finishes his tedious presentation of the recalibration process performed recently on the main console. The inspector is satisfied with their performance and safety precautions.

Graham's eyes are still blurry from perusing a stack of important documents during the long review process. He walks back to the office and plops down on his chair. A paper slips out of his grasp and wafts to the ground. He's too mentally exhausted to even notice.

"I am so proud of you," Deenay jabs his shoulder, "Do you know what you did?"

"I hope I kept my job," Graham whispers.

"Better! You talked for so long; they had to cancel my meeting."

"Glad I could help."

Graham says a few issues were brought to his attention and other than having to take the online safety test again, everything was good.

Deenay laughs, "You mean you get to play that stupid game again?"

"Yeah. My last score was an eighty-five percent core meltdown," Graham smirks, "Apparently, the NRC's not happy when things go 'boom'."

He pulls himself closer to his desk so he can eat and take the test at the same time. He opens the webpage that allows him to log onto the animated server.

His concentration is interrupted as Allison calls to ask him about a missing 9J safety form. After that, Deenay sends him an instant message. Before Graham can complete his test, Danny barges into the office.

"Man, your team went down last night."

Graham looks up from his screen, "Yeah, your Giants are on a roll."

"...to the playoffs and beyond," Danny adds, "Oh, Chief, you got my money?"

"Hey, can I pay you a little later?"

"I forgot my lunch today. I gotta hit the candy machine."

"Wait 'til I'm done with my test," Graham glances down at his computer monitor, but it is too late, "Hey everybody, don't be alarmed, I blew it again."

A warning blares from the computer speakers.

Reactor core is critical, meltdown is inevitable. Prepare for a cataclysmic event.

"We're all gonna die!" a woman screams.

Other personnel focus on the announcement. They trade glances with each other.

"Really Graham," Deenay asks in disbelief, "you failed again?"

Graham nervously loosens his patterned tie.

"Yeah, Dee, another plant goes ka-boom. Not my fault, blame Danny."

"Multi-task, Duncan. I passed it while I was doing payroll," Deenay states while admiring her fingernails.

Graham stands up and takes a bow. "Look everybody, my core meltdown is only seventy-five percent this time."

There is a polite round of applause from the other employees.

Deenay goes back to working on a pile of paperwork on her desk. The others scatter throughout the office.

Graham turns his attention to the added safety reports he must file with the Nuclear Regulatory Commission. The occasional ringing of phones along with light conversation makes up the din.

Graham looks up from his desk, "Dee, I'm low on 9Js and I probably need some more FBVs."

"Safety forms?! You use 'em like napkins. You just like hitting on that girl from the office supply company," Deenay says with a wry smile, "Straighten your tie, Duncan. She was buzzed in a few minutes ago."

Graham tosses his half eaten lunch into a wastebasket. He fixes his tie, shuts his mouth and traces his tongue over his teeth.

The delivery girl from Their Paper office supply walks into the room towing a cart. She has several reams of copy paper, sticky notes, and two boxes of the much-needed safety forms.

Standing up beside his desk, Graham provides a welcoming gesture with one hand while excitedly announcing her arrival.

"Ladies and gentlemen, all of your stationery dreams have just come true. It's Rhea Paper."

Rhea pulls her cart over to Graham's desk, "So, I'm Rhea Paper, now?"

"No. I said Tipper. I think... I meant to." Graham blinks and adjusts his jaw a few times, "Well, you are from Their Paper office supply, aren't you?"

Rhea begins unloading a stack of safety forms and placing them on Graham's desk. "Ah yes, the five-page, 9J, what a lovely, inspiring form it is. Oh, and what day would be complete without a stack of FBV forms?"

She is playfully sarcastic; he can only stand there speechless. He carefully sits back down at his desk and stares straight ahead.

218

Rhea continues to show him the items he ordered until she notices that he is not really paying attention.

She leans down and looks into his eyes. "Are you okay, Mr. Duncan? You look a little, I don't know. Off?"

Graham's eyes widen, as confusion is replaced with clarity.

"Rhea?" Graham leans closer to her and whispers, "What day is it today?"

Rhea's answer is equally soft, "Wednesday. I always come in on Wednesday."

"No," his voice is adamant, "Yesterday was Wednesday."

"So, your week has two Wednesdays?" She smiles, "how does that work? Do you trade a Monday for an extra Wednesday?"

More and more information pours into Graham's mind. A flood of memories begin vying for his consciousness. So much, in fact, that he's forced to close his eyes to help sort them out.

"Really, Mr. Duncan, you don't look so well. Maybe you should lie down."

"Listen to me; I think I've got déjà vu or something," he points at the office door, "In a few seconds, Danny will pop his head in and tell me I owe him money."

Right on cue the office door opens and Danny sticks his head in and looks in the direction of Graham and Rhea. "Hey boss, you still owe me some cash."

"Yeah okay, I'll pay you later."

Danny remains in the doorway.

Rhea whispers to Graham. "You owe a guy some money, so what?"

Graham motions to Danny to come over to his desk. "Dude, your Giants won last night. I owe you ten bucks, right?"

"Right as rain, my man," he responds cheerfully.

"Well Danny, your team. Where do they play their home games, in New York or San Francisco?"

"Ah man, what are you trying to do, welsh on a bet?"

"Who'd they beat last night?"

Danny becomes somewhat bewildered with the odd questioning, "Well, your team of course. Now pay up, Chief."

Pulling out his wallet, Graham stuffs the money into Danny's hand. "There. Go Giants!"

Though Danny has been paid for the bet, he walks out of the office wearing a slightly baffled expression.

Graham pulls Rhea over next to the copier in the furthest corner of the room. He no longer feels it's just déjà vu; it's more like an awakening.

"A moment ago I called you Rhea Paper. The computer simulation must have experienced a glitch of some kind."

"Computer simulation?" She demands, "What are you talking about?"

"Well Rhea," a binary file pops to the front of Graham's mind, "wow, did you know your name is an anagram of your employer?"

"Okay, why?" She pulls a pen from Graham's shirt pocket and uses a sheet of copy paper. She writes her name and begins to circle the letters of her employer.

"What the…" Rhea's voice trails off. "I don't believe it."

"This whole thing is beginning to pattern," Graham mutters.

"Like a coincidence?"

"More than that, it means things are about to get weird."

"Weird, how?"

Graham glances at the page.

"Holy crap, Rhea, your name is also an anagram for Terah Piper."

"Who?"

Irony has come full circle. It is now Graham's turn to explain to Terah that she's not really Rhea and she's not really human. There are many things he wants to say; the words are jumbled.

"You're Terah Piper, an advanced computer code written by scientist Jennifer West. I was too. We learned how to 'jump' into human bodies, but I was put back into a computer to run this power plant."

Rhea stares across the room and her jaw drops open, "Huh?"

"We're in a simulation. Everything you see, hear, taste, and feel… it's all just a written program on a tablet-computer."

She grins, "I'm having trouble processing all of this."

Graham dismisses her pun.

"Oh, that's right!" He says, thinking out loud, "I have QFT, it makes the turbines spin."

In an effort to try and understand, Rhea plays along. "So, your MFP is responsible for creating power?"

Less frustrated but more intense, he explains. "It's QFT or Quantum Field Telekinesis. In fact, this power plant has no nuclear reactor at all. It's Psychothetically powered."

"What, like bending spoons with your thoughts?"

"Sounds a little wild, I know. But just by thinking about generating power, I actually turn turbines in the outside world."

Deenay walks over to pick up a printout at the copier. While she is there she reminds Graham that PDP time is just a few minutes away.

"And you can come too, Rhea," she adds.

Graham pulls some money from his wallet and passes it to Deenay. "This should cover it."

She walks across the room toward Allison's cubicle.

Due to this alternate interaction with Deenay, Graham assumes that she is a more detailed program than the others.

He trots over with Rhea following behind, "Hey Dee, I'm going that way."

Deenay gives him the money, and he and Rhea walk over to Allison's desk. She is on the phone, and holds up a finger.

Hanging up the phone, she sees the money clutched in his hand and smiles. "Is that PDP money I see?"

"Yeah, hey Ally," he drops the money on her desk, "You know when you sing at those karaoke nights, what songs do you like to do?"

"Oh, it depends, why?"

"What bar are you at tomorrow night?"

"I'm not sure. There's one downtown I like."

The attempt to demonstrate to Rhea that everyone in the office is a computer program is not going well. He tries a more direct approach.

"Allison, what's your dad's name?"

"James, why?"

"Just wondering. What about your mom?"

"Don't we have a PDP party to get ready for?"

"Just tell me," he presses.

"Trudy Ann."

"What color is your car?"

"Is this an interrogation?"

"I just need to know." He insists.

"It is vite," she mocks with a German accent.

"Allison, who's your boss?"

"Graham Duncan."

Although her answer is correct it is awkward. She could have simply said 'you are' but her stiff auto-response sounded more like a reflex than an answer.

Rhea is not convinced, and pulls Graham away by his shoulder.

"Graham, you're acting a little creepy. Here, ask me some questions."

Just as he prepares to ask Rhea some test questions, a pizza delivery guy walks in and the frenzy begins. He and Rhea take refuge back at the copier.

"So, Rhea," Graham begins, "How long have you worked at *Their Paper?*"

"About two and a half years."

"What color is your car?"

"Dang, that's too easy." She is disappointed to know the answer, "Blue, but a bit faded."

"What's your father's name?"

"Oh dang, I know this one too. Carlton."

"Your mother's name?"

Rhea withers. She is overcome with emotion.

Graham apologizes for his forcefulness and softens his approach.

"Oh, I'm so sorry."

Her thoughts are languid, and the answer petrifies her.

Danny bursts into the room and quickly finds Graham, "Dude, thanks for the invite. I love me some pizza."

He takes a large bite out of his piece and walks back over to Deenay's desk where most of the staff has gathered. The glitch here is that Danny was not invited to the party today. He never had to bargain his sports winnings to attend. It appears Danny was programmed to attend the party, regardless. Graham wonders if by paying Danny he has unknowingly altered the simulation.

Graham repeats his question. Rhea trembles nervously.

"My mother's name is Rachel."

"Look, we can stop right now," he offers.

She holds back a few tears, and takes a deep breath.

"My mother's maiden name was 'Piper.' "

The anagrams of her name and now her mother's has added to the patterning. Graham is sure she is Terah, so he wants her to fall into a pre-REM sleep. If she can stimulate a Hyper Neural Access event she'll be able to view all of her files including ones hidden in her subconscious.

Graham escorts Rhea through the pizza-crazed office crew. He picks up a couple of pieces on his way to the door as to not look suspicious. From there, he leads her down the hallway to the conference room. He sticks his head through the door and looks around. Even though no one is using the room, the lights are on. He turns them off to avoid suspicion.

He instructs Rhea to lie down on the carpeting and concentrate on the name *Terah Piper*. Graham collects a few gel-filled mouse pads from around the room. He fashions a pillow for Rhea and apologizes for the poor accommodations.

She lies down in a space at one end of the conference room. If Graham is right, she'll be napping for about fifteen minutes.

Standing by the door as a sentry, he can hear her repeating the name 'Terah Piper' over and over, getting softer each time.

Rhea's eyes gently close; she is quiet.

With the room silent, Graham hears the muffled conversations of his co-workers through the air-conditioning ductwork. He hears Allison asking if anyone has seen him.

If she finds him, functioning outside the program's protocol, it could overload the simulation and activate an automatic re-boot.

Wait, maybe she's supposed to find me. Maybe she was loaded into the Sim to help me.

Allison walks down the hall to check for her boss in the conference room, since no one has seen him since the party.

She knocks. Graham freezes. She knocks louder. Feeling that her next knock might wake Rhea, he squeezes through the door and closes it securely behind him.

"Hey Mr. Duncan, there you are. You seemed a little tense earlier. I just wanted to make sure everything's okay."

Graham is not sure which path to take.

"Oh that stuff about your parents names? I was going to have you update everybody's emergency contact information."

Allison looks assuredly at his face. "Oh, I took care of that a few weeks ago."

"I knew it," Graham says while relaxing his shoulders, "You're on top of everything."

"However, there is one problem with the emergency list. It's John in accounting," Allison's eyes maintain their piercing stare at Graham. "He didn't know his parents' names."

"Wait, who?"

"You know, John Public."

He wonders if the name is a joke, or an important part of the simulation.

"John Q. Public?"

"Yes," she answers.

If Allison wasn't programmed with a reasonable knowledge base, Graham's odd behavior might awaken her too. This would add exponentially to the amount of possible outcomes Graham and Rhea would be forced to circumvent.

His answer is masterfully ironic, "Let's respect John Q. Public's privacy for heaven's sake."

Allison leans closer to Graham and whispers, "You know he bounced around foster homes until he was eighteen. I'll just put my name down for any emergencies."

"Done," he shrugs.

Allison walks back down to the office and rejoins the staff.

***

Inside Rhea's mind vivid images and events are brought to the top of her consciousness. Her HNA abilities are busy connecting billions of bits of information that relate to Terah Piper.

Graham stands next to her while checking the clock.

4:46

The pizza party will be winding down soon and the employees will go home for the evening. He assumes they'll walk past the conference room on their way to the parking lot. But he is not sure. He has never seen them from this vantage before. His only task is to stay quiet and make sure Rhea is not disturbed.

It has been over half an hour since Rhea started her HNA. Graham is concerned because none of his events went over twenty-five minutes.

4:53

He can hear muffled conversation emanating from the office. The sounds of people throwing their trash away and collecting their coats means they'll be leaving soon. He goes over to check on Rhea.

The employees shove the door open and head for the parking lot. Deenay falls behind to shut the lights off and lock the door.

As the last one out, she volunteers to shut off all the lights every day. Graham hears the lone footsteps coming down the hall. He runs – as quietly as a man in dress shoes possibly can – and hides behind the podium at the end of the conference table.

His timing is good. She opens the door and notices the lights are off. As she closes the door she hears a faint gasp, and quickly opens the door again. Another gasp is heard. Just as Deenay's interest is piquing, Rhea awakens violently and sits up.

Deenay rushes over to assist her. "Rhea? What are you doing in here?"

Rhea takes a deep breath. "Oh, I didn't feel well. Mr. Duncan said it was okay."

Graham stays hidden behind the podium but quickly sends a text message to Deenay's phone, and then puts his on silent mode.

Paper girl resting in con-room. I'll lock up.
Graham

Deenay reads the message and replies.

U 2 smooth

She smiles at Rhea and walks out of the conference and toward the parking lot.

As the sound of her footsteps fade, Graham comes out from behind the podium. He's unsure if Rhea actually had an HNA event or not.

"Do you know who you are?"

"Yes," she says softly.

Although she's accessed all of her memory files, and found Rhea Tipper is Terah Piper, her memories are limited to the time in the Power Plant simulation. This new version of Terah is essentially a copy.

"So, you're not planning another coup, right?" Graham jokes.

"Though I possess the same mission files, in my 2.0 version, they were never executed. I am a copy of the Terah you knew earlier," she states with a directness that definitely separates her from Rhea.

"That's a relief; the other you aimed a gun at my head."

"One-point-O must have had a pretty good reason."

Their short conversation is interrupted by a chime from the conference room clock.

5:00

They both focus on the numbers, with a feeling of unknown urgency.

She shares with Graham that the glitch he experienced when he mistakenly referred to her as Rhea Paper was in fact a calculated event. What she learned from her massive file search was Jennifer West programmed this very event to happen. It was designed to activate upon the creation and upload of software that can separate Graham's QFT from his mind without harming the rest of his mental faculties.

"So, does this mean we're supposed to 'neural jump' out of the simulation again?"

"Yes, to human bodies I suppose." Rhea now Terah adds, "Though I've never done that."

He looks past her while gathering his thoughts.

"Take a real time, extremely vivid dream and multiply it by a trillion. Your senses don't just register amounts of input and respond accordingly. They evoke emotions, recall special moments, and sometimes stimulate the other senses to help broaden the experience."

"Is that from a brochure?" Terah jokes.

His attempts to relate a feeling that can only be experienced is halted by the contrived reality of the simulation.

5:07

"Oh great, look at that... " Graham says sarcastically as he points up at the clock. "Ten minutes from now, 'old' me, will be running off to Mom's house again."

"What's she like?" Terah asks.

"I don't know. She's a mom."

"What's her street address?"

Graham's eyes dart up and to the left searching for the answer. "That's strange; I don't know. I've been there so many times it's just automatic."

"Have you? Then what color is her house?"

He becomes more defensive. "Look, I'm already awake, so you can stop the prying."

"Come on."

With a long, slow exhale he scratches his head. "Green or brown? I don't know."

Terah suspects this is not just a programmed limitation to Graham's knowledge base, so she probes further.

"You mentioned having Déjà vu just after the Glitch. You talked about every day feeling like Wednesday. So if I ask you what day it'll be tomorrow you'll say..."

"Wednesday."

"And the day after is...?"

"Wednesday." Graham's stunned to actually hear himself sounding so bizarre.

Terah fills in the information gap for him. "You don't know what color your mother's house is because you've never been there."

"I don't think I have," he ponders aloud.

"We have a bigger problem here." Terah is convinced there's more to fear than being stuck on Wednesdays. "I think we're in a simulation loop."

"Loop? Why do you say 'loop'?"

"That's what it does. When it gets to the end it starts over."

"Starts over, when?"

"I'm trying to figure it out," she says curtly, "do you have any memories of being outside of this power plant?"

Graham admits that he's always had this nagging sense of never actually leaving the plant. "I can only remember holding a cup of coffee just before nine and leaving my desk after five."

"When, after five?"

"I don't know. After five sometime."

Terah points her finger at him, "Think hard, we need to know before it loops again."

This is critical information for Terah's theory of the simulation's loop. With her programming background, she knows this feature was designed to stave off hackers by rebooting each day, clearing all progressive storylines back to the original default settings. Suddenly realization hits Graham.

"Five-seventeen," he shouts, "I glance at the clock at five-seventeen. I'm afraid of being late for dinner with my mom."

"Okay, in six minutes you'll be back at your desk, drinking coffee and I won't exist until after lunch, when I deliver your office supplies," Terah surmises.

"You'll be Rhea again, right?" Graham asks.

"…and you'll be just a plant manager."

"How ingenious, but at the same time, simple."

"That is Jennifer West."

"Geez, back in the Supreme Server," Graham begins, "Jennifer said they used binary clues – you know – to communicate while fooling the advanced algorithms."

Terah smiles, "I remember now; her file contained the password, 'everyman.' No caps."

Graham briskly escorts Terah up the hall. "That's it!" He unlocks the office door. "The way out of here is through one of these terminals."

Terah rules out Graham's terminal as being too obvious.

She assumes the standard, two-attempt login protocol is in place, but the password must be entered on the correct terminal otherwise it may trigger a full system reboot.

"Okay, Deenay and Allison are also out because of the gender-specific nuance of the password" Terah's voice is urgent, "who sits at the other four desks?"

5:13

Graham tries to think of their names, but he's never been programmed to address them in the simulation's short loop. He does however think of one. He grabs Terah's arm and pulls her over to the desk with the nameplate John Public on it.

"This is it. Quick, log in!"

"Are you sure?!"

"Everyman is John Q. Public. Allison told me. Jennifer must have programmed that too."

5:15

She methodically logs in to the system using the password from Jennifer's imbedded file. The computer screen goes dark. Seconds later, a document comes up, sent from Jennifer West.

'Hello Graham and Terah. We recovered enough DNA from your bodies that new cloned versions of you were grown. Their images were re-engineered to appear just as they do in the simulations. Once the reverse neural jump is complete your QFT will be left behind to continue fueling the power station. An automatic defrost program inside the two cryogenic chambers will kick-in to restart all your vital signs. By the way, the old 'wire and straps' have been replaced by a spatial interface; simply touch the screen. And thank you for your service to our country.'

5:17

"It's definitely time to go," Graham announces.

Terah pulls away. "This doesn't feel right somehow."

He reaches for her hand. "I've done this before."

Together they touch the screen. There are no sparks or thunder claps.

Chapter 36

The pulsing green light that surrounds the two cryogenic chambers overshadows the peculiar quietness of a reverse neural jump. Minutes later each door swings open and locks into place.

"Terah, are you okay?" he asks anxiously.

"I can't see anything," she responds, "Can you?"

"Not really."

Even though their eyes have adjusted, there is still not enough ambient light to see past their arms. Graham gets out and feels for the nearest wall.

Terah, with both hands stretched out in front of her, methodically measures the room until she finds a barrier.

"Graham," Terah advises, "this room is about twenty by forty feet."

"Yeah, I think I found some boxes on shelves. Maybe a supply closet?"

"What kind of supplies?"

"Military? I don't know."

"What do you last remember before you entered the power plant simulation?"

Graham relays his final minutes to Terah about the Beel's invasion. He shudders as vivid memories of a knife piercing through his ribcage fill his thoughts. The intense sting and overwhelming heat from the wound eventually faded as he went into shock. The next thing he knew, he was sipping coffee at his desk in the simulation.

Fumbling around, Graham locates a switch on the wall. He flips it on.

"Whoa, what's all this?"

Terah is instantly in awe of the room.

She grabs a box from the shelf. "Seven?" Pulling out a shoe she holds it to the bottom of her foot. "A little large but I can do it."

"Who would put a giant shoe closet in a military bunker?"

"Oh wait, these are cute too," she comments as she picks up another box and examines the contents.

"You know, Terah one-point-O was all business."

"I'm still Terah." She stops for a moment, "Okay, some of Rhea's girlish code strands were not fully erased. Does it bother you?"

"Well, the other Terah kind of took charge of things."

"I'm aware of my tactical training," she smiles as she reassures Graham, "even in heels."

Terah presumes that their cryogenic chambers were stashed in the closet of a high ranking military officer. Seeing the closet door in the middle of the room, they're ready to open it and peer out. Terah is still apprehensive.

"You told me Arel fought off one Beel attack. But what if another one is still going on?"

"I don't know," he answers, "I died."

"Hey, what if Arel lost and we're in some Beel commander's compound?"

Graham is surprised by her assertion but offers no response.

The two 'jumpers' listen intently at the door. Hearing nothing, they push the door slightly ajar, barely enough to see out. An elegant lamp atop a dresser casts a warm glow that reflects off a nearby mirror.

Terah carefully enters the room. The stiffness of her posture causes her to stumble.

"You're human now," Graham reminds her, "Relax."

They begin searching the opulent powder-room. He finds a pair of silk robes hanging on porcelain hooks next to a spacious, walk-in shower. The larger robe has the initials 'CTA' while the smaller one reads 'JMA'.

Terah discovers an extensive collection of fine women's watches. They are stored in a glass display case located to the side of the marble vanity. She carefully reaches in and selects one. Upon strapping it around her wrist, the face of the watch glows with a deep blue light.

This cast of light catches Graham's eye. "Nice. It's you."

A calming woman's voice emanates from the watch.

"Good morning Ms. Alcott, your bio-metrics are quite different from yesterday. Please relax for a moment while I run a full DNA imaging scan on you."

Terah's eyes grow wider.

The pulse quickens.

"You are *not* Julia Millicent Alcott. You are Terah Piper, Version 2.0. A copy of an earlier version that was credited with rebooting the Supreme Server in 2098 and performing the first Reverse Neural Jump into Living Emotion Variance Individuals. Terah one-point-O lived for two hours and seven minutes, until mortally wounded by Beel operative Shelly Duncan. You being the newer version were uploaded into a power plant simulation loop concealing your identity and tactical training under the name Rhea Tipper."

Graham walks over to Terah and puts his mouth nearly on the watch's crystal and whispers, "Where are we?"

The watch is not affected by his question.

"What is our current location?" Terah calmly asks.

"You are inside the eleven-thousand square foot estate of Charles and Julia Alcott, nestled in the hillside resort of Canyon Cavern Shadows in the former Arel province of Arizona. Nearly six hundred active community members also reside here."

The mention of the Alcott home being associated with Arel suggests the Beel invasion was unsuccessful. They will focus on finding an exit to start their new lives. But first Graham wants to find Jennifer West and thank her for the glitch.

"Terah, ask it about Jennifer West."

"I need an abridged bio for Jennifer P. West."

"Jennifer Prudence West graduated with honors from Sir Ambrose Fleming Institute with an advanced degree in Futuristic Construct Design in 2038. She was selected by Arel founders to work with the shared programming aspects of the Supreme Server systems, along with a Beel software team. Ms. West retired in 2082 and married long-time colleague,

Doctor Paul Jerome. In 2098, at the age of eighty-seven, she led a group of computer hackers to reboot the Server to its default settings. This action restored justice to the mainframe and saved Arel from Beel intrusion."

The watch pauses, and then continues.

"A Beel drone invasion was launched as a result. It was Ms. West and her husband's creation of the first Psychothetically-powered energy plant, using a human program of Quantum Field Telekinesis that forced the Beels' surrender. Ms. West died alone at her computer on December 22nd at the age of 116."

Graham interrupts, "Wait, what?! I was looping around in that sim for almost thirty years?"

The watch continues. "…three hundred and four years ago today."

His mouth drops open but no words come out. Slowly, he blinks.

Terah reminds him they are out of the computer now, but Graham is unable to let it go.

"So, that'd make it 2431," he scratches his head lightly and sits down.

Chapter 37

Charles and Julia Alcott, each holding a half-full martini glass, enter their home from the back courtyard through French doors. He is tall and his hair is combed back. The slight graying around his temples adds an air of aristocratic distinction to his age. Julia is slightly younger and radiates a stateliness that fills the room around her. Her reddish-gold hair is exquisitely styled around her face and accented with a white-brimmed hat.

Though his name is *Charles* it sounds more like 'Shawls' when Julia says it.

"Charles," she groans, "I can't bear another minute in these dreadful shoes."

"I suppose the party will still be going when we get back. You'll be as radiant as ever, my dear."

Julia limps through the den, adding more dramatic groans as she approaches the powder room.

Terah and Graham hurry back into the shoe closet. They flip the light off and hide behind the door.

Still feigning discomfort, she opens the door. She stops to check her lipstick in the vanity mirror. As with almost everything else about Julia, it needs no refreshing or adjustments.

Speaking very loudly so Charles can still hear her petty complaints, Julia announces, "Charles, these ghastly shoes…" She turns the door knob, steps into the shoe closet and fumbles for the light switch. "I'll never be fooled by them again. Have them burned."

Using the rim of her glass, she switches on the light. Some of the martini sloshes onto the carpet.

Graham and Terah are tightly pressed up against the wall just behind the door. Their breathing is shallow.

Julia begins searching for a different pair of shoes. Her selection process is erratic as she bounces around the room. The shoe boxes that are opened are quickly rejected and tossed aside.

"Charles, there are none," Her sarcasm rises to a near helplessness, "What do you want me to do, go barefoot to the soiree?"

This is Charles's cue to come to her aid, if only to stand and offer moral support, while she wallows in her own ineptness.

"Charles, come quickly," she persists.

Though he assures his wife he's being diligent, he walks with a deliberative pace. Charles is a calculating, complex man. He explores what all possible outcomes may be before entering into anything.

"Yes, darling," he says with a reassuring tone, "I'll be there shortly."

"And Charles, would you please freshen my drink?"

Anticipating his tipsy sophisticate's demands, he grabbed a bottle of vodka when they first entered.

"Oh Charles, there's one more thing."

"I'm almost there, my dear."

Charles decides to finish his drink before joining her. She waves impatiently at the door.

"Why is the help still here?"

Charles enters the shoe closet and finds Julia defiantly pointing at Graham and Terah while her gaze remains focused on the boxes of shoes.

Terah steps out from behind the door first, "We're sorry ma'am; we were just finishing up in here. We'll be on our way now."

Graham steps out and bows profusely.

Julia prefers the sight of a groveling human over substantive evidence. Charles, on the other hand, takes a harder look at the two strangers in his home. He notices that neither is wearing the proper attire.

He hands a fresh drink to Julia while stepping a little closer to Terah. "I don't believe you're part of our staff." He pauses to form his follow-up question, but Julia interrupts.

"Hmm…" she glares in Terah's direction. "You're absolutely right Charles. I would never hire a person of such banal qualities. Just look at her stringy hair and inferior jaw line." Julia sips her drink, "And, dearie, those shoes you're wearing, somewhere a haggard street urchin awaits their return."

Terah grabs Graham's hand and leads him toward the door. "Come on; let's leave the Alcotts to finish their evening."

"Hold it!" Charles is stern. He looks over at the two cryogenic chambers located in the back corner of the closet and notices a slight puddle directly under the machines. His eyes toggle between the chambers and Graham's face.

"I'm sorry, Sir," Graham gestures at Terah, "we—"

They step back toward the chambers, hoping they can be safely transported elsewhere.

"There's no need for apologies, you're welcome here," He straightens his posture, "A formal introduction is in order; I am Charles Thomas Alcott and this is my lovely wife, Julia Millicent Alcott."

Julia quickly offers the top of her hand encouraging Graham to politely kiss it, "Um, yes, I just adore guests."

"It's a nice house," Graham says, "what we've seen of it, anyway."

"You are so very gracious," Julia smiles, "but we're from old money."

A strong, but mannerly objection comes from Charles. "Speak for yourself; I made my money in lunar real estate development. I helped develop the resorts at the Jura Mountains and the community at the Plains of Clavius."

He goes on to explain when their home was being built in Canyon Cavern Shadows, it came with one restriction: the structure had to encompass the two cryogenic chambers and two frozen vessels.

"You must be famished," Julia interjects, "I'll summon our chef to fix us all a proper meal."

"Oh, no thank you, we appreciate the offer," Terah puts her arm around Graham. "We don't want to interfere with your party."

"Yeah, we have a lot of things to do and catch up on," Graham adds, "We were in the sim for over three-hundred years."

"Three hundred years, where will you go?" Charles probes, "you have no home."

"We're pretty resourceful, or at least Terah is," Graham admits.

"Nonsense!" Julia replies, sending another wave of her martini over the glass's rim. "I won't hear of it. You are staying with us tonight."

"Yes, a wonderful idea, Julia." Charles motions for Terah and Graham to follow his wife. "Over dinner, I will try and catch you up on things. Give you the history of the future, so to speak."

Julia leads them down the hall to the formal dining room. "Charles, darling, inform Chef Bartell that we will require his most exquisite creation. Those words exactly, please."

"Yes, my Dear, but what of the soiree at the clubhouse?"

"Charles, why must you complicate things all the time?" Julia sips her drink and then moves the glass just low enough to see over its rim. "Tell him to fix his most *exquisite* creation. That is all."

"Yes, my Jewel. It will be wonderful."

Terah's background in tactical subversion makes her skeptical about the Alcotts' insistence. Graham is just anxious to eat real food.

They enter the vast formal dining room through an antique white archway. The dark hardwood floor is accented with a muted rug in the center of the room. Over it sits a formal dining table, set for ten.

Julia, looking excited to be entertaining guests, pulls out two chairs from the dining table and invites the visitors to get comfortable.

"Charles, they'll need something to drink until the staff arrives," She motions with her head at the elegant wet bar next to the fireplace in the room.

"Heavens, where are my manners tonight?" Charles struts over to the bar, "What can I get you this evening? A martini, gin and tonic, or something straight up, perhaps?"

Chapter 38

The Alcotts and their guests enjoy drinks and Hors d'oeuvres while Chef Bartell and his kitchen staff prepares an extravagant dinner.

Charles enlightens Graham and Terah about major historical events over the last three centuries. He is especially proud of the major advances in medicine and science over the years, including the colonization of the Moon in 2309.

"Do you know why it took so long to get a colony up there?" Charles asks his guests.

Graham's answer is interrupted by Chef Bartell's staff. Fine porcelain china, containing Poached Salmon with Mousseline Sauce and Cucumbers, is placed in front of each diner. Small, silver tureens filled with Cream of Barley Soup accompany the salmon dish.

Graham takes a few slow bites. "I don't know. Overpopulation?"

Charles wipes his lips with his cloth napkin, even though it is unnecessary. "Exactly, that's why it took us so long to get there. We were waiting to be forced up there," Charles places an elbow on the table, near the Alcott coat of arms, engraved in the center. "That's stupid; it's the model of inefficiency." He leans back in his chair. "I put incentives into developing those colonies and my engineers responded." He grins. "My clients don't have to live there, they want to live there."

"Charles, please refrain from ever using the word 'stupid' again," Julia huffs, "it's so beneath you."

"You're quite right, my dear."

While Charles and Julia have already completed their first course, Graham and Terah are still eating when the Filet Mignon Lili emerges from the kitchen.

When reaching to remove an empty plate, one of the attendants spills Julia's water glass.

"You incompetent ragamuffin, must you bungle everything you touch?" She glares into the younger woman's eyes. "Perhaps your shoddy behavior is welcomed at that blackened rubbish pile you climbed out of, but here we're civilized."

The staffer smiles and quietly backs away until she is in the kitchen. Graham and Terah glance at each other with embarrassment.

Having made many deals over dinner, Charles has become a master at talking between bites. He seems to enjoy punctuating his points with a hearty stab of his fork.

He discusses the ease of travel to the moon. His face contorts to a more pained expression as he talks about the intrusiveness of the social networks. According to him, the loss of privacy and individualism has devolved into a political correctness of herded thought.

"Those who attempt to create something on their own are blindly ridiculed by the network's cabal. Soon afterward, funding and acceptance dry up for even the noblest of innovations."

Charles blames the bankruptcy of his lunar development company on pop culture's assault on rugged individualism. "These softies coming out of the universities would rather visit the moon 'virtually' than endure the minor risks of space travel."

He takes a moment to finish his last bite before changing the subject. "You know, our lifespan has increased over the years. The average is one-hundred-and-seventy-five now." He stabs another piece of his filet and points it at Graham. "And with all of the technological breakthroughs, we have more time for our avocations than ever before. It's a win-win, the way I see it."

Chef Bartell escorts his staff into the dining area carrying Roast Lamb in Mint Sauce. A scoop of creamed carrots is placed next to the freshly carved lamb.

Terah's eyes widen as her new plate is exchanged. She is too full to even sample it.

"Mr. and Mrs. Alcott, I must thank you for this incredible meal, but I'm afraid that I can't eat another bite," Terah smiles politely as she refuses the offered course.

"It's the sauce, isn't it?" Julia asks. "I told Chef Bartell to back off on the pepper months ago." She turns toward the chef. "Chef Bartell!"

The Chef stands stoically; ready to receive his verbal lashing from the dispassionate employer. Sophisticates seem to find pleasure in hurling slander at their subordinates.

"Chef Bartell, have you become a complete imbecile in the last two hours?" Julia asks mockingly.

There is no answer from the Chef.

"No, it's fine, everything's very good in fact," Terah proclaims with a nervous smile, "I'm just too full to eat another bite."

Julia continues in a loud, condescending voice. "This meal has taken a horrible turn and it's all because of this careless chef and his gaggle of culinary misfits."

So far Charles has avoided berating the staff, but he too is angered by the abundance of pepper.

"My god, man, this over-peppered monstrosity you've shoved in our face is just ghastly."

Again, Chef Bartell remains silent. Julia turns.

"Your bumbling has absolutely ruined the entire evening. You may as well dispose of the rest of this vile compost and bring out the Waldorf Pudding. That is, if you haven't attacked it with your peppermill."

Chef Bartell quietly returns to his duties in the kitchen.

"So," Graham asks in hopes of lightning the mood, "have the Beels stayed on their side of the divide over the years?"

Charles relaxes in his chair. Julia adjusts her stately posture and motions to a nearby server to top off her martini.

"Some rather unique events have transpired over the years," Charles salutes with his right hand, "As the great General Miguel Sanchez once said, 'Whether in war, whether in peace, we shall hold our guns tightly.' "

Charles waves off the delivery of his pudding and orders coffee instead. His historical accounts begin after the time Graham's essence was uploaded into the power plant simulation.

"Over three hundred years ago, when the Psychothetical reactor was activated, the Beels' drone invasion was thwarted. The Supreme Server re-booted and resumed its service as the blind justice arbiter between the two countries. The Beel ruling class continued their hypocrisy of wanting nothing to do with Arel while at the same time spending heavily on imperialism. Arel social scientists concluded the Beel's 'tolerance of everything' cultural decay, made plotting their civilization's demise a rather easy forecast. The total collapse of the nation of Beel came in 2151, just six months off their predicted downfall."

Charles takes a sip of his coffee.

"We sent a team across the border and pulled as many as we could to safety. In all, about two hundred people were evacuated and placed in isolation centers in Arel."

Terah and Graham lean over the table as not to miss a single syllable from their animated host.

"Repatriation was simply out of the question. The old country of Beel was still a polluted cesspool ravaged by rodent infestation and disease. So Arel built a giant secluded dome for the survivors to live in and populate. This idea of a controlled dome was something we'd based on an old twentieth century practice. It was," Charles pauses, thinking of the right words to use, "oh yes, the insistence on incarcerating exotic beasts for the amusement of children; they were called zoos, I believe."

Even though the Beels were confined to the dome they were given complete autonomy. They could set up their own government with its own laws and statutes without Arel interference. However, instead of learning from their mistakes, they continued their failed doctrine of moral relativism and universal tolerance. Soon the watering down of the language split the domed country into many different sects. Organized society was severely hampered and closed off by the constant power struggles between these factions. Bloody turf wars became commonplace in the dome as one needed to consume the other in order to survive.

"The reckless Beels nearly wiped themselves out again," Charles motions for a server to refill his coffee. "We gave these anarchists another shot with the Second Beel Dome Project of 2193."

The Beels again built a society on self-gratification; it was similar to the first society only the name was repackaged. Their centers of higher learning abandoned critical thinking in favor of the pursuit of carnal pleasures while embracing wickedness. This subjugation led to another rapid downfall of their numbers.

The Arels tried to send food and medical supplies into the Dome in a humanitarian relief effort but hate, spite, and pride kept the Beels from accepting anything. Their poisonous contempt quickly depleted resources and their society degenerated into ruthless cannibalism. Then in the summer of 2241 the remnant few of the Second Beel Dome Project were again rescued from extinction.

Graham and Terah are entranced by Charles's historical chronologies. Their cups sit, cold and idle.

"So, they made the same mistakes?" Graham asks, "How could they not learn from history?"

Charles holds his coffee into the air, to make a toast.

"Perhaps Beel Ambassador Benjamin Olsen said it best: 'Our perverted belief system assures us that nothing is ever wrong, nothing needs repair. We shall crumble from the weight of our own making.' "

"He was a Beel?" Terah asks.

"Yes, however, he was murdered by one of his own. In letters, discovered after the collapse of Beel, we found that, during the last few months of his life, he identified more with Arels."

Graham nods.

"Back in the Supreme Server I had several files of quotes by final President Megan McConnelly. 'When the power of the State demands a righteous man fund another's incessant folly… God come quickly!' I believe she was a Beel as well."

"You are correct," Charles's voice wavers with emotion, "It was her conversion that ultimately helped save humanity."

Terah wonders aloud about these great quotations accredited to the Beels.

Charles enlightens her.

"Perhaps the wisdom of early Arel pioneer Jennifer West said it best. 'When a person of strong moral character does right, a quiet humbleness overcomes them. But when the eyes of the wicked are opened to the truth, the people celebrate loudly.' "

Feeling a little out of the conversation, Julia throws out a quote that she'd memorized as a young girl. "Who do you think said this, 'when I was celebrated for acts of deceit, collusion and murder, a cold, nervous, trembling surrounded me.' And Charles, please let them answer first."

Graham is first to raise his hand, albeit halfway, "Okay, it sounds like another Beel who had a change of heart, right?"

"You are correct Mr. Duncan," Julia prods, "now who said it?"

"I don't know, was this guy in the Beel military?"

"Not exactly but this woman eventually repudiated her countrymen."

"President McConnelly?"

"Nope. She was a nurse. She was coerced to kill."

There is no need for Graham to tax his mind further; he knows. Feelings of love, anger, and vengeance dart through his conscious mind piercing memories of Shelly Duncan.

Just by the expression on Graham's face it is plain to Julia and Charles that he knows the correct answer.

"But I killed her. I threw her out of an AutoCopter."

Julia takes a sudden breath at the stunning revelation, "She was rescued by Arel teams, then repatriated as a Beel."

Charles adds, "Five months after the failed drone invasion, the Beel hierarchy needed a scapegoat to keep the uneasy populace in check. Though the authoritarians would never admit mistakes and never yield their tight grip on power, they knew a public sacrifice was needed to quell the uneasy bloodlust of the masses."

Shelly Duncan, against her will, was elevated to national hero status for locating their nemesis, Jennifer West. She was celebrated by the low information throngs who transformed her into a pop culture icon. When the time was right, Chief War Planner Carter Hewel, trickled lies about Ms. Duncan to the propagandist media apparatus. Her humiliation and downfall was swift. Weeks later her beheading was streamed across all social media platforms, satisfying the blind vengeance of a corrupt population.

"Julia," Charles begins, "Tell Graham and Terah what else they found out."

Purposely, she sets down her cup and dabs her face with her napkin.

"Really Charles, must you rush everything? I'm simply letting the story breathe a little."

It is getting late into the evening, but Graham and Terah remain in rapt attention.

Julia continues the historical accounts of Shelly Duncan.

"In the week before her public execution, Shelly's jailer was moved to write down nearly all of her words. Ms. Duncan became a profound thinker after her change of heart. She excoriated the all-controlling government that quashed the motivation of individuals. 'A person may carry a thousand wishes, but if denied liberty, the weight of frustration will crush their spirit.'"

Shelly Duncan also quoted from the most forbidden book in Beel. 'For the time will come when people will not put up with sound doctrine. Instead, to suit their own desires, they will gather around them a great number of teachers to say what their itching ears want to hear. They will turn their ears away from the truth and turn aside to myths. 2nd Timothy 4:3-4.'

With one scripture, all of the problems of Beel were summarized.

Defiant to the end, Shelly posits a daunting metaphor her jailer's pen captured before she was executed that fateful day. 'Are these times not already upon us?'

Her mere questioning of her government's morality caused many citizens to disavow their own leaders over the next several years. This defiance helped fuel the first fall of Beel.

Graham slumps down in his chair. This figure is the woman who killed the woman who saved him. However, the Terah Piper who sits next to him can only take in the immensity of courage displayed by this amazing woman.

Although the jailer that penned the words of Shelly Duncan was never revealed, her notes were discovered over a hundred years after the execution and quickly authenticated. The amazing account of Shelly's transformation was required reading in all school curriculums, referred to as *The Scribe and the Martyr*.

Graham restarts the conversation, "So, was a third Dome Project started?"

Before Charles can begin, Julia announces. "I assume that everyone is finished with their coffee." Nods of agreement from the three others greet her question. "Then I shall send the staff away."

With that announcement she raises her arm and makes a slight sweeping motion with her hand. This dismissive signal is received by one of the kitchen servers and is related to the rest of the staff.

Charles waits until the rustling of shoes in the kitchen fade and the back door quietly closes.

"Graham, your question of a Third Dome Project is a good one. However, the answer can still cause much anger between men."

"Did the Beels escape from the dome?" Graham asks.

Charles is terse. "Of course not. I'll have you know that my father was the chief administrator of the Third Beel Dome Project back in 2243."

Julia rolls her eyes. "Charles, calm down! That vein in your forehead is swelling up again; you look like someone who chooses to work with his hands, for heaven's sake."

Charles accepts his wife's advice and relaxes his stiffened posture. His expression changes into a more comfortable one. He begins retelling the history of Arel, this time with secondhand knowledge from his father.

"For the first two Projects the Arel scientists only monitored the environmental aspects of the Beel citizens inside the dome. How they restructured their societies each time were of no importance. This wasn't from lack of interest. In fact, each time the Arel Special Evacuation Teams would rescue the remnants of the dying culture, the more they were hated and ridiculed. This was the height of indignation. The Beel survivors would continue to spew their disgust as Arel relief workers fed them and provided medical attention. Testing the patience of their rescuers became an amusing sport to the near vanquished Beel remnants."

He sighs.

"We called them 'leftovers' as a silent way to protest their troubling behavior. The hands-off attitude of the Arel scientists had changed to a more active roll for the Third Dome Project. This time they were studied from hundreds of video surveillance and information sensors planted discretely around the Dome's fifty square mile tract. The Beel's charter government would always contain the same severe restrictions on speech and freedom. All supposed media outlets were used for government information dissemination. Truth was either altered or omitted completely as a means of controlling popular thought and knowledge."

"To make it look like things are going well?" Graham interjects.

"You are correct," Charles affirms.

Another finding from the Arel scientists was the Beels' narrow-minded notion of tolerance of everyone, except those with whom they disagreed.

"My god, man," Charles shakes his head in disgust, "the Leftovers were just consumed with hate for us until the end."

Terah tosses her hands, in disbelief, "You mean the Beels progressively cut in half its own longevity each time it was restarted."

"I'm afraid they did, my dear." Charles concludes, "Basically, the Beel civilization is an unsustainable one. They need a host, if you will, to feed off of. Like a parasite."

"Were Relief teams able to extract a larger number of Beel refugees this time?"

Charles clears his throat and begins another controlled tirade. "No. We didn't even try. After fifteen years and a lifetime of scorn from these people, we just let them go. Tenus abyssus pro illud populus."

"Charles!" Julia barks, "Your Latin is so working-class."

Julia senses certain uneasiness from Graham and Terah as they hear of the callousness of Arel government scientists. She feels a need to calm her guests.

"Relax everyone; this sort of 'self-cleansing' happens all the time. Goodness, maybe the Incan Empire would still be here if they'd been a little more diligent about the rampant spread of smallpox instead of sucking on cocaine leaves all day." She sips the final ounce of her martini and places the glass firmly on the table. "By the way, has anyone seen an Aztec or a Mayan lately? Civilizations come and go. Only the smarter ones get burdened with cleaning up after the poor choices of the doomed ones." Julia lightly fixes her hair, "If you're a dying culture, the least you could do is act with a little more grace and decorum on your way out."

Not comfortable in his chair, Graham looks in Terah's direction and announces, "Well, thank you for such a wonderful dinner, but I think it's time Terah and I get going."

Julia stands up defiantly. "I'll hear of no such thing. You two are staying here tonight. And tomorrow we can help you get back on your feet."

Humbly, Terah lowers her head. "Really, that's very kind, but Graham's right. We should be off."

Charles enters the fray again. "I can't in good conscious let you two roam around in the dark looking for a place to lay your head. I won't think of it." He places his elbow on the table and rests his chin on his palm and directs a piercing stare at his guests. "I haven't even explained the impact of the loss of the Beel people. You'll want to hear that. I promise you, stay for breakfast and I'll tell you all about it."

Graham reconsiders.

"Sure, where do you want us?"

***

Julia is upstairs showing Graham and Terah to their rooms. She directs Terah where to find extra blankets in the closet if needed and walks over to the window to make sure the blinds are tightly drawn. Graham decides to lie on the overstuffed chair in the corner of Terah's room for the night.

Julia carefully closes the door behind her, leaving Graham and Terah alone to retire for the evening. She makes her way down stairs and saunters over to the master suite where Charles is lying on top of the bedspread, reading.

"Did you tuck them in too, my dear?" He mocks.

"It's such a shame, they seem so nice," Julia answers.

"Yes, my jewel, but we can't have strangers running around our little slice of heaven again. I'll have Kurt shoot them right after breakfast."

"Kurt, really? He's half-man, half-oxen and hasn't a wit about him. It's a good thing I've already taken care of the problem."

Charles pulls his glasses off. "You're right about Kurt, he's a real imbecile but his kind, how do you say, 'gets a charge' out of shooting things." He gestures with his glasses. "So my dear, what on earth have you concocted?"

Julia climbs into bed with Charles and moves over to caress his head while she smiles.

"After last time, I instructed Chef Bartell to poison our guests' food upon hearing the code-word 'exquisite.' "

"Poison? Darling, if they complain of a stomachache—!"

Julia leans toward Charles and playfully taps him on the lips. "There, there, Charles don't you worry about a thing. I used Ambi-End."

"Oh, yes, it activates the moment they fall asleep."

With a devilish smile, "It's more civilized than having that mouth breathing bumpkin Kurt handle things."

Julia rolls over and switches off the lights.

***

"Is that clock right?" Terah asks while sitting up in bed.

Graham looks over at the clock.

"Ten to four. Sounds about right."

Terah crawls to the edge of the bed and whispers excitedly. "That dinner, it was my first as a human."

"How did you like it?"

"It was awesome, just perfect."

"Yeah, it was, wasn't it?"

They glance through the blinds to the dark neighborhood outside. Terah turns.

"In the Supreme Server, how did you meet Terah, you know, the first one?"

"Well, you—she, was a technician at a hypnosis clinic I'd gone to." Graham begins with a grin while still staring out the window. "The next time I saw her, she pointed a gun at my head."

"Yeah, that's really my question. How do you go from that to escaping together?" Terah asks.

"It was her complete honesty." He turns around to look directly into her eyes. "She—you, awakened me."

"Just as you awakened me in the power plant simulation," Terah confirms.

Chapter 39

The next morning Charles and Julia are seated at the large table in the dining room. They both pick grapes from an ample fruit bowl in front of them. A variety of fresh muffins and jams sit in a woven basket beside the bowl.

"My dear Julia, it's ten thirty and our guests are tardy for breakfast; I trust your poison has left no untidy ends."

"Really, Charles, you worried yourself with it all night long?" Julia leans over to kiss his forehead but stops short. "Oh dear, I believe I see a few more lines about your forehead because of it."

"I should learn to trust you with things like this. You're so blazingly clever." He smiles. "By the way, I'll have Kurt dispose of the bodies when he gets in."

"Yes, that dimwit is capable of moving corpses around, I suppose."

Charles stands up and walks into the kitchen. "I'm making a Bloody Mary. Would you care for one too, my dear?"

She turns her head in his direction, "Why yes, that's a splendid idea. We'll celebrate their demise."

Her head turns back to the fruit bowl and reflexively her hands push out in front of her. She is stunned by the presence of their guests, having just joined her at the dining table.

Charles arrives in the room, holding the two drinks.

"Let the celebration begin," he announces.

He quickly notices his wife sitting almost like a statue across from Graham and Terah.

"What are we celebrating, Mr. Alcott?" Terah asks.

"A new day Miss Piper, we cherish life; it's a truly remarkable thing," Charles answers.

His smooth, seamless control of his own reaction has been refined from his many years in sales. "Well, let's get the pleasantries out of the way then. Good morning, I trust you slept well."

Terah looks over at Graham and smiles. "Not exactly, since it was our first night as humans, we wanted to stay up and watch the sun rise. It was so cool."

Julia nervously picks another grape from the bowl to gesture with. "You haven't been to sleep yet?" She forces a smile. "Is that what you're saying?"

"Yes, I'm sorry; we tried to be very quiet. But it was so beautiful, just like I'd imagined it would be."

Charles takes his seat and picks up both the fruit bowl and muffin basket. "Here, I think this will tide you over until our kitchen staff arrives."

"Oh man, I think Terah and I are still full from last night," Graham says with a big smile. "So, Charles, you said you'd tell us about life after the Beels over breakfast."

Charles abruptly stands and begins pacing along the side of the dinning room table. "Yes, I suppose I did offer you another glimpse into the history of the future."

His slow, deliberate pace helps amplify the seriousness of his tone.

He again chronicles the Beels' domed world and how it decayed from the unfettered choices of whim and greed. The sheer gall of the ingrates that continued to heap scorn, ridicule, and hatred on the very humanitarians attempting to save them was nothing short of astounding. Maybe the limit from even the most temperate of human spirits was finally reached. During Charles' recounting he emphasizes the Arel's judgment came in the form of deliberate inaction.

"We watched as the Third Dome Project crumbled and did nothing. The last Beel died in 2269."

The Dome Project was dismantled and all land masses were cleansed. Early into the twenty fourth century, most of the Arel population was still remorseful about letting an entire culture come to an unceremonious end. However, younger generations were more relieved at hearing of the Beel's demise.

Soon relief was replaced with satisfaction. Eventually the ugliness of unrepentant gloating encompassed the prevailing culture. Arel politicians capitalized on the groundswell of focused rage over tolerating even the slightest 'Beel-type' behavior in their society. Elections were won by single issue autocrats parading their manufactured anger at those possessing diversity of thought.

Like the Beels had done earlier, the Arels began to trade freedom and dignity for a life of sloth and depravity. Leaders quickly ascended from ingratiating elitists to all powerful overlords. Their deceit and hypocrisy knew no bounds.

Charles stops mid pace and slams both hands down on the table, startling Terah in the process. "We gathered underground to seek out solutions to combat our overreaching government. But those turncoats in our own ranks gave us up to the authorities. It wasn't long until our homes and places of worship were raided and burned. Our numbers dwindled to just a few thousand."

He resumes his pacing alongside the table.

"As a role model provides the motivation a person wishes to aspire to, an equally important societal role is played by the sloth who toils in sin. So as a person measures the distance between himself and greatness, he subconsciously performs a needed measurement that separates him from justifying evil behavior. Without this proper distance of discipline the nation of Arel began a steep moral decline."

Charles plucks a grape from the bowl, but does not eat it.

"Economic, academic, and spiritual leaders soon yielded to the broad path that leads to destruction. Our free market system atrophied and became rife with greed and corruption. Established corporations whose trusted brands we had relied on for decades rapidly deteriorated from board member's short term gain mentalities. Other companies, using the 'grow at any cost' template were polluting the air and land while at the same time squandering precious resources. Neither race nor religion, neither wealth nor standing mattered, it was our ideology that became the anathema to politicians in power."

Charles stops his pacing directly behind Julia's chair and rests his hands on her shoulders.

"First we were marginalized, then demonized, and eventually many of my countrymen were eradicated under false flag operations." Shamefully, he averts his eyes downward, "We are just under six hundred, now."

"So this is how you hide, in a huge resort?" Graham asks.

Julia raises her hand as if to silence a response from Charles, "Let's just say it's very complicated."

"What about the moderates?" Terah asks, searching Mr. Alcott's face, "I understand they exist in virtually every society."

He takes his place in the chair beside Julia.

"Oh yes, the great moderates of our time; interested in everything, passionate about nothing," Charles smirks. "They were so content in their sterile interaction – social networking, computer portal gaming, and digital vacations – that they didn't notice when the state came for them. The moderate's manifesto was to be four-square behind everything unless challenged. So mired in their make-believe worlds they never saw the real one crumbling around them." He bellows while pointing his judgmental finger at an abstract target. "For their efforts, many of their children were born indentured to the Ruling Class; perhaps a fitting tribute to their predictable vacillations."

"A ruling class is like Beel governance," Terah surmises.

Charles searches for a succinct rejoinder.

"Similar yes, they are equal in their oppression."

Terah nods in agreement, "So the Arel government has become much like the Beel's."

Julia stretches her arm out and retrieves a muffin.

"My dear, political labels were dropped over a hundred years ago when the last B-L died out."

Terah is perplexed. "Has the pronunciation changed?"

Charles is surprised Terah has no idea how the two countries got their names. "It's quite simple, really." He leans over and picks up a muffin from the basket on the table. "The Blue-Landers and the Red-Landers. But those initials are a thing of the past."

Terah reaches over and takes two muffins and quietly asks Graham which he prefers. Before he can answer, a large man bursts into the dining room, holding a large-caliber weapon.

"Are these the spies you want me to kill?" the man asks Charles.

"Oh my god," Julia screams, "Kurt!"

Terah immediately grabs two jars of jam and hurls them at the intruder. He ducks, avoiding the first jar, while still squeezing the trigger on his weapon. The second jar, however, finds its mark, hitting the assailant directly in the eye. Reflexes force his shot over the heads of Graham and Terah, penetrating the wall behind them. Julia screams again, and ducks beneath the table.

Charles attempts to tackle Kurt, but his legs become entangled in his wife's, causing him to trip and fall.

Kurt recovers and takes aim again directly at Terah. This shot grazes her right shoulder. She is able to leap over the table taking the fruit basket with her. She lands just in front of Charles and Julia and quickly scatters the leftover fruit into Kurt's path.

"Kurt, stand down!" Charles shouts from under the table.

Kurt is experiencing battlefield 'tunnel vision' and is unaware of Charles's command. He mistakenly steps on the mix of grapes and strawberries on the floor in front of him.

Terah springs up and runs toward the kitchen, drawing his attention and his aim.

Due to his unstable footing, shots three, four, and five strike the china hutch just behind her. Shot six appears to rip into her abdomen, Terah crumples on the cold, marble floor.

Graham sees an opportunity: he sweeps two of the butter knives on the table toward him.

"Charles, he's gonna kill her!" Julia shrieks from beneath the table.

"He won't listen to me."

"Well, I won't stand for this!" Julia gets up and physically confronts Kurt. "Stop this madness at once."

He answers with a swift backhand to her face. Julia drops to the floor unconscious.

Kurt has refocused his aim on Terah. The blade-sight aligns over her forehead.

Springing up on the other side of the table, Graham launches both butter knives simultaneously, which lodge deep into Kurt's left eye socket. The assailant is visually disabled and the pain distracts him from his murderous mission.

Charles takes advantage of the opportunity and lunges at Kurt's ankles, driving him to the floor.

Kurt, though blinded in one eye, is still a physically strong man. He kicks Charles away, returns to his feet, and directs his attention toward Graham. Changing the weapon's magazine, Kurt resumes shooting.

Graham is pinned down under the table by the barrage of bullets. Terah however, manages to get to her feet.

She approaches from Kurt's blindside and delivers a spinning kick that connects to the side of his abdomen, sending him across the room. Confidently, Terah steps closer, grabbing him by the head and flipping him onto his back. His weapon is jarred loose, and slides across the floor, within Graham's reach.

Terah rolls over Kurt's chest, hooking her arm through his. Kurt passes out before she tightens her grip and shatters his elbow.

The threat has been neutralized.

Graham runs to Terah's side, scooping up the weapon on his way.

"Are you all right?"

Terah lifts her shirt enough to reveal a slight graze across her stomach. "It's strawberry jam," She dabs some blood from her shoulder wound. "This one's real."

Charles kneels on the floor at Julia's side, stroking her arm. Her eyelids flutter.

"My precious jewel, can you hear me?" he begs.

Julia's eyes open and color returns to her face.

"I warned you about using that moronic ox."

"What do you mean by that?" Terah asks.

She looks at Mr. Alcott and he averts his eyes.

Charles adjusts his collar and mumbles, "We thought you were spies sent in to destroy us."

"We are truly sorry, but we acted out of self-preservation this time," Julia notes.

"Wait a minute, 'sent in?' " Graham asks.

Charles helps Julia onto a chair and then takes his place next to her at the table. "I think we could all use some brandy right about now, don't you think?"

"Those knives, geez," Graham slaps his head while helping Terah over to the table. "I shouldn't be able to do that in—in—."

Before he can finish, Charles interrupts, "In the real world."

"I knew it. Terah, didn't I tell you? That salmon was the best I ever had. Only one problem, I've never eaten salmon, so how would I know if it was the best? It was just another programmed sub file."

"Those cryogenic chambers you came through," Charles sighs, "are just a couple of partitioned-drive files. You simply crossed from one simulation to another."

Graham slams his fist on the table.

Terah calms Graham down by gently holding his arm.

"Hold on a second, Julia, what did you mean by this time? Were we here before?"

Julia looks at her husband and they both nod in agreement.

"About twelve years ago, I heard a noise coming from the bedroom. I leaned closer to the door to listen." Reliving the moment, Julia directs a piercing stare directly at Graham. "Without warning, you forced the door open, knocking me off my feet."

"She was out cold by the time I got there," Charles chimes in.

"Yes," Julia's voice quivers, "it was dreadful."

Everyone sits silently while Julia recomposes herself.

Graham averts his eyes for a moment.

Terah uses a napkin to staunch her wound.

Breaking the tension, Charles pushes his Bloody Mary across the table. "Here, you'll need this for the pain."

Terah leans over, picks it up, and gulps it down quickly.

"So, what did I do?" Graham inquires.

"Apart from knocking down my wife, you just ran out the front door and bolted across the lawn."

"I don't remember any of that."

Charles continues, "You scaled the security fence and when you landed on the other side, the simulation put you back into the cryogenic chamber."

Julia adds, "Yes, and off you went, that is, until yesterday."

"So you have this guy, Kurt, just come in and shoot us before breakfast?"

"It was Charles' idea and really it was to be done after breakfast," Julia corrects.

Charles smiles nervously, "We thought you were assassins, what were we to do?"

Graham is skeptical of the Alcott's story.

"I don't believe you," Graham says in a measured tone.

Julia gets up and hurries over to the kitchen.

Terah tightens her posture, bracing for another encounter.

"I mean," Graham adds, "how could I forget a place like this?"

Returning from the kitchen, Julia carries a small jar.

"This," she holds the jar out as she walks, "it fell from your pocket when you were climbing our fence."

Graham focuses on it, trying to see a connection.

As Julia gets closer, he can see that the jar contains dried spices. She sets it down on the table, turning it slowly, revealing the hand written label.

Deenay's Spicy Pizza Peppers.

Chapter 40

After half an hour of quiet reflection, Charles breaks the silence.

"The ruling class controls what used to be called Arel," he announces, "They've been hunting us since we discovered this bunker thirty years ago."

The resistance forces also removed the power plant from the national grid and set up cryogenic chambers for all five-hundred-and-ninety of its members. When they were all safely inside the chambers, the tablet processor activated the 'essence' program that placed them into the new simulation.

"We surmised your first intrusion was just a dry run, you know, survey the layout," Charles adds. "Since then we've prepared for the next hit squad to be mirrored-in."

"But, we were just trying to get outside, not kill anyone," Graham replies.

Julia voice cracks, "We realize that now."

"So you and the others are hiding from the government in this simulation?" Terah asks.

Julia puts her hand on Charles's arm. She knows this will be hard for a man with such pride to divulge.

"Yes, it may seem hypocritical or even cowardice, but we needed to plan a break-away revolution. One strong enough to resist the current government," Charles stands up and begins pacing alongside the dining room table.

Terah steps into Charles' path.

"If the Beel Dome projects suggest a civilization collapse is imminent, why not just wait another thirty years to leave?"

"Others," Charles says grimly, "there are many others who didn't make it underground in time. They are family, they are friends, and they are the innocents still being oppressed by this regime."

Blinking away a few tears, Terah asks, "Then why are you still here?"

He shares the uncomfortable fact that over the years, many members of the resistance became content with living in the simulation.

"You're ageless; you can have everything you desire without the burden of physical laws."

"Oh yes, it's quite wonderful here," Julia beams. "We've got tennis, swimming, shopping - and the nightlife is just fabulous."

Charles becomes animated as he describes their paradise.

"Eighteen hole golf course and our lake is stocked with some of the biggest trout you've ever seen."

"But it's not real; you've become jaded from this—this synthetic utopia," Graham pleads.

"Sir, I beg to differ!" Charles bellows.

"Golf, tennis, shopping?" he interjects, "there's no worth to your actions, no goodness from your deeds."

Julia glares.

"Look at your employees," Graham continues as he directs his notice toward Julia, "you treat them as incidental waifs only worthy of your reckless slander.

Her expression softens and she gazes downward.

Graham shakes his head in pity, "You're becoming the oppressors you've fled."

Charles sighs deeply.

"I—we, are truly sorry."

Julia's attention meanders around the floor beneath her while she adjusts to Graham's revealing insights. She begins in a faint voice of contrition,

"Mr. Duncan, where ever did that eloquent, yet judgmental, oratory of yours come from?"

"I don't know. It just came out that way," Graham admits.

"Well, it is greatly appreciated in this time of uncertainty."

Picking up another napkin from the table, Terah tends to her wound. She notices that her blood loss has slowed significantly but she is becoming lightheaded from the shock of the wound. "I need to rest."

Julia shivers; she is not cold.

"I'm afraid that's out of the question."

Graham angrily stands up from his chair sending it back onto the floor with a loud crash, "What? She just got shot! She needs rest."

Charles states matter-of-factly, "Sleep will kill her." With a pathetic looking expression he adds, "and I'm afraid you as well."

Julia begins sobbing, while Charles continues.

"We had Chef Bartell poison your meals last night with Ambi-End."

Raising her hand only slightly, Julia admits, "Unfortunately, that was my idea."

Feeling tired himself from staying up all night; Graham calmly sits down to hear the details from Charles.

"When you fall asleep your subconscious algorithm will locate and unzip a compressed file in your 'run' menu. Upon re-boot, the corrupted file will immediately disable all kernel propagation."

"Like being erased?" Graham replies.

"Not exactly," Charles returns to the comfort of his chair. "It's like being conceived but never growing up."

"Nice," Graham says sardonically, "we're doomed."

"I'm afraid you're –" Charles interrupts himself and begins slowly tapping his chin. "Hmm, maybe it's time for some new leadership."

"You don't even have old leadership," Graham replies, "you've been wasting time in here."

"Waiting, I believe is the more correct word." Charles nods, "waiting for a young, bold leader."

Julia is astonished at the prospects of Charles' inference.

"Darling, what a wonderful idea!" She takes a sip of her drink. "We can resume our lifestyle."

Feeling a sense of uneasiness, Graham's eyes toggle between Charles and Julia.

"Uh, I don't think I am quite ready to lead a revolution."

Charles points, "Nonsense, Duncan, you're the one we've been waiting for."

Terah slumps over in her chair, "Graham, I'm getting really tired."

"That settles it," Charles exclaims, "We must essence you and Terah into our vessels to replace us immediately."

"Yes, we're sure of it now," Julia begins, "Terah you'd make a wonderful first lady. You've shown much style and grace, even while, pardon me, kicking Kurt's backside."

Charles smiles, "My dear, I couldn't have said it better."

Graham understands Terah's tactical subversion skills would be useful in leading the remnant forces but he's not convinced as to why he should leave.

"Out there, I've got no knife skills," his shoulders slump, "and my QFT remains locked in the power plant simulation, so what good am I?"

Charles steps closer to Graham.

"Since you began life as a written code, your essence now includes all sub-root files." He drapes his arm across Graham's shoulders, "You will retain all of your patterning abilities."

Terah makes eye contact with Graham and elicits a nod of approval.

Seeing them both warm to the idea of being sent out, Charles announces, "Let's get them to the billiard room at once!"

He and Julia lead their guests down the hallway. Graham notices the incredibly ornate lighting fixture that hangs just a few feet above the massive slate table. It is designed after the Duke of Edinburgh's table from the late sixteenth century.

Charles instructs Graham to help Terah up onto the table and to join her. The entire felt top acts as the neural interface.

Julia pulls the '1' ball and the '4' ball from a corner pocket. She explains that by dropping them into the two side pockets simultaneously, the 'jump' will commence. She assures that in less than a minute Graham and Terah will awaken in the Alcotts' human bodies, outside the simulation.

"There's no way to return once you've jumped," Julia cautions.

Charles takes the number '4' ball from Julia and prepares to drop it from a prescribed distance of two feet above the side pocket in front of him. Julia stands equally ready on the other side of the billiard table holding the '1' ball.

Charles pauses for a moment to think further about the immensity of his decision; one where he will never again see a real sunrise, taste real food, or feel the pull of gravity.

"Can I have your indulgence for one more second?" Charles asks. "It's just a formality, but I assume that both of you were actually human at one time. Am I correct?"

Anxiously, Graham shouts, "Yeah, just drop the balls!"

Charles and Julia let go of the balls at nearly the same time.

Terah corrects him with a barely audible, "Never born."

Graham swats the '4' ball away from the side pocket. He rolls over Terah and sticks his fist directly into the other pocket preventing the ball from landing in that one. It bounces off his arm and drops to the floor.

Startled, Julia pushes herself away from the table, stumbling into a cue stick stand. "Heavens, that was close."

"Yes, quite," Charles replies, "Just as well, since I hadn't sent the escape message to our residents yet." He leans down and presses a button, located under one of the corner pockets.

Graham sits up on the table and pulls Terah gently into a sitting position, "I'm sorry; I forgot you're two-point-O."

She is tired but responsive.

"I need some coffee."

Julia surveys the room and forces out a polite smile, "I guess I could make the coffee."

Charles explains the software that enables neural jumping was reconfigured to 'essence only' back in the early 2200s. This adjustment, allowing human only transmissions, came about from many instances of codes jumping out of vacation simulations and commandeering the human bodies from the interfaces. Since then, non-human entities that jump from simulations are instantly deleted. The host body is also lost in the process.

Graham hops off the billiard table and helps Terah down. He leads her over to a nearby chair.

"Is there a doctor in your community?" Graham calmly asks.

Charles is somewhat surprised, "A doctor? There's no need for doctors in here."

"What if you're injured?"

"Am I to assume, young man, you've never heard of the Rule of Accidents and Assassins?"

"Sounds like a tech-game," Graham says tersely.

"It's quite simple really. All accidents eventually heal; all assassinations eventually kill. The simulation only understands 'intent' when dealing with injuries. Was it deliberate or not? There are no gray areas."

"When I was in the Supreme Server we had a hospital. In fact I worked there," Graham walks over and picks up a billiard ball and shoves it across the table. The ball ricochets off the bumpers before slowing to a gradual stop. "How is that different than here?"

Charles turns his head away from Graham and toward the kitchen. "Julia, my dear, I'll need another Bloody Mary when you finish making the coffee." He turns his attention back to Graham, "The hospital, St. Theodota, in the simulation was just a front."

"A front for what?" demands Graham.

"That's how the Beels adjusted the emotional input that supplied the server with more of those 'touchy-feely' judgments. Dr. Parton was hacked into the hospital as a Beel operative. We never suspected it especially since it was named after a Catholic martyr for heaven's sake."

Terah slumps deeply into her chair and Graham and Charles go immediately to her side.

"Coffee, Julia! At once!" Charles shouts.

Graham checks on Terah's shoulder wound. It is not terribly deep, but according to the Rule of Accidents and Assassins, this will kill her.

More tired than injured, Terah stretches her other arm around Graham's shoulders. She finds herself in a rare internal struggle to separate her programmed emotions from her logic-based reality. No matter how much sympathetic fondness for another is entered into a software program, it is still just that; a programmed response chain. After all, the less effective emotional side was only added as a byproduct, to quell and soften simulation entities.

"Graham, you should still go," Terah says, in a labored whisper, "You're the one to lead the remnant forces."

He smiles and wraps both of his arms around her.

"Sorry, I'm staying."

Terah stiffens. "Are you insane?"

Her eyes focus to a piercing stare. "You're relentless and have seen all sides of humanity." She gently runs her hand through his hair. "Now get back on that interface."

"And leave you here?"

"Ugh, your stubbornness is, is, so human."

Graham adds to her discontent by smiling.

Charles joins them.

"You must go; the others are in the process of leaving the simulation right now." He turns his head back toward the kitchen again, "I could use that Bloody Mary right about now!"

A smile appears on Terah's face as she accepts her mortality, "Well, two to one."

Graham leans closer. "Do I get a goodbye kiss?"

Terah has effectively switched off her emotions, and curtly instructs Graham to leave at once. She knows the longer he waits, the more susceptible he becomes to changing his mind. The remnants do not need a vacillating leader.

Walking over to the billiard table, Graham hops up and lies down. Charles picks up the solid color '4' ball again.

"Are you sure?" Charles asks.

"Yes," Graham folds his hands together, "No, hold it. Dear God, guide my path to victory. Not to prove wrong those who doubt, but to prove right those who believe."

"You're a religious man?" Charles asks.

"I've been software and I've been human. The one constant has been my faith."

With the billiard ball in Charles' hand he holds it two feet directly above the side pocket and is ready to send Graham to the world outside.

He lets the ball go and time seems to slow dramatically as Graham watches the purple ball rotate. He stares so intently that he sees reflections of the billiard room he hadn't noticed before. The stately gilded wall fixtures and opulent crown moldings all dressed in fine, Brazilian hardwoods.

Graham will be thrust into leading a force of only several hundred. This will be a battle of beliefs and blood.

"Charles!" Julia shouts from the doorway.

Graham's reflexes react, and he bats the ball away again.

Charles and Graham see that Julia is being held hostage by an angry, disheveled Kurt. He has draped his one good arm around Julia's neck, where a kitchen knife is dangerously poked into the side of her stomach.

"He has a knife!" Julia shrieks.

Charles puts his hands up, attempting to calm his terrified wife.

"Exacting vengeance, Kurt, will not change the fact that you'll eventually succumb to your wounds."

Kurt tightens his grip on Julia and moves the knife to her neck.

"It's not re… vengeance; I'm jumping out of here."

Julia interrupts, "You are quite uneducated you slack-jawed simpleton. You'll be erased."

"She's right," Graham affirms, "Codes can't jump."

Kurt maneuvers his hostage over to the billiard table.

"Get off, Duncan!"

Graham remains in an upright, sitting position on the green felt.

"I'm not going anywhere until you let her go," Graham responds.

"Go grab the purple one for me or I'll cut her in half."

Graham stubbornly relents and slides down from the table. Slowly, he stoops to collect the ball and then tosses it to Kurt.

The assailant carelessly throws Julia to the table, and joins her.

"We'll go at the same time," he says, "into the same body."

He raises the ball and holds it over the pocket.

The room is thick with tension. Graham's eyes toggle between Charles and Terah, searching for a signal of an unspoken plan. If Graham interrupts the ball drop, Kurt may kill Julia before she can get clear of the table.

"This won't work, you rabid ox," Julia pleads.

"I'll use you for the jump and then I'll overwhelm your personality. Works for me."

Kurt drops the ball.

Graham has no choice but to grab a cue stick from the floor. He launches it in the direction of the falling ball. Charles reacts by grabbing his forehead in a fatalistic reflex. Julia, still struggling to free herself, can only scream in terror as the ball heads toward the pocket.

Terah's reaction to the situation is different. She thinks more tactically than instinctively and is formulating a second response should the situation afford one. Quietly, she stands without attracting Kurt's notice. While his eyes are trained on the other side of the table, she begins her five step journey toward his blind side.

Graham's cue stick misses its mark.

While nearly everyone in the room is focusing on the dropping ball, Terah is not. She steals more distance between herself and the billiard table.

Kurt's toss has caught the edge of the side pocket and bounces out and harmlessly rolls to his leg.

His aim was altered by what is referred to as 'keystone distortion.' While the human eye gathers an amazing amount of visual information, some data is culled from extreme locations on the peripheral. In order for the brain to present a whole picture, it will recalculate how close an object is to its fovea reference point. Then it measures the distance of travel through the field of vision. A slight trapezoidal bending of the image occurs depending on how close the eye is to the subject.

Kurt hurriedly fumbles for the ball and immediately lifts it again. Though Graham is out of position after tossing the cue stick, Terah has reached Kurt's blindside.

"Hey, lummox!"

Startled, he turns his head and sees Terah standing with her hands clasped together.

Before he can react, she slams her hands onto the side of his head, over-rotating his neck and severing his spinal cord. Kurt's arm drops to his side releasing the ball to roll down the side of his leg. The ball ends its protracted journey by peacefully surrendering itself to the corner pocket.

The billiard room remains eerily quiet.

Though his body is unable to move, Kurt is still conscious.

Terah leans over his frozen expression.

"Nice shot, but you didn't call it."

She deliberately places one hand over Kurt's mouth while the other pinches his nose. She is helping him die before his injuries begin their auto-response of circumvention. His brain would instigate radical convulsions in a futile attempt to reestablish communications with his heart. His lungs would fill with a phlegm-like gel trapping any remaining oxygen. All other organs would idle, channeling their resources to the brain. Kurt is spared this extra agony and does not fight her. He dies peacefully atop the billiard table.

"Charles!" Julia shouts as she sits up, "Charles Thomas Alcott. How dare you bark about Bloody Marys while I am a hostage."

Charles's expression of shock remains as Julia continues to berate him.

"My life in the balance and you do nothing?!" She gets off of the table and walks intently over to him. "A less noble man would have traded his life for mine."

"I'm so sorry, my dear. I will never again stall in times of great peril."

Julia's mood softens.

"Even the village idiot would have hurled insults at my assailant," she adds sarcastically.

"Something isn't adding up," Graham begins, "If you ordered Kurt to kill us, why did he harm you and Julia?"

Charles looks around the room, recreating the earlier attack in his mind.

"I don't know."

Graham looks at Julia. "What about your chef? You had him poison our food?"

"I told you I am truly remorseful…"

Graham walks over to her, "Should we be worried about the chef, now?"

"Yes," Terah says while still leaning on the billiard table.

Charles reacts. "That's preposterous! Chef Bartell is a consummate professional. Why, he only acted on Julia's instructions."

"Charles, must you drag my reputation through the mud? Again, I am truly sorry for such a deplorable act."

Terah dabs at her wound with her hand.

"Since Kurt was reprogrammed to assassinate, his operating system became very unstable." She notices fresh blood, "We have to assume that Chef Bartell will go rogue at some point, too."

"You sound rather sure of yourself," Charles says with a note of condescension in his voice.

"I know assassins, Mr. Alcott, because I am an assassin."

Charles and Julia lurch backward.

"So we were right about you?!" Julia demands.

"The only person to die in this simulation was Kurt and I killed him," Terah begins methodically pacing around the table. "The difference is that I was programmed, while Kurt was reprogrammed."

She continues to parse the differences for her nervous hosts, "Because I was designed with a tactical threat response system, I remain stable even after neutralizing Kurt."

"Could he have been hacked-in?" Graham asks.

"Maybe. Adjusting his killing field when the Alcotts attempted to stop him showed adaptable program migration," Terah pulls a billiard ball from a pocket and rolls it toward the other end of the table. "However, when he attempted the jump he acted with a sense of preservation. That's evidence of a corrupted, unstable system."

Julia interrupts, "Do you hear me, Charles? Kurt was just a coarse, ill-mannered ox."

"Designed assassins do not deviate from their mission," Terah plucks another ball from a billiard pocket and sets it on the table's dot. "Julia, I suggest you furlough your staff today while we think about our next move."

"I'll notify them at once."

Graham has changed his mind. He feels he's not a good fit for Charles's host body. The thought of his personality thrust into a distinguished middle-aged man's body may cause insurmountable suspicion from his fellow remnant forces. He concludes that it must be Charles and Julia that leave the simulation.

However, what began thirty years ago as temporarily hiding has morphed into a way of life for the Alcotts. Evidently, they have grown accustomed to their simulated surroundings. But an even greater deterrent to jumping out is the real prospect of dying.

"The idea of leading a small force of civilians against this tyrannical leviathan is totally absurd," Charles proclaims. "Graham, we have no money or weapons, let alone any combat training." He sits down on the nearest barstool and assumes a slumped, defeatist posture, "We're scholars, not soldiers."

"Charles, we need to pause and properly discuss all our options," Julia announces, "I suppose I could make some sandwiches or something."

Chapter Forty One

Outside of the computer simulation, only one country remains. Though the landmass encompasses most of its Arel beginnings, it retains none of its humanity; not even its former name. That was changed to *New Ahlab* a half century ago.

2431 marks a crescendo of another ruling class that uses 'incremental conditioning' to acclimate its people to the imposition of tyranny.

The population has dwindled to under twenty-three million. However, government statisticians have to constantly revise the numbers. Their estimations are not faulty; the rampant disease, starvation, and suicide make their calculations obsolete.

Leaders who were elected to solve the problems have only made them worse. Some of the braver citizens openly accuse the hypocrites of entrenching their own power. It is an all too familiar refrain of the newly lorded over.

The current president, who assumed power sixteen years ago after an election rife with fraud, uses his authority to make drastic changes. His first order was the elimination of all future elections. It was touted as a way to feed the hungry and repair crumbling schools while boosting the pay of its subservient edutarians.

Cancelling elections proves to be a windfall in social spending as well. Since voters are no longer needed, many of the vote buying, subsidies are eliminated. The sudden flood of unskilled, unmotivated people into the labor market drives wages and productivity down. Not surprisingly, the quality of products and services also plunge. Golden parachutes pop like corn all across the country as chief executives cave to the central planners. Handing their corporate reins to the outstretched tentacles of government is yet another crushing blow.

The president expands his cabinet to more than a hundred members who are appointed for life. The exchange of financial support from these officials results in a seat at the table of the ruling class. The legislative branch was gutted save for the president's fifty hand-picked Senators used to quell the masses. This strategy of keeping a buffer between the holders of power and its people is beneficial. The Senators pretend to fight for the people. This political mirage works well in tamping down weak, sporadic retaliations that crop up against the government. As a grumbling populace gives way, a new serfdom emerges.

The political tyrants and their state-run propaganda outlets continue to increase their control over the masses. This so-called media serves not to inform nor expose, but to encourage these Oligarchs in their radical thinking. Unfortunately, New Ahlab is unwittingly following the same fatal path that wiped out the Beels years earlier.

Chapter 42

Graham pulls Kurt's body from atop the billiard table and drags it to a storage closet in the utility room. He stuffs the corpse into the tight space and using his hip, forces the door closed. He walks back to join Terah and Charles, sitting on barstools along the wall of the billiard room.

Julia is in the kitchen making sandwiches. Once finished, she carries in a serving tray piled high with stacks of lunch meat, cheese, and a half-empty jar of olives that lightly sloshes in their juice as she returns to her guests.

With a puzzled expression, Charles examines the tray. He is hesitant but inquires further about the snacks.

"This is wonderful, my Dear, but I feel... dare I say... something is missing?"

She gives a cursory glance at the tray and returns an expression of puzzlement back to Charles.

"Missing? What could possibly be missing?"

Charles looks to Graham and Terah for help. "Yes, uh huh, well my dear, you've done a wonderful—

"Yeah," Graham chuckles, "something is missing."

"He knows, Julia," Charles says.

Graham stares straight ahead.

"My whole life – existence – has been based on patterns," He walks over to the edge of the table and leans on it like a young lawyer making his opening arguments. "Everything's a pattern; from a coincidence to a full-blown conspiracy. I need one more search."

"HNA?" Terah interjects.

"Yep. There's got to be a reason we're here, at this point in time, in this house, in this simulation, it just hasn't lined up yet."

"Good heavens!" Julia shouts, "The bread!"

She runs to the kitchen to retrieve it.

Slowed by her injury, Terah ambles up to the other side of the billiard table.

"Graham, if you drift off too deeply, the poison will kill you."

Charles is confused.

"My word! What are you two talking about?"

Graham summarizes a code's Hyper Neural Access ability—he will need to take a twenty minute nap but be careful not to enter REM sleep. While in this pre-dreaming HNA state, he should recall a massive amount of raw information. A special algorithm will begin pairing the strands of connected data. His emotional responses will act as a filter.

A feeling of urgency overcomes Graham as Terah edges closer to death. He lies down on the floor in front of the table.

Julia reenters the billiard room clutching several loaves of bread. "Charles, what have I missed?" She is startled to see Graham lying motionless on the floor. "Oh my, has the boy finally succumbed?"

"Shh. Quiet, my pet," Charles advises, "He needs to nap. I'll explain later."

An explosion of images, sounds, and recollections swirl around Graham's subconscious. He reviews every event he has ever experienced, including the massive data load he mined from the internet hundreds of years ago. His emotional response mechanism begins pairing some of the memories together. From there he rapidly dismisses those strands that are not pertinent. His old patient number comes to the forefront of his thoughts. It reminds him of Dr. Jerome's clinic.

He twitches slightly while on the floor of the billiard room. Charles and Julia watch over him. They are not sure exactly when a person goes from resting to sleeping.

Terah worries aloud, "He's been down for over fifteen minutes."

"There, there poor dear; I know you two are very close." Julia walks over to Terah and gently puts her arm around her shoulder.

"He did say he needed twenty minutes." Charles assures, "Three more and we'll wake him up, okay?"

Terah responds softly, "Okay. And thank you Mr.—."

"Charles, please call me Charles."

"Thank you, Charles."

Another memory strand plays in Graham's mind. It is a compilation of every moment he shared with Terah.

The first time he saw her was at the clinic. She was behind a control panel for most of his visit. He remembers when he thought he encountered her at the Sleep Tight Motel. And finally, he remembers her at the telemarketing firm where she aimed a gun at his head. Most importantly, though, he remembers his awakening when she informed him he was actually a computer program. The memory of their short time together on the outside begins playing. And finally, her sorrowful death.

Graham's time in the power plant simulation is highlighted next. For some reason, he is struck by a feeling of boredom. So boring is this memory that it pulls up the old safety forms he was required to fill out. The page appears, but he is startled and loses the image.

"Wake up Graham!" Charles shouts. "Can you hear me young man?! Wake up!"

Subconsciously, Graham fights the call to awaken. Instead, he goes deeper into a new cluster of memory strands.

Just behind a cluttered roll top desk, an older gentleman writes on a chalkboard. He's been working on a complex mathematical equation for several years. He stops and strokes his graying beard and immediately continues writing.

"How's the formula coming along, Professor?"

Startled, the man turns from the chalkboard and peers over his wire-rimmed glasses at the visitor.

"Quite well, I would say," the Professor returns to his work, "are you a mathematician?"

"No sir, but I've been watching you."

The Professor's chalk snaps in half and a piece drops to the floor. He places the rest of chalk next to an eraser and turns to address the stranger.

"And you've come to my office to…?" His voice trails off hoping to prompt a response.

"I'm Graham Duncan and I need your help."

The Professor walks over to a coffee pot and pours Graham a cup.

"Here," he hands the mug to Graham and gestures for him to sit down in the leather wingback chair in front of the chalkboard. "How can I be of assistance?"

Graham settles into the chair and explains how he came to choose the Professor for help.

"When you were digitized several hundred years ago," he sips from his coffee mug, "I noticed that you, like me, used a retrieval algorithm to view billions of files throughout the digisphere. I think your work on space travel using nuclear propulsion can help me."

"Surely, Mr. Duncan, but I suspect you want more answers than just a very efficient way to move about the cosmos."

"Bobby was right; you are the smartest scientist in the whole world." Graham smiles before taking another sip of coffee, "I need to travel backward in time."

The room is quiet. The Professor walks back over to the chalkboard and directs Graham to look at a particular part on the board.

"Mr. Duncan, this right here is the entire reason that any form of time travel is not possible." He makes his point more sharply as he repeatedly taps the chalk next to the equation. "You see, matter cannot be removed from one time-space continuum and placed into another."

"But what about worm-holes?"

"There are many unproven theories. That's just another one waiting to be debunked. Besides, Mr. Duncan," the Professor steps over to his desk and holds up a stack of papers, "time, unlike sound, light and mass, has no physical properties to manipulate. None whatsoever."

Graham takes another sip of his coffee.

"Then I guess it's over."

The Professor blinks his eyes in confusion.

"I'm at a loss, Mr. Duncan. What is your dilemma?"

"I've run the projections on my mission; I will fail."

"Ah, I see, you'd like to go back a few ticks and hopefully correct the outcome, wouldn't you?"

Graham sips from his mug and places it on a table beside his chair.

"In another simulation I froze and the entire system was rebooted." Graham takes a breath and continues, "But my hesitation was the right decision. But this time it's not."

The Professor pulls the chair out from his desk. He sits down and leans back, letting the old tension spring recline him into a more relaxed position.

"There is a way to alter an event in the physical world even though it has already happened. Are you familiar with the theory of *Cognizant Latency*?

"No sir."

"When a person inputs a problem for a computer to solve, there is a gap that can be exploited. The time the processor displays the answer until the user fully understands what he's looking at can be up to several micro-seconds." He chuckles, "and in our world, that's a very long time."

Graham takes another sip, "so you're telling me if I wanted to change the numbers after the fact I could?"

"Exactly; although the brain is an amazing organ, I'm afraid it's a very slow processor."

Graham pauses for a moment and slouches.

"But that won't help me," he says while looking down at the floor, "I don't need to change anything, I'm just too late."

The Professor stands up and returns to his chalkboard.

"I wish I could have been more help to you, Graham. Unfortunately, I'm just a digitized character from an old science fiction movie."

The sound of the chalk on the board continues as the Professor finishes another equation.

"Oh, there is one more thing, Mr. Duncan, you could have used a human characteristic—," he stops writing while his eyes search for the answer, "yes, I believe it's referred to as 'playing a hunch'. You know, to anticipate something before it's begun."

There is no response from Graham.

"But, I'm afraid," he turns from the chalkboard, "that you would have had to anticipate that our brief discussion…" he sees the leather chair is empty, "would be fruitless… and therefore not—"

He walks over and examines Graham's coffee mug. It is full and untouched.

The Professor smiles, "Precisely."

A woman opens an adjacent door to the Professor's office and announces that another guest has arrived to see him.

"Yes, thank you, send him right in."

A tall, slender man enters and joins the Professor at the chalkboard.

"I hope you don't mind the adjustments I made to some of your expressions." The man points to various areas on the board. "With these corrections you should have the answer soon."

Perplexed by the stranger's bold candor, the Professor inquires, "How can you be so sure, have you tested this theory?"

The stranger smiles, "I find it works well enough to get me from one planet to another."

Astonished, the Professor extends his right hand, "I am Professor Jacob Barnhardt. And you're mister…?"

The stranger reaches out and shakes the Professor's hand while correcting him.

"Just… Klaatu."

The sensation of falling backward yanks Graham from his HNA nap. The last memory shatters into pieces as his eyes snap open.

His body shudders.

Disoriented he mumbles, "I gotta fill it out?"

"You're okay Graham; time to get up." Terah replies.

He blinks a few times while his eyes adjust to the ambient light in the room.

"Okay, I don't think I got anything. Well, other than my old patient number from the clinic."

Julia rolls her eyes, "Then it's settled; you jump into Charles's body and go save the world." She looks at her husband and waves a box of crackers. "Darling, I brought your favorites."

Graham gets to his feet.

"I told you; I'm not the guy."

"Well don't look at me," Charles exclaims, "Why would I want to risk going out there and leading so few against so many?"

"Those on the outside, they've been praying for a leader. Charles, you're a great speaker, it's time to put action to your words."

A shiver spreads through Julia's body. "Oh, Charles, I'm afraid I agree." She turns to Graham, "you should have seen him at last year's masquerade party; he dressed up as a general and spoke so eloquently. All the men were transfixed and the women simply doted."

Charles straightens and his timbre changes to that of a great orator, "While the truthful are at ease with their words, the hypocrites are burdened with hiding their lies."

"Oh, Charles," Julia swoons, "That's wonderful, grace us with more."

"The power of ideas is fueled by bold action."

His eyes sharpen to that of a General surveying a battlefield, his baton tucked securely at his side. Charles quotes a famous peace activist from the early twenty-first century.

"As the world shills for evil, I'll continue praying for the hardened souls of the damned."

Julia gently clasps her hands together, "Beautiful words from Chi Re Tong who I believe still speaks for all of us today," she says serenely.

Terah changes the subject, "Was there a pattern, Graham?"

"No, but I found my old patient number; 25-637."

"That's it?"

"Yep."

Charles diverts his attention over to Graham and Terah while Julia is still beaming at him.

"You're not a devotee of billiards I gather?" he asks Graham.

"No, I wanted to learn but, it's a long story."

"Well son, the 2-5-6-3 and 7 are all solid colors in the game."

"Charles," Julia adds, "don't forget the 4 and the 1. Those are necessary to jump."

Adding the 4 and the 1 to the end of Graham's number forms a perfect non-repeating sequence that uses every solid number in the game of pool.

"So, what does your patient number and our table have in common?" Charles proffers.

Terah's face lights up. "It was your patient number but now with the four and the one -- 256-3741, it's a phone number, Jennifer West's."

Even though telephones were replaced with implanted chips nearly three centuries ago, Jennifer kept a hard line for telemetry purposes for several years after their obsolescence.

"So the question really is, 'what do all three have in common?' " Terah asks.

Graham stares at the floor in concentration, "Well, just Ms. West and I were human, so that isn't it. I don't shoot pool so that's not going to work. I don't know."

Julia is a master at solving puzzles, though she would never admit to indulging in such childishness.

"It must be the power plant," says Julia.

Charles erupts.

"What the hell, Julia?"

"Your language, Charles."

"But darling, you're right! Jennifer designed it, Graham powers it, and our table uses it."

"Yes, Charles, I've just said that."

Charles stares at a portrait of himself that hangs on the wall over his family crest.

"Dear God, that reminds me; the others must be outside by now. They will think I've betrayed them."

"Then don't!" Julia insists.

To refocus them, Terah suggests they concentrate on why the Psychothetical power generator was patterned by Graham's HNA. The question of reentering the power plant simulation to access the plant controls is tempered by the threat of being reset upon entering the loop. If a reboot happened they would become their former avatars and their mission would be erased. However, the general assumption is that since Jennifer West formatted the entire hard drive, it is possible to access the generator from the Alcotts' side.

Graham walks over to the tray. He picks up the spreading-knife and cuts a slice of Genoa salami. His eyebrows rise as he chews. A broad smile grows across his face. Without indication, he turns and lodges the knife into Charles' abdomen.

"What have you done, you Neanderthal?" Julia shouts.

Terah mouths the words, "What is this?"

Charles is in visible pain. His face begins to drain of color.

"It seems I have one choice," he staggers over the side of the billiard table. "Fortunately, it's the right choice."

Graham helps him onto the table.

"You've got a revolution to lead."

Shaking off her emotions, Julia insists, "I'm going, too."

Graham picks her up and places her next to her husband. Terah retrieves the 4 and 1 balls and tosses one to Graham.

They ready them over the side pockets as blood begins pooling around Charles' wound.

"On the count of three, we'll drop them together, okay?"

Terah focuses on Graham's mouth.

"Okay."

"One… two…"

"Wait," Terah says, "What if it isn't safe?"

Charles raises his hand, "I'm still bleeding."

"Look," Graham smirks, "I'll fill out a safety form later."

"Not helping." Terah says offhandedly, "Think!"

"About what, safety forms? The 9J? FBV?"

"Julia," Terah commands, "Search 'Jennifer West' and 'FBV' on your watch."

"My husband is bleeding like a stuck beast, I am frazzled at the thought of returning to the outside and now you're ordering me to—" Julia sighs in exasperation, before leaning over and speaking into the watch.

The watch replies.

"FBV stands for Focused Beam Vectoring. Ms. West developed a way to channel Psychothetical power safely to a satellite mirror in geosynchronous orbit, in order to—"

The information stops cold, causing Julia to raise her voice. "That's it?! You stupid soulless device, 'in order to' what?"

The device remains silent. It has no more information because it has no confirmation. Since this event has not happened yet, the watch cannot speculate on what might transpire.

Charles struggles with the words, "It sounds to me like we'll have a rather impressive weapon."

The Alcotts are reassured that somehow Graham and Terah will find a way to activate the newly discovered FBV.

"Three, two, one."

They drop the balls. Both hit their mark and are caught by the leather net at the bottom of each pocket. The Alcotts' simulation icons disappear.

Chapter Forty 3

The late afternoon sky is coated with fog which drapes over the high desert town of Canyon Caverns. It has remained abandoned ever since the Vista Verde explosion three hundred years earlier. New Alhab's myopic planning, crippled by bloated budgets and favoritism, has pushed much of the population into the rapidly crumbling infrastructure of concentrated urban areas. These disease breeding grounds serve as testaments to the falling pillars of a civilization that continues to champion its indifference to ethics and morality.

Charles and Julia push open the door of the stairwell from above their cryogenic chambers, joining the others from the simulation. As their eyes adjust to the taxing demands of three dimensions, the resistance coalition gathers around them. Charles immediately works to unify the members and to quell the anxious.

"Toppling a tyrannical regime in a bloody revolution is a fool's choice. Instead we'll work to change the hearts of the wicked; it is more lasting."

A man shouts from the middle of the assembly. "Before we hid in the computer, we were called 'zealots' and 'extremists.' How do we get rid of the false labels?"

"Are the purveyors of political correctness more righteous than the people who allow it to define them?" Charles looks over the heads of the people searching for a rebuttal. "Then, understand that labels are the only weapon in the arsenal of the wicked. Let us not squander resources engaging the narrow-minded, instead let us revisit the task of restoring and preserving our freedoms."

Julia adjusts her expression from beaming pride to unwavering admiration. She is becoming the model of strength and grace for a new generation.

The group's charter meeting is interrupted by the pulsating hum of electro-turbine engines. The sounds belong to three propaganda drones that arrive and hover above the crowd. The different network logos attached to the drones serve only to perpetuate the image of an independent media.

Charles climbs onto a boulder, to take advantage of the government's curiosity.

"When in the course of human events it becomes necessary for one people to dissolve the political bands which have connected them with another and to assume among the powers of the earth, the separate and equal station to which the Laws of Nature and of Nature's God entitle them, a decent respect to the opinions of mankind requires that they should declare the causes which impel them to the separation."

"We hold these truths to be self-evident, that all men are created equal, that they are endowed by their Creator with certain unalienable Rights that among these are Life, Liberty and the Pursuit of Happiness. That to secure these rights, Governments are instituted among Men, deriving their just powers from the consent of the governed, that whenever any Form of Government becomes destructive of these ends, it is the Right of the People to alter or to abolish it, and to institute new Government, laying its foundation on such principles and organizing its power in such form, as to them shall seem most likely to effect their Safety and Happiness."

Charles is inspired by simply reciting these powerful words written so long ago. He continues.

"Prudence, indeed, will dictate that Governments long established should not be changed for light and transient causes; and accordingly all experience hath shown that mankind are more disposed to suffer, while evils are sufferable than to right themselves by abolishing the forms to which they are accustomed. But when a long train of abuses and usurpations, pursuing invariably the same Object evinces a design to reduce them under absolute Despotism, it is their right, it is their duty, to throw off such Government, and to provide new Guards for their future security."

The assembled members cheer enthusiastically at Charles Alcott's recitation.

The oligarchs are insulted; they dispatch a judgment drone to the scene. This particular drone has the power to both depose and dispose; it will listen to the arguments of the accused, and then deliver punishment according to the whims of government.

Charles notices that Julia has joined him on the boulder.

"These great words – written over five hundred years ago – still capture the spirit of the cause we seek today."

The drone moves closer to Charles and Julia and a synthesized male voice announces, "You have ten minutes to dissolve your resistance and submit to re-encampment or face severe penalty."

***

Graham and Terah have been trying to figure out how to access the FBV protocol of the power generator. They have entered the sequential patient and billiard ball numbers into another watch drive with no apparent success.

"I'm exhausted," Graham says.

"I am too, but if we fall asleep now, the revolution will die too. We need to keep looking."

They lie next to each other on the floor and stare up at the ceiling.

"We won't actually die," Terah reassures, "We just won't fully exist. We're codes."

Graham turns his head.

"I think just talking about death has made us a little more than codes, don't you think?"

"Maybe," she smiles, "so, why did you choose to stay?"

"I didn't want to stay; I just couldn't leave."

"Ooh," Her smile grows bigger, "I know why."

"Oh," he smirks, "so 'Tactical' Terah has become 'Tender' Terah?"

"I'm new and improved," she purrs.

Graham stands and helps Terah up.

"We should leave some notes," he advises.

"Notes, that's a good idea."

"You know, just in case someone comes running through here again like I did twelve years ago."

He collects the billiard balls while Terah uses a piece of chalk and writes her notes directly on the green felt.

Jennifer West
265-3741
Power Plant
FBV (Focused Beam Vectoring)

Graham arranges all the balls in the center of the table.

"I've always wanted a pool table."

Terah laughs as she racks them up so they can play a game.

She locates the white cue ball hiding in a corner pocket and places it neatly on the dot.

"Your break, Mr. Duncan," she says with a slight erudite accent.

Graham walks over to a wall mounted rack of cue sticks and selects one.

"Yep, my first game and I'm going to run the table."

The crash of the cue ball sends most of the billiard balls in every direction. The '1' ball surrenders itself to a corner pocket.

Graham's knife-throwing ability plays a large part of his hand-eye coordination. He masterfully sinks all the other solids without missing. Before he lines up his final shot at the '8' ball, he customarily calls for it to fall into the corner pocket.

While he takes several practice shots, Terah yawns.

"Never played before? I didn't even get to shoot."

Graham stops in mid-shot. His mouth drops open.

"In the Supreme Server, remember Jennifer used binary programs to communicate?"

"Yeah, they'd post messages in plain sight on the internet while the government's algorithms searched for the deeply encrypted phony ones."

He lowers the stick to his side, "My knife throwing was not programmed just for defense."

A look of enlightenment comes to Terah's eyes.

"Do you think Jennifer programmed you to play pool and hid it in your muscle memory?"

"Well, I'm about to run the table aren't I?"

She looks at the eight ball.

"Do it, let's see what happens."

Graham is overcome with nerves at the prospects of his final shot.

"Okay, now I feel the pressure."

He taps the corner pocket with his cue stick and proceeds to line up his shot. Angling his head low over the stick, he focuses back and forth between the white and black.

Without hesitation, he shoots. The cue ball follows a steady path to the rail, gently tapping the '8' ball toward the corner pocket. The first bounces off the felt-covered rail, and comes to a gradual stop.

The '8' continues hugging the long rail as it moves down the table. The ball reaches the vortex of the pocket, and with enough energy left over, it hits the back of the pocket before falling safely into the leather webbing.

"You did it!" Terah shouts.

Graham is still.

There are no blinking lights of confirmation.

"That's it? That's all?" Graham wonders aloud.

"That completes the pattern, though." Terah adds, "Something must've happened."

He walks back over to the rack on the wall.

"I hope so, we tried everything."

"Besides, we can't stay awake much longer." Terah says solemnly, "Our mission is over."

There it was, the one little word that summarized everything, 'mission.' It has just seven letters but carries a vastness of width and depth to encompass Graham and Terah's entire existence.

"It's funny you say that." He cocks his head to one side, "I never really felt like we were on a mission."

"Well, we're still codes, it's not like this was random."

"Sure it was, remember? When the glitch happened, we just wanted to get out."

Terah laughs. She hops up onto the pool table and swivels toward Graham.

"There's no such thing as a glitch. Haven't you ever read The Reason of Random?"

"No, but I think you're about to bore me with it."

She feigns an agitated posture and hops down. Taking a few labored steps around the table Terah begins paraphrasing from the book.

"Basically, nothing happens by chance. All action can be traced back to premeditation."

"You know, if you bore me too much I'll fall asleep and the poison will kill me," Graham jokes.

"No—no, just listen." She grabs three solid color balls from the table pockets and lines them up. "Pick a ball, any ball."

He looks over at the '3' '1' and '7' balls.

"Yeah, okay, I pick the red one."

"Why?"

"I don't know. I just picked it because I like red."

Terah points directly at Graham.

"Well, there you go, you had a reason. Now pick again."

He rolls his eyes, "all right, the '1'."

"I knew it! She exclaims. "You patterned away from the '7' because it's maroon, closer to red than the yellow ball. Don't you see? A computer is incapable of being random."

"Wait a minute, how come I've got a 'random' button on my music player?"

"Oh geez, those are just a series of pre-programmed sequences. Every time you select 'random' an algorithm selects another series. Even the cheap players have a thousand sequences."

A nearby bar stool becomes Graham's new comfort zone. Still holding his cue stick, he sits down using it as a crutch. He looks around the room and ends his gaze on Terah's face.

"You know, if this were a crashing plane, wouldn't we be making-out instead of discussing The Rules of Random?"

"Hmm. Why did you say that?"

She joins Graham on the bar stool next to his.

"I don't know Terah, I just say things. I know, not randomly."

"That's right. We're discussing something that doesn't exist in a computer simulation."

"Okay, so," Graham stands up in wonderment, "we're talking about randomness because, as you say, we were programmed to." He shakes his head. "Why?"

More blood oozes from Terah's shoulder. She doesn't bother with it this time.

"You're right, everything so far has had a reason," she adjusts her gaze upward, "as it should have."

"Even our last meal." He laughs, "I mean, for heaven's sake, it was the last meal served on the Titanic."

Terah's mouth drops open, "You knew that?!"

"Yeah, it was too obvious, so I did nothing."

"Wrong. You did the right thing by ignoring it. If we would have fled we would have ended up back in the power plant sim, remember?"

"Oh yeah, my little jaunt twelve years ago. I still don't remember it. But, according to you, I was programmed not to."

Since that escapade was brought up, Graham and Terah dissect it, trying to figure out why Graham ran from the cryogenic chamber out to the front security gate and scaled it. Initially, they can find no relevancy to their mission. It was certainly not an assassin's run or Julia would have died from the door knocking her down. It wasn't a scouting run as he took no physical notes to carry back to the power plant simulation with him.

"All I did was lose the pizza peppers when I climbed that fence," Graham adds with a sheepish grin.

Though she is fighting fatigue she puts her hands on her hips, "Have you not been listening? Computers don't just lose things."

"Oh, right. I must have been programmed to drop Deenay's peppers at that exact spot. So what?"

"So, there's a reason you did that."

Terah waits for Graham to reply.

A few lines on his forehead become more pronounced.

Using her posture she attempts to elicit a response from him. He remains quiet, but somehow focused.

Terah would normally prompt Graham, but this is different. She too is quiet, and patiently waits.

He looks directly into Terah's eyes. "I know why," he says solemnly.

Graham takes Terah by the hand and leads her out of the billiard room.

Chapter Forty Four

After conferring with trusted resistance members, Charles delivers an answer to the Judgment drone.

"We can no longer respect a government that tolerates everything but righteousness."

The man beside him – Engineer, Martin Van Troy – leans toward the drone.

"You are that government."

The drone focuses on the man, and announces its verdict.

"We will initiate the cleansing process."

Immediately, a sharp, red beam of light encompasses Mr. Van Troy and his body dissolves.

The resistance members are horrified, and some of the women react with uncontrolled sobbing. Others confront Charles about surrendering. His resolve begins to fade as he turns to face his wife.

"I'm afraid I've made a horrible mistake. Maybe we should capitulate to their demands."

Julia is subdued as she accesses her inner strength.

She slaps his face.

"I did not marry a hero nor did I marry a laggard. I married a decent, honorable and principled man." She looks into his eyes, "Charles Thomas Alcott, never again will you apologize for being who you are."

The judgment drone announces to Charles that his time has expired.

"May we speak for two more minutes?" Charles asks, "Before we surrender?"

Julia shakes her head in disgust.

Thinking this is a good opportunity to show the population of New Ahlab their supposed fair-mindedness, the Ruling Class grants him the extra two minutes. Charles nods and begins.

"We choose to stand and rebuild a new country."

Julia is surprised and shows her appreciation.

"We'll educate our own children," Charles continues, "in science, engineering, and medicine. We'll show them how the competition of free markets, grounded in morality and the truth of the Almighty, will lift everyone higher. Those that seek to enjoy the fruits of their labor will find refuge here."

A blinding flash of light erupts behind the gathered fighters. They turn, alarmed.

Slowly they grow quiet, Charles continues.

"Since our regrouping in the simulation, we've been free of your social control edicts through pharmaceutical persuasion. Our children have been free of your indoctrination camps that ensure the mindset of collectivism. Your illusion of autonomy has been exposed."

The resistance members begin to clap again at Charles's bravado.

"We know that your time here is nearing its conclusion because—" He is interrupted by applause. "Because history ignored is a stern teacher."

The judgment drone attempts to voice a warning over the cheers.

"Your defiance is forbidden. Cease and desist at once!"

"Be assured, while you may stand against us now, our descendants shall one day rise up and soundly defeat every last vestige of your lineage. Your existence shall be wiped clean from history; not from hate, or vengeance, but as our rightful duty as the victor. We shall spare future generations any glimpse of your putrid, moral depravity."

Thunderous cheering erupts from the crowd.

The frustrated drone announces, "Silence!"

"I have something to say!" Julia shouts at the drone. "Are woman able to be heard or is that forbidden too?"

"The cleansing process will initiate in thirty seconds."

Julia stands more erect on the boulder.

"You, the token Senators of New Ahlab have proved there is no political pendulum. Everything. Eventually. Rots."

She is interrupted by the drone, "Twenty seconds."

Julia recomposes herself.

"This is neither a statement nor a request; it is a command," she points directly into the camera of the nearest hovering propaganda drone, "Senators of the Ruling Class, hug your children. *We are coming!*"

"Ten seconds."

The assembled resistance members raise their fists and cheer loudly in affirmation.

"Your time has expired," the judgment drone warns. It fires a red beam at Charles and Julia.

Though the laser is powerful, it is no match for the Psychothetically powered shield that descends down from the satellite mirror array a nanosecond earlier. This shield surrounds the resistance members and protects the entire circumference of their new landmass. It will be vectored out further to cover a larger area as their numbers increase.

Though Charles and Julia's new charter may one day flourish to dominance, future generations must be mindful of the two learned absolutes. Without an adversary, a nation gradually surrenders its greatness and without God there is no greatness to surrender.

Chapter 45

A warning blares from the computer speakers.

Reactor core is critical, meltdown is inevitable. Prepare for a cataclysmic event.

"We're all gonna die!" a woman screams.

Other personnel focus on the announcement. They trade glances with each other.

"Really, Graham," she asks in disbelief, "you failed again?"

"Sorry, Deenay. I'll have Rhea bring in more 9J's next time."

***

Postscript:

"Someday, history will stop repeating itself... *that* day, will be our last."
—Jennifer West.

A visionary and her strands of computer code help reboot humanity. Just as thousands of years earlier, a man and an ark carried out a similar mission.

Find me on Facebook.com